MW00940856

MEN OF SIEGE BOOK ONE

ROGAN

BEX DANE

All my love,
Bex Dane

BEX DANE

Rogan (Men of Siege Book One) © 2018 by Bex Dane.

All rights reserved. In accordance with the U.S. Copyright Act of 1976, the scanning, uploading, and electronic sharing of any part of this book without written permission from the publisher is unlawful piracy and theft of intellectual property.

This book is a work of fiction. Any resemblance to actual events, persons, or locales is coincidental.

Published by Larken Romance

First Edition February 2018

Cover by Elizabeth Mackey Designs

Chapter 1

KABUL PROVINCE, AFGHANISTAN

Rogan

"You ready to get some, Boggs?" Falcon asked as he peered into his scope from his prone position beside me.

"Hell yeah. He's an hour late."

A silhouette of a man, glowing iridescent green in my night vision, exited the front door to the compound and sauntered over to his waiting comrade. Four years since my wife's death, and only two guards separated me from my ultimate target, Mustafa Ahmed Hakim Osmani. Jericho.

I settled into position on the boards and focused my sight on the relief guard's temple. "Ready."

"Send it."

I pulled the trigger and sent one sailing. The relief guard's head jerked, a green mist of blood exploding from his skull.

"Got him," Falcon said. "Above the right eye."

The guard on duty lowered the body of his dead associate to the ground. He bobbed and dodged, trying to escape the invisible sniper fire. If he would just stay put for one second...

When his forehead stilled, I pulled the trigger.

"Hit," Falcon said. "Dead center."

The second guard stumbled and dropped to the dirt.

"Moving," I called through the comms.

The five men on my team and my dog followed me as I descended the stairs of the unit we were using as a hide.

We jogged silently through the moonless night in Kabul, taking cover between mud huts as we advanced. I checked the bodies of the guards outside Jericho's dwelling to make sure the bullets did their job. Yep, two bullets, two dead terrorists. Excellent. Now to the high-value target.

Diesel and Ruger scaled a wall to access the dwelling from the roof. The remaining three men took up positions around the perimeter as Blaze rigged the door to blow. "Fire in the hole!"

I pulled Takoda to my chest. Two simultaneous explosions blasted us, one at the front door, the other on the roof. The element of surprise gone, we had sixty seconds to get in, clear the building, and kill Jericho. I pinched the scruff of Takoda's neck and spoke in her ear. "Be careful, girl." I released her. "Search!"

She charged into the settling dust of the disintegrated door. When nobody shot her and nothing else exploded, we entered through the debris. Two women and three children huddled against the far wall. Oz and Blaze tied their hands behind their backs and forced them outside.

As I marched to meet Ruger and Diesel on the second floor, Takoda stopped and sniffed at a girl the guys had missed. She cowered on a cot with her arms over her head, her knees tucked under her. I grabbed her bicep and yanked her up.

"Ahh!" Nylon rope bound to her wrists pulled her back to the bed frame.

"Oh, dear God. Save me. Dear God. Watch over me. Please. Please," she chanted in a weak voice.

"Are you American?"

One wide eye peeked up at me over her shoulder. Patches of light skin showed through the dirt on her face. She nodded. "Help me."

The long sleeves and scalloped collar of her dress, while filthy and wrinkled, appeared to be Western-styled.

An American hostage? How the hell did we miss her during recon?

The first crack of a firefight sounded from upstairs. "Taking fire!" Ruger's yell echoed through the comms.

"Stay down. I'll come back for you." I released her arm.

Three men and I scaled the steps to the second level. From the stairwell, my mirror sight showed one enemy combatant firing wildly through the hole Ruger and Diesel had made in the roof.

"Mrasta!" I called *help* in Pashto. "Mrasta."

The gunfire stopped and the shooter poked his head out around the banister, looking in the direction of my voice.

I shot him in the chest. He hit the floor with a thud. I took point as we advanced to the second level. Ruger and Diesel dropped in from the hole in the roof and got in line.

We slipped into position on either side of the door that led to the only bedroom on the second floor. Lying prone, I used a corner scope to identify three insurgents in the room. "Open fire."

A hailstorm of shots flew through the doorway in both directions. When the firefight ceased, at least two enemy combatants lay dead. One man stumbled and swayed with his weapon pointed toward the ceiling. I shot him in the head. He rocked and dropped to the floor.

We entered the room to assess if we'd hit our target. I approached the closest body and pulled him to his back.

"That him?" Blaze asked.

"Not sure yet." I knelt beside the body, pouring water over his face to clear the blood. His hair was black, not the gray we were looking for, his nose wider than the target's—the forehead too large. Not tall enough to be Jericho. His features matched Musab Al-Sayed, Jericho's oldest brother, the one we called Zulu.

"Not him."

"What the hell?" Blaze came up behind me.

"Not Jericho. That's Zulu."

"You gotta be shitting me."

I inspected the second body. "Not him either."

The third body was too short to be our target.

"You check the one on the stairwell?" I asked Blaze.

"Not Jericho." He grunted and turned away. "Damn."

Fuck. We didn't get him. "Move out. Blaze, rig it to blow."

He proceeded to set a charge in the corner of the room.

I ran for the door, stopping at the American girl. With a flick of my bowie knife, the rope snapped free from her wrists. I scooped her off the cot and charged to the exit.

"Sixty seconds!" Blaze called.

"Koda, come!"

We filed out of the dwelling and raced the three hundred yards to the extraction point. The impact blasted our backs and propelled us forward. The helo touched down, and the entire six-man team boarded like clockwork.

I set the girl on the bench at the rear of the helo and whistled for Takoda out the door.

"Stand by. My dog isn't here."

The pilot held up his hand, indicating he'd heard me.

"Let's move," Blaze said as I leaped to the ground.

"Not without Takoda." The rotor wind pummeled me as I ran five yards east, scanning the horizon for any sign of her. Nothing.

"Koda!" My call died in the void. Where the hell was she?

There. Fifty yards to the west, a pair of eyes glinted and bounced. Is that her? Yes! Takoda galloped full-tilt toward me, the wind blowing her fur at a sharp angle away from her flanks. We hopped in the helo.

"Go!"

The pilot lifted off. Falcon slammed the door shut, cutting down the rotor noise with a sharp thud. I stowed my weapons and strapped Takoda's harness to a belt. "Where were you, girl?"

She panted, her tongue hanging.

"Good dog." I patted her head.

At least I didn't lose her.

I pulled off my headgear and inspected my team for injuries. Diesel sat on the floor, his face and neck smeared with blood. Ruger kneeled in front of him with his medical kit open.

"How is he?" I asked Ruger.

"Shrapnel grazed his cheek. It's not too deep." Diesel winced as Ruger pressed gauze to his face.

"You got lucky, my friend," I said to Diesel.

"Not a big deal," Diesel replied. "Yolanda's gonna kill me."

"Nah, she gets you back alive, she'll be happy."

"What the hell is *that*?" Blaze pointed to the girl cowering on the bench.

I glanced at her. "She's American." Trembles wracked the girl's body. I grabbed a blanket and covered her.

"You don't know that."

"Look at her. She spoke English to me. We had to get her out," I replied.

"Sure we did."

"We don't leave hostages behind. We don't leave our dog behind. You're amped up and talking nonsense."

"No. You got fucking issues with female hostages."

The movement in the cabin stilled. Five pairs of eyes zeroed in on me.

"Don't go there, Blaze." I towered over him.

He rose to his feet and sneered. "A weakness. Puts us all at risk."

"Rescuing her was low risk. I made the call."

"She ain't her, ya know."

My bones hummed with righteous fury and all my muscles coiled, ready to strike down this insolent ass. Our vests mashed together as I pushed right up in his stupid face. "Shut the fuck up! You're outta line."

"She ain't her, Boggs. Eden's dead. She's been dead four years."

Through the red haze filling my vision, I nailed his chin with a vicious right hook. He didn't expect it, didn't block. He rubbed his jaw and squinted at me.

"Go ahead, Blaze. Hit me back. Let's see who's left standing at the end."

Falcon wedged a shoulder between us. "Hey! That's enough. Sit down."

Blaze broke eye contact as Falcon forced me to sit.

With my elbows on my knees, I peered down at my boots.

I would not lose my shit.

We didn't get Jericho.

Failure. Unacceptable.

I tugged at the straps of my flak vest and anchored myself in the armor.

At least we got Zulu. And a fucking hostage.

She ain't her.

Eden's dead.

This girl wasn't Eden. She didn't die at the hands of terrorists. This girl will live.

"Fuck! Fuck, fuck." The image of Eden's bloody corpse in my arms threatened to rob me of my sanity again.

"Lock it down, Boggs."

I lifted my head and linked eyes with Falcon. "I got it," I gritted out through my clenched jaw. I tucked the image away in a storage pocket and locked the snap.

Gone.

Falcon stared at my fists until I released my grip on my vest.

The girl shuddered under the blanket and snuck a furtive glance at me.

"Ruger, check her condition," I called.

Ruger grabbed his kit and walked to her with his shoulders down and knees bent.

"No! No!" She recoiled against the seat and pulled the blanket up to her face.

I held my hand up for Ruger to back off. He stopped and headed back to his seat.

"Hey." She shrank down when I tapped her back through the blanket. "Are you hurt?"

She shook her head.

"How old are you?"

No answer.

"Why were you in Afghanistan?"

She chewed her lip, her gaze darting around the cabin. "Are you soldiers?" She glanced at my unmarked fatigues then focused on my beard.

"Yes. You're safe. We won't hurt you. You need to give me some info, so I can get you back where you belong."

I could barely hear her weak voice. "I... My church..."

"You here with your church?"

She nodded.

"Where are they based?"

"Karachi."

"We can return you to Pakistan. Are they still in Karachi?"

"I don't know."

"Where's your family? The States?"

She nodded again. She needed to get home. We couldn't leave her here.

I surveyed the faces of each of my men. "She's coming with us."

"You gotta be kidding me. You're gonna blow the roof off this whole mission for her?" Blaze was a pain in my ass tonight.

"She doesn't know who we are. We return her to her family in the States anonymously. She'll keep quiet."

Chapter 2

THE HELO TOUCHED DOWN at Kabul International Airport after a twenty-minute flight. The girl stayed in a tight ball with her head tucked into my chest as I carried her onto the unmarked jet the CIA had arranged for us to take nonstop to Boston Executive Airport. I set her down in the aisle seat and took the window seat next to her. She huddled under her blanket, her wide eyes peeking around the cabin, bouncing to each man as he settled his gear.

Blaze stopped in front of us and gave me his repentant look. "Boggs. I'm sor—"

"Not now, Blaze." He stirred the wrong shit tonight.

"No, man. Your mission, your call."

"It's done. Tonight was challenging for all of us." As always, after action, we forgive each other and forge ahead. "It's all good. Let's get home."

"Right." Blaze glanced at the girl before walking to his seat.

I removed my flak vest. Time to take off the armor.

The shaking in her shoulders subsided as we reached altitude.

"You need to let my medic see to you."

She glanced at Ruger. "I'm fine."

"Ruger!"

Ruger came over with his kit. "Do you hurt anywhere?"

She shook her head.

"How many?" He held up his fingers.

"Two."

Her gaze traced his fingers back and forth as he shined a light in her eyes.

"Can you stand for me?"

She placed her fingers in his outstretched palm. Red marks circled her wrists where she'd been bound. Ruger helped her rise to her feet. Based on the ten inches Ruger had over her, she must be about five-foot-seven. Taller than I thought she'd be based on her weight when I carried her. Her blonde hair, dark with grease and grime, curled in messy twists on her neck. She poked it with her fingers.

"How old are you?" Ruger asked as he checked her vitals.

"Twenty-three," she answered in a shaky voice.

Huh. I would've guessed sixteen by her thin frame.

"When's the last time you ate?" Ruger asked.

"Yesterday morning."

"Try to drink this. Take it slow." He handed her a bottle of electrolytes.

She sipped the drink, keeping her eyes closed.

"Your stomach queasy?"

She shook her head.

Ruger applied ointment to her wrists and repacked his kit. "She looks okay. Malnourished, stressed, but no obvious injuries."

"Good."

"I'll walk you to the bathroom to clean up." Ruger angled his head toward the small door at the rear of the cabin.

She hesitated, her gaze flitting to the back of the plane.

"Go ahead," I said.

Ruger held her elbow as she made her way down the aisle. The door clicked shut behind her, and Ruger walked back to kneel by my seat. "She'll need an internal exam when we land. Testing for pregnancy and disease."

I shook my head. "Black ops stay black start to finish. We're putting her on a plane and sending her home. Her family will have to see to her medical care."

Ruger nodded and returned to his seat.

The girl's footsteps approached ten minutes later. She'd washed her face, revealing lightly freckled pale skin. She'd worked her hair into a loose braid that hung five inches past her waist. She looked down as she slumped back into her seat and pulled her blanket up under her chin.

"Better?" I asked her as she buckled in.

"Yes."

She swiped a loose strand of hair off her forehead. Her eyes held the vacant stare I'd seen many times on shell-shocked prisoners we'd rescued and released. Most of them had been men. None had delicate features like this girl. The last woman we'd extracted had been Eden...

I handed her a protein bar. "Eat slowly."

She took the bar and nibbled at it, finishing it fifteen minutes later.

"The food staying down?"

"Mmm-hmm."

"Leaving Afghan airspace," the pilot called over the speakers.

The tension in the cabin dropped as we all began the familiar transition into post-action mode. Six hours into the flight, the plane's engines buzzed beneath us as the girl rested her head against the back of her seat and peered out the window into darkness.

"What's your name?" I asked her in a calm, non-threatening tone.

She pursed her lips.

"Need your name so I can find out who might be looking for you."

"Vanity," she said in a scratchy, small voice.

"Pardon?"

"Vanity."

"Alright."

I booted my laptop and pulled up the CIA database.

"Last name?"

"Barebones."

"Vanity Barebones?"

The named seemed odd, but the database pulled up three deceased Vanity Barebones in Utah. Two alive in Idaho. One Vanity Barebones in Caldwell, age twenty-three.

"Caldwell, Idaho?"

She nodded.

I searched the latest news from Caldwell to see if she'd made the papers.

Caldwell residents protest the rapid growth of the polygamous Brotherhood of God fundamentalist church.

The break-off sect established in Idaho ten years ago after the Utah-based church was broken up by scandal.

Ervil Jeters, the church's former leader, is currently serving life plus twenty for child rape and molestation. Key evidence included DNA proving Jeters fathered children with three juveniles. Jeters maintains control of the church from prison and asserts the end of the world is upon us.

"You said you were there with your church?"

"Yes."

"A missionary?"

"Humanitarian aid."

Fuck, those idiots thought sending her could help?

"How'd you get captured?"

"In Pakistan, outside a street market in Karachi. Three men grabbed me and shoved me into a van."

"I found you in Afghanistan. Kabul."

"Oh."

"Did your kidnappers contact your family?"

"Yes."

"And?"

"My father said he wouldn't pay the money they wanted."

"He call the police? Washington?"

"No."

"What's your father's name?"

She answered me with a stubborn shake of her head.

"Alright." If she wasn't sharing, I'd find out myself.

The database listed Jebediah Barebones as her father. Two Jeb Bare-bones resided in Caldwell. I turned the screen to her and showed her my image search results.

"See him here?"

She peeked over and pointed to a picture of a white-haired man in a field. His tall, lanky frame towered over thirty or more women and a shitload of children gathered in rows in front of him. Their old-fashioned dresses and weird hairdos made it look like a scene from a time long past, but the photo date said nine years ago. None of the women smiled. Several of them held their hands below bellies swollen with unborn children.

A beautiful blonde child stood directly in front of her father. She wore the same clothes as the others, and her hair was styled the same, but she had a shimmering golden braid over her shoulder. She stood out as the prettiest of the group. Her dazed eyes and vacant expression looked a lot like the one I'd seen on the girl sitting next to me.

"Your dad could've called the government without telling you."

"No. He wouldn't want anyone in his business."

Takoda stood and sniffed Vanity's knee. Vanity's cheeks rounded, and a hint of blue shone in her eyes as they lightened with the grin she offered Takoda.

"Hey there. Is this your dog?"

"Yes, Takoda."

"Hi, Takoda. Nice to meet you."

Vanity placed her frail hand on Takoda's scruffy head and gave her a rub. "Boy or girl?"

"Girl."

"She's a friendly one."

Takoda nudged Vanity's hand, urging her to continue giving the love. "Are you a brave girl? You rescue people with these big guys? What a hero you are!"

Takoda wagged her tail and gazed into Vanity's eyes. My faithful dog just abandoned me for this girl.

I deepened my search into the shit going on in Caldwell.

The Brotherhood settles in economically vulnerable communities, creating competition for already scarce jobs, and takes control of local commerce.

The pictures churned my stomach. Before Jeters went to prison, he'd accumulated seventy-three wives and hundreds of children.

From the FBI classified files: Brotherhood of God Church, Caldwell, Idaho: Ongoing investigation for allegations of human trafficking across state lines, rape, and WIC fraud. On hold until undercover agents penetrate the compound.

Nothing about a hostage. Doesn't mean they don't know about her, but a promising sign.

Falcon glanced at me as I approached him at the back of the plane. "What?"

The seat next to him creaked as I sat down. "What are the chances this was a set-up?"

"A set-up how?"

"The CIA could've fed me bogus intel about Jericho's location knowing I'd get her out and kill Zulu."

"Improbable. Too many variables. We saw Jericho there three times during surveillance. Unfortunate he wasn't there tonight, but not a set-up."

"You're probably right."

"Is the girl in the database as a hostage?" Falcon's gaze flicked to where Vanity slept in her seat.

"Nope. She's off radar."

"Good. Less mess."

"Yep. We should be able to put her on a plane and send her home. Never happened. I gotta run it by Brightman to get clearance, but I think she'll go for it."

"You find out where she's from?"

"Idaho. Some fucked up fundamentalist sect."

"No shit?"

"She says she was in Karachi as a missionary. Jericho must've captured her there and taken her to Kabul Province where we found her."

"Huh." Falcon scratched his head. "Is it safe to send her back to Idaho?"

"Don't know. We can't get involved. Too risky." I pressed my hand to his shoulder. "I wanna go back for Jericho. I think Brightman will back it."

"Fuck. We're still on the plane home, man." He swiped his hand from his forehead to his chin.

"Operation Devil's Gate is not complete till the coward who raped and killed my wife feels the wrath of my rifle."

"How the hell are you gonna find him? Jericho has already caught wind of the raid and crawled under a rock."

I held up the flash drive I'd snagged from a computer during the raid.

Falcon's eyes lit up, and he grinned his crazy-serial-killer smile as he pulled three cell phones from the pocket of his pants.

"That's how it's done, bro. You in?"

"You know it."

I slapped him on the shoulder and headed to the back of the plane to ask the other guys.

"Hey. I want to go back for Jericho as soon as possible. The longer we wait, the harder he'll be to find. You up for it?"

Diesel spoke first. "I got a wedding in two weeks plus a honeymoon where I won't be thinking about any missions except nailin' my wife and burying my toes in the good kind of sand. After that, sure, I'm game to finish the job."

Blaze, Oz, and Ruger all tipped their chins.

"That's how Alpha Squadron rolls. All in or nothing," Blaze said.

"Appreciate it, my brothers. I'll be in contact."

WE SPLIT UP AS SOON as our feet hit the tarmac at Boston Executive Airport. No big goodbyes. Just a nod from Falcon as he left for his connecting flight to North Carolina. Ruger and Oz casually headed to their flight to Virginia. Blaze and Diesel waited for me by the doors to the terminal. We'd done this plenty of times and knew it was best not to draw any attention.

I handed Vanity a boarding pass and five hundred in cash. "You'll board a plane to Boise in an hour. Use the money to get home. Tell your family you escaped on your own from the terrorists. The U.S. military got you a flight home. You don't know who arranged it or what they looked like."

She took the pass and the cash from me and nodded.

I pointed to the gate she'd need for her flight. "Go wait in the chairs in front of that gate."

She turned slowly toward the gate.

"Goodbye," I said to her.

"Bye," she answered. "Thank you."

Thank you she said in her sweet, innocent voice. Thanking me for what? Sending her off on a flight to Idaho to a father who kept wives as prizes, to a commune where children were forced to marry and have kids with old men? All this after whatever hell she'd endured as a hostage?

"Wait." My voice cracked. "Wait," I said louder.

She paused but didn't turn around.

"You ever consider not going home?"

Her mouth dropped open as her gaze met mine. Yes, definitely blue eyes—a striking cobalt blue offset by her fair skin.

"What? I have to go back."

"You're an adult. You don't have to do anything you don't want."

She shook her head and stared at her feet.

"Your daddy a preacher?"

"Yes."

"He treat you well?"

"Why?"

"Just wondering what kind of father sends his pretty young daughter to a war zone then won't even make the call to Washington to save her."

She fiddled with loose strands in her braid. "My father has pressures on him."

"Like what? Keeping up with all his wives?"

Her head snapped up.

"You haven't thought of leaving?"

She bit her lip, wetness shimmering in her eyes. Oh yeah, she'd thought of it and she wanted it.

"You don't have to go back."

"But... my family. They expect me to—"

"As far as they know, you're still being held for ransom. You gonna tell me you don't wanna get away from that shit?"

"No. I do. I mean I dream of leaving."

Like I thought. She wanted out.

"But where would I go?"

"Is there someone back home who could help you?"

"No."

"Then stay here, in Boston."

"I don't have any money. No ID. Nothing."

As I stared into her vulnerable eyes, a conviction stronger than any vow staked its claim in my soul.

Vanity Barebones would never return to Caldwell.

"I'll take care of that."

"You'll take care—"

"I'll help you get settled somewhere. Make sure you're safe from your father."

"I don't even know you."

I lowered my head and pinned her with my gaze. "I'm offerin' you a way out. Be smart and take it."

"Why would you do this?"

I gave her an honest answer. "I don't know." Why the hell would I take on a complication like her? Maybe Blaze was right. I was trying to satisfy the unquenchable need to rescue Eden. Maybe if I saved this girl, Eden's death would be vindicated. Of course it wouldn't. She wasn't Eden. Just another poor girl who found herself in a similar predicament. But since the situation stood before me, I had a choice to make. Instinct overrode all logic. I couldn't leave her here any more than I could leave Takoda. I'd get her on her feet somewhere. Then I'd let her go.

"Who are you?" she whispered.

Good question. Too late to lie to her, I told her the truth. "Master Sergeant Rogan Saxton, U.S. Army. The offer stands. You wanna start a new life?"

"Yes," she said with a breathy burst of air. Her face scrunched up, and her lips jutted out as she pressed them together. "Yes. I want a new life."

The desperation in her voice and the tear trickling down her cheek confirmed my suspicions about how bad things would be for her if she went home. My hands shook with an urge to wrap an arm around her back, but that wouldn't fly at the airport with Diesel and Blaze three yards away, pretending not to watch.

I grabbed my gear and walked to the guys. "It's not safe for her to go back to Idaho. She'll stay with me till she gets on her feet."

"You're taking her on?" Diesel asked. "She's a complete unknown."

"It's temporary. She doesn't know anything about the unit or our mission. Dallas Monroe will help her, and then we go back for Jericho. But if we send her back to her parents, she'll be worse off than she was in Kabul."

They scrutinized Vanity with skeptical eyes. The fragile smile that grew on her lips must have affected them too because they grinned back at her and relaxed their tensed shoulders.

I waved my hand for her to follow us. She took three hesitant steps toward us and paused.

"Let's go then. I'm hungry as hell and need some American welcome home food." Blaze lifted his gear and walked to the terminal exit.

She bit her lip, her gaze darting around the space.

Come on, Vanity. You can do it.

An unseen force pulled her spine straight, and she strode toward me.

Pride surged through me as if she were mine. With her hair and clothes a disheveled mess, her body skinny and tired, the beauty of her courage struck me dumb.

When she reached me, I tilted my chin and bent low so only she could hear. "Well done."

Chapter 3

VANITY

Sergeant Saxton opened the door to an apartment marked 2B. A high-pitched beeping stabbed my ears. He pressed something on the wall inside the door, and one long tone silenced the noise. He lowered his luggage to the floor and swept a hand into the room. "Come in."

I clutched the bag of toiletries he'd bought me on the trip from the airport and peeked down the narrow corridor. The other two men with us had entered a different apartment. He'd have me alone in there. He could hurt me if he wanted to, but his calm and confident demeanor didn't raise any warning flags for me. As I'd done at the airport, I trusted the strong sense of security I felt from him and stepped through the doorway.

"Have a seat." He pointed to a black leather couch, the only furniture in the room except for a wooden coffee table. The cushion squeaked as I sat on the edge with my new bag of belongings in my lap.

He bent his knees and crouched down to my eye level. "Shower and change. Bathroom's there." He pointed with his thumb to a door to his left.

"Thank you, uh... What should I call you?"

His forehead scrunched. "Rogan. Call me Rogan."

"The guy on the plane called you Boggs."

"My men call me Boggs."

"Oh."

"Go ahead."

I checked the bathroom lock twice before peeling off my putrid clothes and stepping into my first warm shower in nearly three months. My skin turned red from all the scrubbing, but I had to get every particle of the powdery desert sand off my body. After four shampoo rinses, the grease finally came clean from my hair.

Alone for the first time in months, the terror of it all poured out of me in wet streams. Why had God been so cruel to me? Freeing me from my father's grasp only to toss me into the hands of terrorists. Was he punishing me for rejecting the Brotherhood and planning to escape?

My mother's voice echoed in my head.

I'm sorry I didn't see this sooner. Get out as soon as you can. Do not keep sweet. Keep strong. Make sure they are safe. Fight till you find joy.

With a fortifying breath, I stemmed my sobs and straightened my shoulders. I'd been rescued, and for the moment, I was safe here in this stranger's apartment. A chance at freedom hovered within my grasp and crying wouldn't do me any good. My hollow eyes and stick-thin figure peered at me through the mirror. In my mother's dying words, I found my courage. The time had come to keep strong, and I would do it for her.

I braided my wet hair and dressed in the white cotton underwear and sports bra Rogan had purchased for me. The tears threatened again as I slipped into a heather-gray T-shirt and matching sweatpants. After weeks suffocating in my dress, the cool fabric caressed my skin like silk. Never again would I take for granted the simple pleasure of clean clothes.

In the living room, Rogan waited for me with his hip propped against the back of the couch. He scrutinized me in the clothes, his gaze stopping on the braid over my shoulder. "Drink those to gain your strength." He pointed to a six-pack of vanilla Ensure and two bottles of green Gatorade on the coffee table.

I sat on the couch and twisted the cap off a vanilla Ensure. My first sip tasted overly sweet after only drinking water and tea for the past ten weeks, but the second and third sip went down easier.

Takoda trotted up and sniffed my knee. A greasy residue remained on my hand after petting her. "Hey, girl. You need a bath too."

Rogan watched our interaction with a scowl, like Takoda shouldn't have approached me.

"Is she a German Shepherd?"

"Belgian Malinois."

"Isn't it dangerous for her out there in Afghanistan?"

His eyebrows rose and mashed together. "Yes, it's dangerous. That's why you never shoulda been there."

He peeled off his jacket and dropped it on his pile of bags next to the door. His sweat stained T-shirt stretched tight over his muscular chest and arms.

"When shit gets hairy downrange, the best weapon to have at your side is a trained working dog at the top of her game."

I couldn't pull my gaze from the tattoo on his massive bicep. Two perpendicular stark black lines, one disappearing under the sleeve of his olive-green T-shirt. It looked like a letter.

"Her senses are off the charts—better than any human." He sat on the floor and unthreaded the laces to his boots with mechanical efficiency. "She wouldn't hesitate to throw herself on an IED for me." He aligned his boots next to the door and stood to his full height. A chain around his neck trailed inside the shirt, ending at a bump in the fabric between his pecs.

Affection shone in his eyes when he peered down at Takoda and gave her head a pet. "She's good at it, and she loves her job."

Takoda stood squarely on four legs and peered up at him with eager faithfulness on her face. Her ears flicked as he entered the bathroom and shut the door behind him.

"Wow, Takoda. You *are* a hero." She came to me and arched her head to get my fingers behind her ears. "But please be careful out there. I'd hate to lose you."

Her eyes squeezed tight as she relished my head rub.

―――――――――――

TEN MINUTES LATER, a misty cloud preceded Rogan out of the bathroom. He'd changed into a royal-blue T-shirt and black cargo pants that hugged his trim waist.

I leaned against the arm of the couch and eyed him as I sipped my protein drink. His sandy brown hair spiked up in dark points as he rubbed it with a towel. He'd shaved his beard. Tiny red dots peppered the sharply angled line of his jaw.

Wowza, they sure didn't make men like him back on the compound. I'd never been in the presence of a man with Rogan's staggering build and rugged handsomeness.

A hint of humid air hit me when he sat next to me on the couch. "You need to choose a new name. Vanity Barebones died in Afghanistan."

"She did?"

"Don't pick anything that will lead them to you."

"Give me a minute to think about it."

"Alright."

How should I choose a name for myself and this new life? I needed a secular name, something meaningful.

"Harlow," I said.

"As a first name?"

"No, a last name."

"Could they trace it to you?"

"I don't think so. It's a name I saw in a book."

"What kind of book?"

"I babysat for a family in town. The Jensens. They had old encyclopedias I liked to read. Harlow was a scientist." Rogan's eyes had unfocused while I was talking. "Would Harlow work?"

"Sure."

"What first name would you pick for me?"

He slid his gaze from over my shoulder and studied me. I hadn't seen his eyes before in the daylight, but oh my, gold and brown whorled in them like wheat in a summer field.

"Sunshine," he answered solemnly.

"Sunshine? Why?"

"Found you in the desert." He pointed at Takoda. "My dog smiles at you like she's looking into the sun."

"Oh."

He cleared his throat. "But how about Tessa?"

"Why Tessa?"

"It's a name a pretty girl like you would have."

I pressed my hands to my cheeks to hide the warmth growing there.

"It's also common enough it won't draw any attention if someone is looking into you."

"Um, okay. So could I be Tessa Harlow?"

One edge of his mouth turned down, and the skin around his eyes crinkled. "Yes, you can be Tessa Harlow."

"Oh my goodness. Thank you."

"No problem." He strode to a card table in a breakfast nook beside the kitchen, opened a laptop, and sat down to type.

No problem. Who was this gorgeous man who marauded across the globe without sleeping and could make me Tessa Harlow with no problem?

A new identity terrified and excited me at the same time, but it was the first step in fighting for my joy, so I'd embrace it and make the best of it. Like Rogan said, *Vanity Barebones died in Afghanistan.*

I finished my drink and rested my head on the arm of the couch.

———————

MY FATHER'S WEIGHT dipped the side of the bed. I shrank deep in my sheets and curled in a ball, trying to become invisible. But it didn't matter. He always found me and slithered in behind me whether I welcomed him or not. With his reptilian arms snaked behind my back and knees, he hauled me from my hiding spot and carried me to the edge of a raging fire pit.

"In you go," he snarled as the flames of the burning inferno licked my shoulders and legs.

"No! No! Let me go!" I pounded my fists on his chest and swung my feet to break free.

"Hey, hey. It's alright. You're safe."

The jagged voice speaking to me sounded nothing like my father's monotone drivel.

"It's just a dream, Tessa."

When I opened my eyes, my hands clutched Rogan's T-shirt as he held me in the air.

"A dream. Oh yes. I'm sorry. Please forgive me."

"Nothin' to forgive." His nose crinkled as he squinted at me. "There's only one bed in this place. I'll be on the couch."

As I peeked down at the bed, he stared at me as he waited for some kind of reply. My awareness shifted to the heat where my side touched his rock-solid torso, and under my legs where his powerful arms supported me.

"Uh... Thank you."

Rogan lowered me to the bed and stayed close for a split second longer than he needed to before straightening.

"Okay, then. There ya go." He turned and left the room in a blur, like a vortex of fine sand in a windstorm.

Chapter 4

TESSA

Rogan's immense body spilled over the edges of the narrow couch in the living room. One foot rested on the floor, the other hung over the arm. His hands were folded on his chest. Rogan half opened his eyes but didn't move.

"I don't mind taking the couch. That can't be comfortable."

"Trained to sleep on rocks, Sunshine. A couch is a fuckin' luxury." His gravelly voice rumbled from his throat.

He sat up and rubbed his eyes before walking to the kitchen. "Coffee?" he asked as he filled the pot with water.

"Yes, please."

After we watched it brew, he handed me an Army mug and took a sip of his own. "No limits on coffee on the compound?"

"No. When my father took over he lifted the ban. His wives needed the caffeine to get all the work done with so many kids."

"Still doesn't sit right hearing you talk about one husband with many wives."

"I grew up in a plural world. They tried to convince me it was normal, but I always knew it wasn't the way the outside world lived. Hey, at least we had coffee." I savored my first taste of life juice in months.

He leaned his hip against the counter and peered at me over his cup. "When did you fly to Pakistan with your church?"

"Beginning of March."

"And when did you get captured?"

"The first week."

He gulped down a sip, and his sleepy eyes popped fully open. "Shit. They had you ten weeks?"

"Yes."

"Did they hurt you?"

I took a deep breath and told Rogan the truth. "They called me dirty. Seemed like it was the only English word they knew. Dirty."

"Go on."

"This man with a white turban... He beat me the first day. They took pictures of my battered face and sent them to my father."

Rogan gripped his cup so tight his fingertips turned white. "And your dad didn't even pretend to negotiate with them to keep you alive?"

"He said *no* and disconnected the call."

"And we know he didn't call the government to send a team for you."

"No. He wouldn't do that."

"Fuck." His cup clanked on the kitchen counter.

"I'm just telling you how it happened."

He rolled his hand for me to continue.

"The women kept me on the bottom floor of the house with the kids. I thought for sure I'd die there. I'd never see my family again or get a chance to say goodbye."

Rogan pressed his palms to the top of the sink with his elbows straight. "They rape you?" he asked gently as he peered out the kitchen window.

"No. The man with the white turban tried, but..."

"What happened?"

"I fought and screamed *dirty* and pointed to myself here." I pointed to my crotch.

"You did?"

"Mmm-hmm. And I told the one woman who spoke some English that I had a disease. If anyone raped me, his manhood would turn green and fall off."

His eyes crinkled when he grinned. "That was... creative."

"I had lots of time to think."

"It was also risky. They could slice your head off for that."

"Luckily they didn't."

"Yeah." He shifted his gaze to the window again. "I'm gonna set you up with a doctor to check you out."

"No. I'll be okay. My body's not broken." My head spun with all the challenges ahead of me, and my heart fractured at the thought of abandoning my family, but at least I had my health. "I'll be fine."

"Do it anyway. As a precaution."

"Okay."

He rinsed his cup in the sink and placed it in the dry rack. "You have a cell phone back home?"

I nodded. "My father gave some of us cell phones. It was too difficult for him to communicate with all his families without them."

"Did you have access to the internet?"

"No. But I worked at the drugstore in town and could get WiFi access at the library on my breaks."

"I'm surprised your dad allowed all that."

"He didn't know I had internet. I cleared my history every day."

"So, you babysat and worked at a drugstore?"

"We needed money so we worked wherever we could."

"But the drugstore was outside the compound? Sold the things an ordinary drugstore would sell?"

"Yes, they sold magazines, alcohol, cigarettes. We shopped at the Costco in Boise City. We weren't Amish. We were exposed to the outside world, just taught to reject the excess and gluttony or we'd go to hell."

"But you didn't believe it?"

"No. I was fascinated with the outside world and always wanted to be a part of it. The possibilities were endless. So much color and music and art. I didn't see the harm in it."

"Follow me." Rogan walked to the living room. He dropped a shiny rectangular box on the coffee table. "For you."

I picked up the box and opened the packaging. I lifted out a thin cell phone and earbuds.

"It's a smartphone registered to Tessa Harlow. No limits on data. My cell is programmed under *R*. Don't give out any personal information. Trust no one."

Wow. "Okay."

"No contact with your family."

No contact? But my little brother Milo would be waiting to hear from me. I agreed with a nod of my head. "Thank you so much. For all of this. If you hadn't rescued me—"

"And you can stop thanking me." His voice hardened like I'd offended him.

"But I'm so grateful."

"Got that. Just accept it and make the best of it." He sat down at his card table and opened up his laptop.

I tucked the phone under my armpit and strode toward his bedroom.

"One more thing." Rogan's voice stopped me mid-step.

"Hmm?"

"There's a shit ton of ebooks loaded in the reading app on your phone and a credit at the bookstore website. Get whatever you want," he said casually and looked back at his screen.

Get whatever you want. For him, this was probably a normal thing to say. For me, it meant the world. Never in my life was I allowed to get what I wanted. I'd only heard *no, you can't have that.*

I plopped on his bed and opened the reading app. Romance novels, mysteries, classics, and memoirs. So many memoirs.

How I Escaped Polygamy

The Scarlet Sister

Life on the Outside by Gracelynn Jeters

Gracelynn Jeters! Ervil's ninth wife had written a book? I'd met her once on the compound in Utah. I flipped to the foreword.

With this book, I hope to reach the thousands of religiously oppressed like my former self. Never give up on seeking freedom from the emotional and physical captivity of polygamy. There is light on the other side. And it's beautiful.

The room grew darker until the glow from the screen projected an isolated cloud on my sheets. The rolling hunger in my tummy finally roared so loud it couldn't be ignored.

I placed the phone next to me on the bed and wept. I was no longer alone and invisible. I had sisters in spirit who'd fought for their right to be seen and heard. Other women had gone before me and made it through. They were scared. They'd feared the isolation, the loss of their family, the threat of eternal damnation. Yet they'd stood strong and risked their lives to escape.

A soft rapping on my door interrupted my sobs. "Come in." I wiped my cheeks, and my muscles protested as I moved from the position I'd sat in all day.

Rogan poked his head around the door and held up a white paper bag. "I brought you Roxy's."

"Sounds good." Whatever Roxy's was, I'd eat it. "I'll be right there."

I washed my face and met him in the kitchen. Takoda sat at his feet, her tail wagging double speed, her nose pointed at the food Rogan arranged onto plates.

"Koda, down."

She lowered her chest and rested her nose on her paws.

Rogan handed me a plate loaded with a hamburger wrapped in white paper, a pickle, and a heaping mound of thick-cut potato fries.

"Oh my gosh." A full plate of food. Another thing I'd never take for granted. "It smells so good. No wonder she's begging. Can I give her some?" I picked up a fry, ready to hand it to Takoda. Her ears perked up and she began to rise to all fours, but Rogan pointed one finger at the floor and gave her a stern look. She settled back into her down position.

"No. She's on a special diet." He pulled out a chair at the kitchen table for me. "If she sits quiet while we eat, I'll give her a treat at the end. But you give her a fry now, she'll be begging at every meal."

I set my plate on the table and sat in the chair Rogan offered me. "Sorry, Takoda. I can't share."

Rogan took the seat next to mine. "What'd you eat there?"

"Rice. Some fruit. I wouldn't touch their rancid meat."

He looked from the food to my face. "You think your stomach can handle this?"

"I think so."

"Take it slow."

My first bite was so delicious, I moaned through a full mouth. "Mmm!"

He pointed to a cup and straw on the table. "Triple chocolate shake."

I gulped down the food in my mouth. "Triple chocolate shake?"

"You wanna put on weight, Roxy's is the way to go."

I managed to eat half the burger, a quarter of the shake, and a few fries. Rogan collected the plates and tossed the uneaten food in the can.

"Shouldn't we save the leftovers?"

Seemed so wasteful to throw away all that good food.

He looked at the can and back at me. "Fast food doesn't keep well. I'll fetch Roxy's for you anytime you like."

"Oh, okay."

He pitched a jerky treat in the air. Takoda caught it in her teeth and scarfed it down.

My chair scraped across the floor as I stood and tucked it back under the table.

"So, the books helpful?" he asked me.

"Yes."

Rogan leaned with his back against the counter and focused on me as he crossed his arms over his chest. "How many wives does your father have?"

"Thirty when I left for my mission."

"And your mom is?"

"She *was* his fourteenth wife."

"She pass away?"

"Yes. Diabetes."

"Diabetes is usually treatable."

"We had no medical insurance."

"So, what? He just let her die?"

"Yes." My eyes stung and filled with tears. "He said God was calling her to him."

He stared out the kitchen window over the sink. "Your father is a piece of shit."

"He says he's God's messenger."

When his gaze returned to mine, a stone-cold hardness filled his eyes. "You know that's not true."

"Before she died, my mom said she'd changed her mind about the plural life and keeping sweet, like they tell us to do. She warned me my father misled us, and I should escape."

"And what'd you think?"

"I believed her. She was never happy. Always pregnant and struggling to feed us. It's hard to go against what you're taught, but my heart always knew it wasn't right. She told me to fight for my joy."

The stern line of his lips softened. "Is that why you were crying?"

"No. I cried for my siblings. I have to get them out too."

"How many?"

"There were eight of us total. Five are still at the compound. Three girls, two boys. The oldest, Temperance, is sixteen." I swallowed back tears, thinking of them there without me. "Milo is six now. He'll be devastated when he hears about my death." I buried my face in my hands. "I have other half-siblings and cousins... I need to go back."

"You can't."

The finality in his voice ripped a sob from my throat. I couldn't move on and leave them behind.

I gasped as his arm encircled my back and pulled me to his chest, enveloping me in his sculpted frame. Rogan was hugging me.

He smelled like buttermilk biscuits. I tucked my forehead into the planes of his solid pecs. His palm skimmed over my head and warmed my back as he smoothed my braid along my spine.

I hadn't been held like this since I was eighteen and Zook hugged me under our oak tree. He'd caress my back in the same loving way Rogan was doing, although his hand was a lot smaller and more tentative. Rogan's touch was confident and reassuring, as if comforting a crying woman was second nature to him.

The two precious years Zook was my boyfriend were a long dead memory. The only joy of my childhood killed by my father when he caught us kissing and sent Zook away forever. After that, confusion and misery reigned when my mother died and my father started sneaking into my room. I forced my brain to halt the memories and focus on the present.

Right now, Rogan Saxton held me in his arms. How long he held me was my choice. No one would stop us and call us sinners. My life had changed. The embrace of a man could be meaningful and good again like it had been with Zook. My long-forgotten dream of being someone's only wife could come true now. Probably not with Rogan, since he was larger than life and merely helping me get on my way, but I would meet new men. They wouldn't even know about me and my messed up past. It could all work out, like Zook had promised me.

"Please let me go," I whispered.

"It's not safe for you to go back."

Rogan thought I was begging to go home, oblivious to the vivid maelstrom of memories his touch had incited and the shocking revelation that my life was open to love again. I stiffened in his arms and lifted my shoulders, raising my shaking hand to his pec.

Rogan stilled, and as he pulled away, static crackled between us like socks fresh from the dryer.

I exhaled slowly and pressed my hand over my stuttering heart. I shouldn't get attached to Rogan. He hadn't expressed any interest in being friends with me or even contacting me after I got on my feet and left here.

He bent at the waist and squinted as he looked into my eyes. "You afraid of me?"

I glanced around before meeting his gaze. His eyes were the color of raw maple syrup. The cast of his pillowy lips reminded me of wild huckleberries on the river banks back home.

Yes. Terrified of how much I liked it.

"No. You just surprised me." I shrugged. "I guess I'm not used to being hugged."

A muscle twitched in his neck. "Let's sit down."

I followed him to the couch. He let me sit first, then chose a spot leaving two feet of space between us. "I want you to get rid of any ideas about going home for the younger ones."

"I promised my mom. Before she died. She begged me to take care of them."

"That's too much responsibility for you."

"No, it's not."

His jaw worked, and he took a deep breath, blowing it out slowly. "How the hell were you gonna get five kids out if you couldn't even get yourself out?"

"I had a plan." His brows scrunched together. "I saved a portion of my earnings in a jar. After a few years, I had enough for a bus trip out of town. I'd sneak them out through a tunnel in the middle of the night. It would've worked if my father hadn't sent me to Pakistan."

Rogan huffed out a sigh. "Ridiculous."

"What? The plan to escape or my mission?"

"Your suicide mission."

"They said it was safe."

"It's not."

"I know that now."

"Clearly." He ran his hand over his head and scratched behind his neck. He glanced at Takoda, where she'd curled up in her bed outside the kitchen.

"Have you ever cared for a child?" I asked him.

"No."

"There's nothing like the love you feel for them. Stronger than any heavenly love, tighter bond than you have with your brothers in arms. You'd give your soul not to disappoint those trusting little people who've placed all their faith in you. When my mother died, I grieved for them as much as her. When my father would go on a tirade, I fought to protect them from him, no matter the consequence. Even though I'm not their mother, I love them as if I were."

As I spoke, his shoulders lowered and his eyes gentled. Hopefully I'd convinced him how important this was to me.

"Listen, I would very much like to go to Idaho and plant one in your father's forehead—"

"Plant one what?"

"A bullet."

"You mean you'd kill him?"

"It'd be my pleasure." Rogan's eyes gleamed with frightening intensity.

"Oh. That's not what I—"

"I know, but as much as I'd like to, I can't get involved. I've already put my life on the line bringing you here."

"What? Why?"

He looked at the ceiling, and when he returned his gaze to mine, he spoke slowly, like each word was guarded. "I have enemies with long memories. I can't tell you the details. But I gotta lay low. Just give me your word you won't contact your family."

"I promise."

"Good."

He leaned forward with his elbows on his knees and chewed on his lip. He nodded as if he'd come to a decision and turned to face me. "You didn't hear it from me, but the FBI is looking into it."

"They are? I never saw anyone."

"Jeb Barebones has been under surveillance since Jeters went to prison. They'll have him soon enough. I understand you want to help them, but it's best if we let the law handle it."

The authorities were investigating my father? What could they have found out? No one on the compound would dare break the "tell them nothing" rule.

"Your word mean anything to you?" The bitter crease of his eyes and the distrust in his voice carried the sting of rejection. Rogan was a good man, and even if we weren't going to keep in contact in the future, his acceptance mattered to me.

"Yes. It does. I'll keep my word." Honoring the promise would wreck me, but he'd saved my life and given me my freedom. Now he was asking for my compliance to protect his own life.

I owed it to him. But we'd talk about this again soon because I'd also given my mom my word as she lay on her deathbed. I had to go back for Milo and the others. They deserved a chance to find joy too.

"Good." He stood and grabbed Takoda's leash. Her ears perked, and she bounded to him as they left for her walk.

Chapter 5

————

THE NEXT MORNING, ROGAN wasn't home, and I gave TV a try. The news struck a raw nerve in me, so I stopped on a reality show where the woman had her choice of twenty-five handsome bachelors to find a husband. The girl had all the power, and the men fought over her instead of vice versa. I was laughing when Rogan burst through the door in a blast of energy.

"Hey." He dropped his gym bag by the door, and I stared at his backside as he set the alarm. His skin glistened with sweat, and his workout clothes clung to his sinewy muscles. His butt under his tight shorts was firm and round like cantaloupes. Yum.

He glanced at the TV then looked back at me. "You watch TV on the compound?"

"No, but... I've watched TV before."

"How's that?"

"When I babysat, I watched TV there."

"Your parents know this?"

"No. They wouldn't have allowed it if they knew. They believed TV was sinful."

"Huh. It might be, but it's not hurting anyone." He turned and headed for the kitchen. "Hungry?"

Um, yes. I'm suddenly craving ripe melons. "Yes."

He tilted his head for me to follow him. I leaned a shoulder against the doorframe as he hunched over the fridge to look for ingredients. His T-shirt rode up over the top of his shorts, and the band of his briefs peeked out. I could almost make out the lettering...

"Eggs alright?"

"Uh. Sure." I shifted my gaze to the wall. "I can cook. I worked in the kitchen on the compound."

"Don't need you to cook for me, Tess. Need you to eat, gain your strength."

My new name sounded even cuter shortened to Tess.

"How are your injuries?" The eggs he'd cracked sizzled in the skillet.

I rubbed the sores at my wrists. "Getting better. Not as red. I feel stronger today."

"Glad to hear it." He placed two plates of steaming eggs on the counter, pushing one toward me. I stood next to him and burned my tongue on the first bite. "They're good. Thank—"

He stopped me with a raised eyebrow.

"They're yummy." I smiled with my mouth full.

"Got a friend coming over this morning to see you." He shoveled a forkful into his mouth.

"To see me?"

He nodded as he chewed. "He'll get you set up."

"Okay..." Whatever that meant.

Rogan poured us each a glass of orange juice. "He's aware of your history. You can trust him."

"I thought you said trust no one."

"Exceptions. You can trust me, the five other men on that plane, and Dallas and Brock Monroe. That's it."

"Including Blaze?"

"Yes, why?"

"Seems like you don't like him."

"Blaze operates at a level of intelligence beyond what most of us can comprehend. He stirs the pot to entertain himself and throw people off, but he wouldn't betray you."

"And I'll meet Dallas and Brock today?"

"Brock today. Dallas next week."

As Rogan cleared the breakfast dishes, a rat-a-tat-tat sounded from the front room.

Rogan opened the door to a tall figure looming in the corridor. He wore all black and held a bulky manila folder in his left hand. The threat I sensed from him forced me to take a step back as he entered.

Rogan greeted him with a head tilt. "Tessa, this is Brock Monroe."

My worry dissipated when he smiled. An alluring dimple appeared in the scruff on his chin, and he spoke with a mellow voice. "Hello, Tessa."

My hand felt small in his as he wrapped it around mine and gave me a palm-to-palm handshake. "Uh, nice to meet you."

There must be something in the water in Boston because this man had flawless bone structure, long legs, and an athlete's build. Women everywhere must stammer and drop their jaws in adoration like I'd just done.

Rogan coughed to bring our attention to the card table in his nook. He shifted his laptop to the kitchen counter and motioned for us to sit.

We all took seats, and Brock pulled out a compact leather clutch purse from the manila folder. He withdrew a card and held it up for me to read.

Tessa May Harlow

"Your ID."

The Massachusetts driver's license had a recent picture of me smiling at the camera. I didn't remember anyone taking my picture.

"For me? I'm Tessa May Harlow?"

"You are now. Your new birthday is July tenth. You'll be twenty-three this July."

"Again? I turned twenty-three when I was in Afghanistan."

His russet eyes flashed in the morning light coming through the window. "Let's hope the second time around is better."

His tone held compassion like he knew I'd spent my last birthday tied up and frightened.

"You were raised in Wilmington, North Carolina. Your cousin Seth Hendrix lives there, goes by the name Falcon. I suggest you get yourself up to speed on Wilmington and North Carolina so you can be convincing if it comes up in conversation."

The name Falcon sounded familiar, but Brock talked too fast for me to process any of this.

"You came to Massachusetts to go to UMass Boston, my alma mater. You'll get a quality education there."

"What do you mean?"

"You're registered as an undeclared major. Summer session starts end of June."

I'd be going to school in a month? I was nobody. Invisible. "I- I never graduated high school."

"Tessa Harlow earned her GED three months ago."

"What's a GED?"

"It's equivalent to a high school diploma."

My hands shook, and my heart hammered in my chest. A high school diploma? This couldn't be happening.

Brock continued matter-of-factly like this was indeed happening. "Your parents are Dale and Sandrine Harlow from Wilmington. They're a typical working-class couple, devoted to their only daughter. They don't exist, so no inviting friends home for Christmas."

"Of course, no. Uh..."

He held up a large key and fob on a simple ring. "The key to your new truck. Automatic transmission, security alarm." Brock slid his gaze to Rogan. "Fully armored, run-flat tires."

Rogan responded with a slight nod.

I had no idea what armoring and run-flat tires were or why I would need them.

"If you find trouble, stay in your truck and call Rogan or me. Can you drive a truck?" Brock shifted his gaze from Rogan to me.

"I drove the old Chevy around the farm and into town for work sometimes."

"This is a top of the line special edition Sierra Denali. A lot more fun than an old Chevy."

"Oh." I clapped my hands together and held them over my mouth.

Brock watched my reaction with assessing eyes as he handed me the fob. "If you want, we can take your truck out for a break-in run. Leave the city, head up to the mountains? I can give you a four-wheel drive lesson."

"I- I'm not sure." I looked to Rogan, but he'd frozen solid, his face blank. "I haven't thought about leaving Rogan's place."

"When you've been confined in a cage for a long time, it's daunting to venture out, no matter how eager you were to escape. Your shackles have been removed. You're free to fly away."

Why hadn't I considered the possibility before? "You're right. I am." With a phone, a car, and this identity, I could go anywhere I wanted with no one to stop me except myself.

"Then yes!" Brock and Rogan sat motionless as I stood and bounced on my toes. "I'd love a driving lesson. Thank you, Brock." I couldn't hold in the tiny squeak from the back of my throat.

"You come alive like this over a truck, I got a new bike to show you."

"Ooh, I like bikes too." I placed my hands flat on the table and smiled at him. "We had a Schwinn on the compound, but we all had to share it."

He chuckled and wiped his hand along the table top. "Not Schwinn, sugar. I'm talkin' Harley. Even better, take you for a ride on the back of my Ducati. You like to go fast?"

Motorcycles? I'd never even ridden on a moped. "I don't even know. But yes. I'd love to find out!"

The prospect of riding a motorcycle with Brock had me so enthralled, I'd forgotten Rogan was even in the room. When Brock cast his gaze over to Rogan, I looked too and saw he'd turned to stone. He shot a dark look at Brock.

Brock cleared his throat and gathered his hair in his fingers as he ran his hand over his head. Wow, he had long fingers and silky brown hair. He pulled a blue document from the purse and placed it on the table. "Passport." He pointed at two cards in the folds of the purse. "Social security card and a debit card connected to a bank account. You have five thousand dollars in there to get you started."

"What? I mean... Why? You're giving all this to me?"

Brock grinned. "Courtesy of Dallas Monroe. Help you get your feet off the ground."

"Is he your father?"

"My little brother. You'll meet him next Monday. Be at Siege in Somerville at noon. You now have a job at the hottest nightclub in the city."

"I can't..."

"You're a Siege employee now. Dallas takes care of the people who work for him."

I blinked away pending tears. "Please tell him I'm so grateful. I can't wait to meet him. I'll pay him back for all of this."

"No worries." He stood and strode toward the door. "I have to get going, but good luck to you, and I'll see you at Siege."

I waved goodbye to him as Rogan walked him out.

"Thank you," Rogan said to Brock as he shook his hand. "And I'll teach her how to drive the truck," Rogan said more quietly.

Brock ducked his chin to his shoulder and lowered his voice. "Sorry, man. I didn't know. I'll hold off on the bike ride too."

Rogan grunted.

Brock left, and Rogan set the alarm behind him. We stared at each other as I processed the deluge of information swimming in my head. A guilty smile twitched on his lips.

"Did you do all this for me?"

"Nah. Dallas Monroe is a generous guy."

"He doesn't even know me."

"He knows you're a friend of mine. That's enough." He looked around like he was missing something. He swiped his keys from his gym bag by the door. "I'm going to the store. You need anything?"

"Ooh, could you pick up some cornmeal?"

"Cornmeal?"

"Mmm-hmm, with flour and salt, some butter. I wanna make cornbread."

He stared at me like I'd spoken in French.

"And I'd like those Ensure drinks in chocolate, if they have it. Maybe some ice."

His eyes crinkled, and the corner of his mouth turned up. "Why don't you come with me? We'll take your new truck."

I smiled and ran to grab my shoes and my new purse. "That'd be so much fun."

He chuckled under his breath as he opened the door and pushed the buttons of the alarm. "Yes. Fun."

I HAD TO CLEAN OUT the cobwebs and dust from Rogan's oven before I could use it, but the cornbread came out with a crunchy brown crust, and the dome didn't flatten when I set it on top of the stove.

As it cooled, I moved to the bathroom to shave my legs. I spread the shaving cream over my shin and carefully drew the razor up to my knee. Removing ten weeks of hair from my legs was like shedding a second skin.

The front door clicking open and the alarm beeping let me know Rogan was home.

"What's that smell?" his voice called from near the front door.

"Cornbread. Spoonbread, really." Standing on one leg with my foot up on the counter, I had to arch my neck and twist my torso to see him in the living room. I gasped as I took in his new haircut. His square buzzed cut highlighted the thick cords of his neck and made him look more like a soldier.

"Where do you get your hair cut?"

"Why?" He cocked one knee as he looked at me.

"Next time, let me do it for you. I just need scissors and a comb. Do you have an electric razor?"

"You are not cutting my hair."

"Why not? I did it all the time back home. I'm good at it."

He shook his head and walked to the kitchen.

"Let me cut your hair next time," I called to his back. "You don't need to pay a barber when I can do it for free."

The silence of his reply was a firm no to that idea.

As I finished up my right leg and switched to my left, Rogan returned and stood in the bathroom doorway. His eyes darkened as he stared at my bare leg angled above the counter.

"That doesn't taste like any cornbread I've ever had."

"It's spoonbread. It has cheese, sour cream, and all kinds of mushy goodness. You can eat it with a spoon. Did you like it?"

"Fuckin' loved it."

I smiled, and his gaze focused on my mouth. "If you eat all that, I have enough ingredients to make more."

He grunted and nodded as he turned to walk to his computer. Over his shoulder he said, "And close the bathroom door, Sunshine."

Chapter 6

I WOKE UP AND PEEKED into the living room. No Rogan spilling off the couch meant he must be at the gym or walking Takoda.

With the place to myself, I cranked up Taylor Swift in my ear buds and danced to "Shake It Off" as I made my way to the kitchen. I'd heard the song the first time over the radio at the drugstore. I looked it up on my phone and listened to it whenever I could get time alone with an internet connection.

Near the fridge, I chanted the words and wiggled my butt like I really had girlfriends and ex-boyfriends I could sing about, pretending I could shake off whatever life threw at me.

At the other side of the kitchen, I looked through the opening in the far wall. In the nook, Rogan and two men sat at his card table with their guns held motionless in the air, all three sets of eyes focused on me.

Rogan's gaze skimmed over my face and torso. He snapped his head away and shoved a long rod inside the barrel of his gun. Bottles, cloths, and tools were scattered between the dismantled parts on the table.

"Hey, girl." Blaze lifted his chin to get my attention.

He offered me the smile of an old friend, even though I'd barely met him. He wore a black tank top which showed a stark tattoo on his left arm, two arrows crossed at an obtuse angle. Unlike Rogan, he hadn't shaved his beard or cut his hair, and he still looked like a rugged warrior from the desert.

Rogan stopped cleaning his gun and tilted his head to him.

"Tessa, you remember Blaze. His real name is Gavin Turner."

"But no one calls me that."

Rogan nodded at the man across the table from him. "Dirk Legend, known as Diesel."

"Uh, hey." They didn't see my ridiculous Taylor Swift moment, did they? "I actually don't remember much from that night, but hello, nice to see you again."

"How're you doing?" Diesel asked. His hair curled over a small bandage on his temple. His voice struck me as deceptively soft for a man I knew was in the middle of explosions and gunfire just a few days ago.

"I'm doing well, thank you."

"Boggs treating you okay?"

"Yes."

"You look better, Swift," Blaze said.

"Swift?"

"Your little song and dance." He wagged his finger in a circle and pointed at me. "Taylor Swift."

Shoot. I guess they did see me. "Oh. I, uh, love that song."

I smiled at him and he grinned back. Leaning my elbows on the counter, I watched their hands work with casual intention. "Do you guys clean your guns over breakfast often?"

Blaze stopped working and looked up at me. "This is my rifle." He pointed to the gun on the table. "This is my gun." He grabbed his crotch. He raised his rifle in the air. "This is for fighting. This is for fun." He gave his dick a squeeze.

"Oh." I hid my giggle behind my hand.

Rogan narrowed his eyes at Blaze without lifting his head from his work.

Blaze ignored the warning in Rogan's glare and bellowed a rich belly laugh.

Rogan returned to shoving small cloths inside the barrel of his gun, but I could swear his lips twitched and his head shook in laughter.

"LATER, SWIFT," BLAZE called. Diesel waved behind him as they walked out the door with their guns and supplies in cases slung over their shoulders.

I turned off the TV and peered up at Rogan. "Do they live close?"

"Next door."

"I thought I saw them going in the apartment next to this one."

"Hmm-mmm."

"Guns all clean?"

"Rifles."

"Right."

He took a seat next to me on the couch. "What'd you do on that compound when you weren't babysitting, working at the drugstore, or cooking in the kitchen?"

"I woke up before morning prayers and did my chores in the barn. Most days I'd ride my horse before anyone woke up." *And some days Zook joined me.*

"So you worked three jobs and shoveled horse shit?"

"Everyone helps out. We had an Appaloosa mare named Traveler. Beautiful pearl-white with chestnut spots."

"Solid horses, Appaloosas."

"She was sure-footed and fast. I'd ride her through rivers and trails for hours. She never let me down."

"What else did you do?"

"I taught the younger kids." I stared at the black flatscreen, remembering my hours in the schoolroom with my sisters and brothers teaching them to read and do arithmetic. I didn't want Milo to find himself in the same position as Zook and some of the other boys who worked construction for my father. "We raised them as a community. It wasn't all bad."

"You spent your childhood shoveling shit and taking care of kids."

"What's wrong with that?"

"Young girls should be out doing stupid things."

"Like what?"

He crossed one ankle over his knee and wrapped a hand over his calf. "Chasing false hope. Believing in fairy tales."

"And you don't believe? How old are you?"

"Thirty-three."

"Oh yes, old man. Life is miserable, so why try? If you live to be ninety-three, you still have sixty years left, almost a lifetime. Are you going to live those years believing there's no hope?"

"One day some bastard is gonna get the best of me. Maybe when I stop to rescue a hostage"—he winked at me—"he'll plant one in my back. The way I'm living, I'm not gonna make it to ninety-three."

"So stop living that way."

"Not that simple. I've trained my whole life to get where I am—made immeasurable sacrifices. I'm called to be a soldier."

"Called? I'm not buying that called stuff anymore. My father felt called to have thirty wives. My whole family believed they'd been called to live a life that caused children to suffer. If your calling hurts people, you need to find another way to answer that call."

Rogan grunted.

"You don't need to seek out war zones, battling the worst criminals in this world. Life is what you choose to focus on. Focus on beauty."

"And ignore war?"

"Yes. Choose not to dwell on it."

"I'm not the kind to pretend it's not happening."

"I have two sisters I'll never see again. I could sit around and grumble about the unfairness, or I can tackle the day in front of me."

"What happened to them?"

"Pride and Sin disaffiliated when they returned from their missions. They're supposedly dead to me as I am to them."

"Pride and Sin?" He shook his head. "How'd they get out?"

"Someone outside the Brotherhood sponsored them. I don't know who."

"And you didn't have a sponsor?"

"No. I don't think my dad would let me go even if I could find someone willing to sponsor me out."

Rogan nodded.

"Anyway, lots of horrible things happened to me. My point is, I don't ruminate on the pain, I choose to rise above and enjoy the beauty right in front of me." I raised my hand and motioned to him from head to toe. "Like you, Rogan. You're a beautiful person."

He rubbed his hand over his head and turned his gaze to the floor. His golden eyes tilted up to me, but he kept his head down. He raised one eyebrow, and pulled his lower lip with his teeth. The raw lust smoldering in his eyes sent a hook careening into my chest. It reeled me in toward him, urging me to lean over and... kiss him. I wanted to tug his shirt off and dig my fingers into his pecs. What would his skin taste like on my lips? Um. Whoa.

"I took a ruby necklace," I blurted out.

"What?"

The deep breath I took barely calmed me, so I rambled. "At the drugstore. We had a countertop display. A shiny red square surrounded by little fake diamonds on a sparkling silver chain. It wasn't expensive, but I couldn't buy it even if I could afford it. Jewelry from the outside wasn't allowed, and red is the color of the devil."

Lines creased in his forehead.

"While my manager worked in the stockroom, I slipped the necklace in my pocket. My heart was beating so fast, I thought Satan would appear and strike me down. I never even wore the necklace. I twirled it in my pocket, played with the flat and sharp edges of the stone, pressed it as hard as I could and marveled at its strength. I expected it to heat up and singe a hole in my dress. My manager would see me as a thief. I'd be fired and my father would discipline me."

My head shook in disbelief.

"I didn't burst into flames. My soul wasn't damned. I enjoyed my time with that necklace while I had it. I appreciated its beauty, the person who designed it, the workers that created it, my manager for selecting it as an item the people of the town might like to spend their hard earned money on. At the end of my shift, I put it back in the display. But the loss churned in my stomach. I had held precious color in my hands, given it back, and returned to my dreary life at the compound. Before bed, I would dream I wore that necklace in the crook of my neck. Then I cried myself to sleep, praying my father wouldn't sense the sin of my thoughts."

Rogan turned toward me and pressed one palm into the couch. "Coveting a necklace is not a sin." His voice dropped and became scratchy. "It's normal to find something attractive and want to own it." He cleared his throat and broke our eye contact. "Besides, holding a necklace in your pocket for a few hours, then putting it back is not stealing, so stop beating yourself up about it."

He was right. I didn't actually steal it, and I shouldn't feel guilty for admiring it.

"You want a ruby necklace? Go online and buy yourself one. Clothes, jewelry, school supplies. Get whatever you need."

"Just order all that online? And what? Have it delivered here?"

"Sure."

"I don't... Okay. I'll try."

"You're sweet."

"Don't call me sweet." I stood and glared down at him. "Sweet makes me sick. Sweet shackles and gags me till I can't breathe. My mother died trying to keep sweet."

His head snapped back, and his brows drew up. "Fair enough. No more sweet." He chuckled and turned his gaze to the floor.

Chapter 7

I SLAMMED MY PHONE down on the coffee table. "I give up."

Rogan looked up from his laptop. "On what?"

"Shopping online. How does anyone choose? I have no idea what size I am or what kind of clothes I even like. And it's all so expensive."

Rogan stared at me for a moment before picking up his phone and swiping the screen.

"Dallas, calling in a favor. T needs shoes, clothes, stuff for school."

Oh my gosh, Rogan's generosity knew no limits.

"Remind her, discreet." He paused. "Just taking precautions. Thank you."

He hung up and looked at me. "Mrs. Monroe's coming to take you shopping tomorrow at eleven a.m."

"Mrs. Monroe?"

He slipped his phone into his pocket. "Dallas's wife. This is your chance to practice your public story. You came out here to go to school. You're starting at Siege on Monday. She isn't aware Dallas Monroe provided you with cash, a truck, and ID."

"Okay." I hated to lie to people I'd just met, but lying and keeping quiet were second nature after growing up fearing outsiders and appeasing my father. I could do it if it protected Rogan and prevented my father from finding me.

"And she thinks I'm retired military. Do not even allude to me and my team being in Afghanistan—best to avoid discussing me at all."

"What about Blaze and Diesel?"

"She doesn't know them, but to everyone else Blaze is a fireman. Diesel is a cop."

"Okay." Why did he keep such elaborate secrets from his friends? "What if I mess this up?"

"You'll be fine. If she figures out you're lying, it's not critical, but it means you need to work harder on putting up appearances."

"Okay."

"And don't worry about the price. Dallas pays generously. Just get what you want."

"Did you work for him?"

"Yeah."

I looked around at his sparsely furnished apartment. Nothing in his place appeared to be new or expensive. He glanced at me and walked away.

―――――――――

I CAME OUT OF THE SHOWER and heard music from the living room. I opened the bathroom door and found Rogan sitting on the edge of the couch hunched over an acoustic guitar. The silver beads of his dog tag chain circled his neck and dipped behind the guitar at his chest. His bare shoulders shined in the light from the lamp. The tattoo on his right arm was an elaborate letter *E*.

Takoda slept near his feet as his fingers strummed a mellow song with a sad, thoughtful lyric. I leaned against the door jamb and absorbed the notes, as if I could learn more about Rogan if I just knew the words to the song. How could this rough and tumble man who was forged from stone play such a tender melody without breaking the strings?

Without looking up or moving, he stopped playing. The vibrations of his last notes dissipated in the room.

"Don't stop. It's beautiful. What is it?"

"Pearl Jam. Look it up." He set the guitar down next to him on the couch and stared at it. I couldn't help checking out his bare chest. Stark, jet-black stars and stripes decorated his pecs.

"I didn't know you play." I took a step closer to the couch.

"I don't."

"I just heard you."

"I don't play. Not anymore. It was a way to pass time on base."

I rested my hip on the arm of the couch. He turned his head with a tilt of his chin and perused my body from the bottom up. My legs were shaved and smooth. I was wearing a white T-shirt but no shorts.

His eyes stopped on my chest. My hair had made a wet spot near my boobs, and my tee had become see-through. My nipples poked the fabric. Darn. I should've worn a bra.

"Got towels for your hair."

I crossed my arms over my chest, causing my shirt to hitch up. His gaze cut to my thighs, and his eyebrows scrunched. My hips had filled out, and the underwear we'd purchased that first night had grown tight. The tingling I felt earlier when he looked at me returned. Rogan and I were no longer rescuer and freed captive. Somehow we'd become man and woman.

Oh gosh, what was I thinking? I barely knew Rogan. He'd told me nothing about himself, and yet his eyes claimed my body like it belonged to him. I belonged to no one for the first time in my life. Before anything more developed between us, he'd have to divulge some of his secrets.

"Why were you in Afghanistan the day you rescued me?"

His back stiffened and his face hardened into steel. "That's classified."

"Why? Did you know I was being held hostage?"

"No. I knew those men had a history of taking American women hostage. I knew you were in grave danger the second I saw you. Don't talk about it to anyone, hear me?"

"I won't—"

"And don't ask any more fucking questions." His voice went from controlled to harsh. "We need to get you your own place."

My heart plunged into the pit of a bottomless well. He wanted me to leave now? I was just settling into life in the outside world. I'd enjoyed the time we'd spent together and our conversations. And despite my efforts to keep Rogan at a distance, I'd developed a crush on him and fooled myself into thinking he might like me in return. But he considered me a nuisance, a charity case he couldn't wait to get off his hands. I didn't fit into his life at all.

"I'll start looking for a place tomorrow."

I walked into my room and leaned against the closed door. The crash of mangled guitar strings striking the wall resounded through the apartment. Followed by the dull thud of wood hitting the floor. I flinched, cupping a hand over my mouth.

THE NEXT MORNING, I hid in my room and got ready for my shopping trip. I couldn't face Rogan after our tense discussion and guitar smashing last night. A message beeped on my phone.

R: Playlist for you

I clicked on the link and it took me to a Spotify playlist titled "Beyond Taylor Swift."

The first song was the Pearl Jam one he'd played last night. "Better Man." The singer had the sexiest voice I'd ever heard. I scrolled through the list. Some artists I'd heard of like The Doors, but lots I hadn't like Zac Brown Band and Dusty Springfield. I sat down on the bed to listen, but Rogan's knock on the bedroom door startled me.

"Mrs. Monroe's here to take you shopping."

"I'll be right there."

My hands shook as I tucked my hair behind my ears again. No braid for me today. Meeting my boss's wife and going on a real shopping trip might be commonplace for other girls, but for me, it was monumental.

As I made my way to the living room, Rogan opened the door wide and a curvy brunette walked straight toward me. A second woman with long, red hair lingered in the doorway by Rogan. He glanced at her but didn't change his stern expression. She took a deep breath and joined her friend next to me.

A bulky man stood outside the door instead of coming inside. He turned sideways, clasping one wrist with the other hand. His jeans stretched tight on his legs as he widened his stance and pulled his shoulders back. Rogan gave him a slight nod and closed the door.

"Tessa, this is Mrs. Monroe," he pointed to the brunette, "and Tori."

Tori looked back at Rogan, and he met her gaze. I could not read a darn thing on their faces, but some understanding passed between them.

"Oh please. I'm Cyan. Nice to meet you." She embraced me and brushed her cheek against mine. Her vanilla perfume tickled my nose. "So, I hear you're new to Boston and looking for a bargain?"

I nodded because even if Rogan said not to worry, I needed to be careful how I spent the money.

"Have you been to Burlington Mall yet?"

"No."

"Oh, girl. You gotta go to the promised land. Do you need shoes? Please say you need shoes."

"I need shoes."

She clapped her hands. "Excellent." She took my arm in hers.

I picked up the purse Brock brought for me and followed my new friends out the door.

"Later, Rogan." Cyan waved over her shoulder.

"Uh, bye," I said as the man outside trailed behind us down the corridor.

"That's Lux. Don't worry about him. He's the quiet type." She spoke casually like all women in Boston had a burly guard follow them when they go shopping.

―――――――――

FAST MOVING ESCALATOR teeth nipped at my ankles, and sleek floors squeaked under my sneakers as I scurried behind Cyan and Tori, who were clearly in their element and felt no need to slow down to admire a flower arrangement or window display. These two women were on a mission and knew where to go and exactly how to ignore distractions. Somehow Lux managed to keep up with our mad dashes from store to store.

At the first store we entered, I held up a sparkly T-shirt with gems appliqued into fun swirls and scrolls. "I like this one," I said to Cyan.

Her eyes bugged out. "Oh, you like the diamanté? Me too! A girl's gotta bring her own sparkles sometimes, liven up boring everyday old life!"

Once Cyan realized I liked sparkles, she picked me the perfect pair of skinny jeans with rhinestones in fancy designs covering the pockets and trailing down the legs.

"These fit. Size seven. But those fit too and they're size six," I said to Cyan, holding up two pairs of jeans.

"Don't you hate how sizing isn't consistent?"

"Mmm-hmm." I had no idea sizes weren't consistent, but I guess I was right about the internet being confusing. If the sizes were different, I'd have to try them on. I encountered the same dilemma with the shoes. My feet fit snugly in a six and a half or had more room in a size seven.

Cyan spoke quickly and added shoes to her cart without even trying them on. "You never know when you might need pink heels, or purple gym shoes, or golden sandals, and you always need killer boots. Oh, look, these are on sale!"

Tori nodded her agreement as she followed behind Cyan like Cyan was speaking the gospel.

"Let's get new makeup," Tori declared as if women got new makeup every time they went shopping.

"I don't, I mean, I don't really wear much makeup."

"And you don't need it. You're so pretty. But, let's do it anyway. For fun."

Cyan and Tori marched into Sephora and purchased a complete set of all the "must haves" of the season, unaware this was my first season ever.

"Can I do a free makeup application for you?" the attractive girl at the counter asked me.

"Sure."

I watched as she dabbed foundation on my face making me look paler than I already was. Then she slowly stenciled brown liquid eyeliner, dusted rose on my cheeks with a soft fluffy brush, and applied three layers of light pink color on my lips. "You have gorgeous big blue eyes. I'm just outlining them with a little smoke. Your cheekbones are exceptional. Just add bronzer here to accentuate them."

When she was done, I tried not to act surprised, but I didn't recognize the girl in the mirror. She hadn't gone too extreme or dark. I was still me, but fresh and light and happy and colorful.

Cyan's smile held mischief, as if she knew how much this meant to me. She hugged me like my sisters used to hug me, loving and warm. "You look incredible."

They took me through the jewelry department at Neiman Marcus. "Ooh, Tessa. Look at these." Cyan held up a set of chandelier earrings with blooms of dainty rubies and diamonds dangling from invisible chains. The price tag said twenty-five hundred dollars.

"Wow, so beautiful." I rubbed my earlobe. I couldn't imagine wearing crafted art like the earrings Cyan held up. They looked like something a princess should wear. "I don't have pierced ears."

"What? Do you wear clip-ons?"

"No."

"You mean you've never worn earrings?" Tori asked.

I shook my head.

"Do you want to?" Cyan asked with her eyebrows pulled together.

Did I accidentally say something to tip them off about me? Was getting your ears pierced a rite of passage in the outside world?

"I don't know. Yes. I think so."

Cyan marched me straight to a piercing counter.

"It'll hurt initially, but after a few days, you won't feel it at all. You wanna do it?"

"Yes."

"What kind of earrings would you like?" The technician pointed to a display of silver and gold balls and rings, but my eyes glued to the colored gems.

"These are birthstones. What month is your birthday?"

My real birthday or my fake birthday? Fake, of course. "July."

"July is ruby." She pointed to two sparkling red stones rounded with silver edges.

"Then I'll take ruby, please."

Cyan and Tori smiled with anticipation like I was their child getting her first piercing.

The technician marked my earlobes with black dots and showed them to me in a mirror. "Like that?"

"Yes, looks good."

She loaded the rubies into a device that looked like a staple gun. "I'll put some alcohol and a little numbing gel. It'll sting for a moment."

"Okay."

She pressed the cold metal to my ear. With a snap, a sharp pinch struck my ear, and I squeezed Cyan's hand.

"One more."

I anticipated the pinch on the other ear and didn't flinch as hard.

"All done."

She held up a mirror, and my fingers rubbed the sensitive skin on my lobe and the hard stone now residing there. This color was mine and

I was free to wear it. I felt the sting of tears before my eyes started blinking.

"Aww. What's wrong? Does it hurt?"

"Huh?" I dropped my hand from my ear and focused on Cyan. "No. I'm just happy."

"You always remember your first earrings."

I nodded and dabbed at the corner of my eye, trying not to mess up my makeup. I'd never forget this moment.

"I remember mine because I slipped them in my purse and walked out of the store without paying," she said matter-of-factly.

"You stole them?"

"Mmm-hmm. Got caught. The store manager said she wouldn't call the cops if I promised to leave and never come back. I felt terrible."

Oh, Cyan. I took a necklace. I know how you feel.

I held my words in. I couldn't give away more than I already had by not wearing makeup, or earrings, or knowing how to shop.

We passed a hair salon. "Want to get your hair cut?"

I imagined the tears I'd cry through the cutting of these locks I'd been forced to wear my entire lifetime. "Not today."

At Victoria's Secret, Cyan bought garters and stockings that looked uncomfortable and useless. She explained most women don't wear stockings anymore but she liked them because they're sexy—and her husband was crazy about them. I splurged on thong underwear, nighties, and colorful bra and panty sets.

My final purchase of the day was for my dad. To piss him off, I bought the shortest pair of cutoff jeans I could find with bright red sparkles on the pockets. I tried them on with heels, but I was too wobbly to walk in the mall, and I didn't want Cyan and Tori to see my lack of experience, so I wore a pair of chocolate suede boots with a low heel and strutted out of the store with a smile on my face.

Come get me, Satan.

"Oh, girl. Those shorts are to die for on you," Tori said as we walked to lunch.

Ha! If she only knew my father would actually kill me for wearing them.

———

"HE'S NOT GOING TO JOIN us?" I pointed my thumb at Lux who stood at the bar of the sports themed restaurant Cyan had chosen for lunch.

"No. He likes to watch hockey from the TV in the bar," Cyan answered.

I glanced over my shoulder at Lux. He stood with his back to the screen and scanned the restaurant with the same alert caution I'd seen in Rogan's eyes so many times.

"Why do you have a bodyguard?" I asked Cyan.

She shared a look with Tori before leaning forward. "My husband is a little, uh, overprotective," she whispered.

Tori chuckled and exchanged a knowing grin with Cyan.

"Are you comfortable with that?" Was she under the thumb of some tyrannical dictator like my father?

She shrugged and peeked over at Lux before returning her attention to me. "It took some getting used to. I've been alone most of my life, now I have constant company. But Dallas feels it's necessary to protect me and it eases his mind. It's a small concession on my part compared to all he gives me in return." She twirled the rocks on her left ring finger.

"Can I ask you another question?"

"Of course. What's on your mind?"

"Is he faithful?"

Her eyebrows rose, and she shared another look with Tori. "Yes. We hit a few bumps in the beginning, but he's proven his trustworthiness to me. There's no one else for either of us. It's easy with the right person."

"I'm excited to meet him on Monday."

"Now his brother, on the other hand, is another story."

"His brother?"

"Brock."

Hmm. I wasn't sure if I was supposed to tell Cyan I'd met Brock already. Probably not. "He's not faithful?"

"He has so many women, he doesn't know which way to turn. I bet if he had a chance, he'd legalize bigamy just so he wouldn't have to choose one woman for a wife."

They'd laugh more if I shared the inside joke with them, but Rogan trusted me, so I kept my mouth shut.

"So how was it with Rogan at his place? Seemed awkward," Cyan asked Tori.

"A little weird seeing him for the first time since your wedding."

A green haze blurred my vision. Tori dated Rogan? She didn't seem like his type. I guess I didn't know him very well.

"Did he call you or say anything?"

"He sent a get well card after I got shot, but I don't expect Rogan to talk about us. He's not that kind of guy."

The waiter arrived and served us our drinks with a big basket full of breadsticks. I took a sip of my iced tea and swallowed my jealousy. Rogan wasn't mine anyway.

"You seem over it," Cyan said.

Tori nodded. "I learned my lesson and moved on."

So it was over between them? "What lesson?" I asked Tori.

"If a man is into you, he lets you know. I'm not chasing anyone around who doesn't want me like crazy." She narrowed her eyes at me and looked down at my hands fidgeting with my napkin. "So, Tessa. Tell me about you. You're cousins with a friend of Rogan's?"

Oh no, Tori had me on the hot seat. "Yes, Falcon's my cousin. Our mothers are sisters." There, that was convincing, right?

"Interesting." Tori's gaze remained focused on me while I glanced around the restaurant to avoid eye contact. "Why're you staying with Rogan? Couldn't get into the dorms?"

"Uh... This was a last minute decision."

"What about off-campus housing? You couldn't get an apartment?" She was clearly savvy and smart, and her tone conveyed she wasn't falling for any of my bullpucky.

"I'm looking... now. I just..." When the waiter arrived with our lunch, I caught Cyan's eyes and cleared my throat, giving her my *please help me* look.

Cyan sat up straight in her chair and reached for my hand. "You'll have to excuse my friend. Tori's an attorney, always digging for a juicy hidden angle. Even if there isn't one to be found."

"I'm sorry. I shouldn't have interrogated you like that." Tori finally pulled her sleuthhound eyes off me and turned her attention to her food.

"It's fine. Honestly, I sort of fell into this situation, and I'm not exactly sure what will happen next."

"I totally understand." Cyan gave my hand a squeeze. "When I first came to Boston, I was a mess. I'd gotten myself arrested for prostitution in Atlanta and owed some bad dudes a lot of money. I ended up at Siege in a failed attempt to worm myself out of trouble."

"And then you met Dallas?"

"Yes. I was there to spy on him, but he blew my cover the first night!"

"Wow. You must be brave."

"Not brave. Desperation will drive a woman to do crazy things."

"So Dallas helped you?"

"Yes. He put me under his protection. He said they'd never come after me again."

"I'm so happy it worked out for you."

"It did. And it will for you too. If you want to talk to someone, we're here whenever you're ready."

"Thank you."

MY BAGS RUSTLED AS I plopped them on the couch in Rogan's apartment.

"Whew! Shopping is hard work." I flipped my hair back from my face.

Rogan appraised my appearance from his place at his card table. A sly grin grew slowly on his lips. "Looks like it went well."

"Yes! Burlington Mall is a shopping utopia. I love Cyan and Tori. I stuck to the story, but I think they knew something was fishy."

He stood and walked slowly toward me. "Maybe someday you can tell them. But not now."

"Okay. It's difficult lying to them and wanting to make friends with them too."

"I know, but you'll get used to it. You got your ears pierced?"

"Umm, yes." I fiddled with my new ruby stud.

"Makeup too?"

"Yes."

"First time for both?"

Insecurity washed over me. Was the makeup too dark? I must look ridiculous trying to be a city girl when I'm nothing but a farm girl who's never seen the world. "Yes. Maybe I shouldn't have."

I picked up my bags and walked toward his room.

"Your cheeks are hanging out."

I stopped and turned back to him. What the heck? Why was Rogan acting this way? "No they aren't."

"Sunshine, if I can see the crease of your ass, your cheeks are hanging out."

I'm not letting his judgmental tone ruin this for me. I'm wearing my first pair of earrings, and I think I look fabulous with my makeup done. He needs to keep his trap shut. The bags swayed as I propped my hands on my hips. "Are you my daddy now approving my clothes?"

"I'm not your daddy." His voice was deep and his lips twisted like he found this funny.

"Good. Even if you were, I'm not living for his approval anymore anyway. I think I look awesome."

"You're stunning. You know you're beautiful without all this, right?"

"Um..." Wow. Rogan threw compliments out so easily.

"But with it, Christ, I reckon you were gorgeous with your hair braided and no makeup, walking around on that compound, a few cute freckles on your nose. Your curves hidden under a dress the color of sherbert. I bet every guy there wanted you but they couldn't touch the preacher's daughter. If those men saw you today, they'd curse

God's name and kick themselves for not breaking through the walls and stealing you away when they had a chance."

"Oh." Warmth fluttered up from my belly to my cheeks. Did Rogan really see me that way?

"So yeah, you should have done this."

"Um, thank you." Oh, darn. He said not to say thank you. Did that apply to effusive compliments that made my breath catch in my throat? Oh well, I'd already said it. I spun quickly to pick up my bags and escape.

I took one step before Rogan's front door burst open. Blaze walked in and punched the console of the alarm to stop the beeping. "Boggs—" As he turned, his eyes landed on me and popped wide open. "Swift?"

I dropped the bags in one hand and waved three fingers at him. "Hi, Blaze."

He circled around me and whistled. "Holy shit. You look hot. You're fuckin' on fire. I mean you were a chili pepper before, but now... Whew! Ha-ban-er-o." His hand punctuated each syllable with a swish in my direction.

I stared at my boots so he couldn't see the crimson color my cheeks must have turned. "Thanks."

"I'm serious. You just made a huge deposit in my spank bank."

"You got a reason for bustin' in my door, Blaze?" Rogan's angry voice suddenly sounded close. When I looked up, he was standing on high-alert between Blaze and me, shoulders taut, face red, and fists clenched, as he stared Blaze down.

Rogan's calm demeanor was incredibly appealing, but when he got intense like this, holy moly, sexy overload. His testosterone filled the air like thick smoke.

Blaze stepped back with his hands up. "Diesel sent me, man. Calm down." He looked down and wiped the sweat from his palms on his jeans. "Yolanda wants to invite Swift over for drinks tonight."

Rogan grunted and unwound his fists.

"Whaddya say, Swift? Wanna consume a little brain grenade with us?" Blaze leaned sideways to make eye contact with me around Rogan's massive body.

"Brain grenade?"

"Just a little beer. Chance of tequila."

"Oh, sure." I tried to sound casual. Sure, Blaze, I drink beer and tequila with hot Army guys all the time.

"Come over at seven."

"Okay."

"Later." His gaze traversed my bare legs one last time before he tilted his chin at Rogan and walked out. Rogan glared at the closed door before returning to his work.

Chapter 8

————

I SPENT THE REST OF the afternoon practicing my walk in the ice-cream cone wedge heels and getting used to my earrings. At seven o'clock, Rogan was gone, so I tottered the few steps down the hallway to Blaze and Diesel's apartment. I knocked on the door and held my breath. I could do this. My first party in the outside world. Rogan's friends must be nice guys, right? Even if they cleaned their rifles at breakfast, they'd been nothing but kind to me. This would be easier if Cyan and Tori could go with me, but facing this alone would be good for me too.

When Diesel opened the door, his warm smile and open arms immediately calmed my nerves. "C'mon in." I followed him to a small kitchen. Blaze waved to me as he walked in from the balcony carrying a plate of cooked meat.

"Uh, hey, Blaze." His faded blue jeans fit him snug and his long-sleeved black T-shirt hugged his bulging shoulders.

"Swift." Blaze placed a platter of barbequed meat on the table.

Diesel sat down next to a striking woman with straight brown hair and blunt bangs. "This is Yolanda."

Wow, Yolanda was showing lots of cleavage. I thought I was being daring with my low-cut blouse, but she wore a shirt made of two triangles that tied behind her neck. I could see the bottom of her perfectly shaped breasts. She must know Victoria's Secret because there's no way I could get my breasts that round even with a miracle bra.

"Hi, Yolanda."

"Hi, Tessa." She offered me a pleasant smile.

"Have a seat." I sat down opposite Diesel.

"What's your poison? Beer, wine, tequila?" Blaze asked me.

"Um... Wine?"

"Sure." He went to the kitchen and returned with a wine cooler. He winked at me as he twisted the cap and handed the bottle to me.

Yolanda chatted about the wedding, and the guys remained quiet as we ate a delicious meal of steak, potatoes, and corn. The wine cooler tasted fruity and bubbly.

After dinner, Blaze opened a box and placed it in the middle of the table. He pointed to the assortment of sweets and dried fruit inside.

"No, thanks. I'm stuffed."

He tossed what looked like a chocolate coconut cluster in his mouth and sat down opposite me. "Let's play I never."

"How do you play?" I asked.

"You say something you've never done. Anyone who has done it has to take a drink."

"Okay." I kept my voice even, but stifled my laugh. Blaze was trying to get dirt on me.

Good luck, Blaze. There's not much for me to tell.

"I'll go first," Blaze said. "I've never had sex in an elevator."

Diesel and Yolanda smirked and drank at the same time, but Blaze didn't take a sip of his beer. Oh, this should be interesting.

"Your turn, Swift." Blaze popped another cluster in his mouth.

The door flew open and Rogan strode in. He snatched the box of treats off the table. "Don't steal my mail."

Blaze laughed as he chewed the lumpy treat. "Your mom rocks the exotic care packages, Boggs. She'd want her little prince to share with his loyal subjects."

"Fuck you." Rogan sat down on the couch in the living room and tossed the box next to him. He put his feet up on the coffee table and clicked on the TV.

"As I was saying... Your turn, Swift." Blaze tilted his head at me.

Hmm. Obviously they expected me to say something about sex, but I didn't want to announce my virginity to the whole table.

Following Blaze's lead, I said, "I've never had sex in a car."

They all took sips of their beers and looked at Diesel for his turn.

"I've never sucked cock." Diesel kept his eyes on Yolanda.

"Ugh." Yolanda groaned. "So unfair." She took a sip of her beer.

Diesel swiveled his gaze to Blaze and raised an eyebrow. Blaze took a casual sip of his beer. What did that mean? Did I understand the rules correctly? Did Blaze just admit to being gay?

All eyes came to me to see if they had me. The truth is Zook and I had experimented with it a few times when we were out at the reservoir. His dick was in my mouth when my father caught us. I took a sip of my wine cooler before the horrid memories and pain of that day showed on my face.

Rogan glanced at me when I pressed the bottle to my lips. He masked his expression and turned his attention back to the TV. Why did it always feel like he knew what I was thinking?

"I've never tasted pussy," Yolanda announced to the table.

Diesel and Blaze smirked as they raised their beers again.

"Would you like to?" Diesel asked Yolanda.

She peered at him with a twinkle in her eye. A naughty grin lit up his face as he trailed one hand up her thigh, the other curling behind her neck to pull her in for a kiss. I squirmed in my seat and searched the room for something else to focus on.

I stopped on Rogan's eyes locked on me. His tongue ran over his top teeth under his lip like he was chewing on something. The hunger in his face sent a tremor from my chest to my belly. My hand slid down the bottle of my drink, and I gulped back the lump in my throat.

"Knock that the fuck off, you two," Blaze said.

What? Huh? Did he catch the heated look Rogan and I were sharing?

"Diesel, you need to move your ass into Yolanda's place tonight. I'm sick of this shit."

Whew. He wasn't talking to us.

Diesel pulled away from a dazzled Yolanda. "You can wait a few more weeks. Make her mama happy."

"Yes, because making her mama happy is such an important part of my life. God, Diesel, you're so whipped."

"That I am." Diesel gazed lovingly into Yolanda's eyes.

The passion painted on their faces was so tangible, watching them intruded on their privacy.

Blaze started talking and gave me an excuse to look away. "Hey, Swift. You should come live here when Diesel leaves. Got two bedrooms. You'd have your own bathroom. It's not the Bel Air, but it's a decent place to crash."

From the corner of my eye, I saw Rogan stand.

"Ooh, I love that idea." My father would absolutely hate me living with a male roommate. "When's the wedding?"

"Two weeks," Yolanda answered my question.

"Cool. And, Swift," Diesel chimed in, "you're coming to our wedding."

"What? No. I can't. I'd have no idea how to get there."

"Boggs'll take ya," Diesel said.

"Oh please. I'd love to have her there," Yolanda begged.

"That settles it. My bride wants her there. You'll bring her to watch me tie my can to Yolanda's bumper."

Yolanda slapped him on the bicep.

"I'll take her," Blaze said with his beer raised over the table.

"No. I'll take her." Rogan's voice boomed from behind me.

"Okay, Boggs, whatever. My turn again. I've never taken it up the ass." Blaze focused on Diesel, who held his gaze and defiantly didn't raise his beer. Blaze tipped his bottle toward Diesel and... took another sip. Okay. I totally didn't understand the rules to this game. If Blaze was following them, he'd totally admitted to sucking cock and um, taking it up the ass.

"Damn you, Blaze." Yolanda took a sip of her drink, oblivious to whatever the heck was going on between Diesel and Blaze.

As I shook my head and laughed, Rogan's firm hand wrapped around my upper arm and yanked me up from the table.

"Hey! What're you doing? We were having fun." Blaze stood to stop Rogan, but we were already at the door.

"Uh, bye..." I said to the group as Rogan hauled me out of their apartment.

My ankles twisted in my heels as he dragged me through the corridor and into his place. Good thing he held me up because I must've looked like a drunken scarecrow.

He ignored Takoda's greeting and pegged his gaze on me. "How drunk are you?"

"Not at all. I was winning that game before you pulled me away."

"Why're you walking like that?"

"I can't walk in heels, drunk or sober."

As I talked, he dipped his chin and crowded me backward. "Moving in with Blaze is not a good idea."

"Why not? I need a place, and he'll have an empty room in two weeks." My legs bowed out as I wobbled on my heels.

The weight of his big hands squeezed my hips and forced me back till I hit the wall. "You can do better than that place."

"It's just temporary. I'll look for an apartment of my own eventually, after I get more settled."

My awareness shifted from our conversation to the heat of his body invading my space. Standing close to Rogan was like being right up next to Traveler. A powerful beast that could smash your skull in with one kick of a hoof, but you know she won't because her shrewd eyes communicate with your soul.

"You wanna tell me how a girl who grew up on a fundamentalist commune has... sucked cock?"

Sweat beaded on my skin, and the air between us thickened. "If you think that place wasn't sexually charged, you're wrong."

"Really?"

"Mmm-hmm. There's an undercurrent of sex to everything. Girls know real young they'll be getting married, and they wonder who they'll get. They dream of having sex and making babies. We're taught all about intercourse and making sure the man is pleased."

"Hmm."

"One husband is sleeping with eight, ten, thirty women. Sometimes he takes two or three at a time." I lowered my voice to a whisper. "It's all about the sex."

"Huh." He stared at my mouth as I teased my bottom lip with my teeth.

"Did you have a boyfriend back home?"

I nodded, keeping my eyes on his. "We kept it secret."

"How long?"

"Started when we were both sixteen."

He pressed his palm flat to the wall over my head. "You have sex with him?"

"Rogan..."

"Tell me."

"No."

"No you won't tell me, or no you didn't have sex with him?"

"I didn't have sex with him."

"When did it end?"

"When I was eighteen. My dad caught us and sent him away."

"What was your boyfriend's name?"

"Why does it matter?"

"Want his name."

"Zook Guthrie."

"Did you love him?"

"I don't know. He was my only friend when I was a teenager."

"Do you still love him?"

"No. I haven't seen him in years. I rarely think of him. It came up because of the game." *And because you're much sexier than him, and I want you more than I ever did Zook.*

His gaze dipped to the cleavage above the buttons of my blouse and dropped to my feet. His lips mashed into a crooked line. "You got ice-cream cones on your shoes?"

"Aren't they cute?"

"Mmm-hmm."

My breath caught in my throat when he leaned in close to my ear. "Cute." His earthy scent drifted to my nose. I closed my eyes and inhaled, holding a piece of him captive in my lungs.

His lips skimmed along my ear. They felt as smooth and soft as I'd imagined. I angled my head to press his mouth to my temple.

A magnetic force drew my hands up to settle on his stomach. My fingertips only grazed his abs, but his raw strength charged through my arms.

He dipped one shoulder and weaved his fingers into the hair at the base of my scalp, tugging till my head tipped back. "Tempting."

My breath left me and my frame went weak. He supported my weight with his arm and trailed his nose along my raised jaw. "So fucking hard for you right now."

My fingers curled into his shirt.

Come closer. Kiss me.

A frustrated growl emanated from deep in his chest. He clenched then released my hair and inched away from me like he was fighting a fierce wind.

He tilted his head down and glued me with his golden eyes. "Goodnight, Sunshine." His voice softened.

With each step he took backward, the kinetic energy between us cooled. I pressed my hands to the wall to ground myself.

I teetered to the bathroom on shaky legs and closed the door behind me. The cold water I splashed on my face did little to douse the fire Rogan had started out there. My hands shook as I brushed my teeth.

I finished up in the bathroom and changed into the cute silk nightie I'd bought at Victoria's Secret on my trip with Tori and Cyan. The lavender lace at my thigh and around my breasts had sparkly swirls of sequins that made it my favorite purchase from that day.

I crashed in Rogan's bed and closed my eyes. My skin still sizzled from his breath on my ear, his nose on my jaw.

Fap. Fap. Fap.

A subtle noise from the bathroom thumped through the wall.

The sound sped up and got louder. I recognized it from the nights my father slept with me and from the time I'd spent with Zook. Either Rogan was brushing his teeth vigorously in the bathroom on the other side of my bedroom wall.

Or he was masturbating.

Like my father had done. No, not deviant and evil. Easy, like it had been with Zook. As natural as breathing, we'd released the tension between us during our time under our oak tree.

But this felt more extreme than the innocent interludes I'd shared with Zook. The smoldering fire in my belly turned molten at the thought of Rogan being so turned on he needed to touch himself, possibly thinking of me. I shouldn't masturbate at the same time, should I? My hands reached into my panties.

It's all in fun, not hurting anyone.

Exactly. Who would it hurt if I pleasured myself right now? I used to do it on occasion after Zook showed me how. I stopped after my father started coming to my room, but Rogan had awakened my sexual desires again. Only this time it was magnified a million times by Rogan's powerful body and the intense connection between us. Unlike before, now I was free to explore my feelings. No one would punish me if I got caught touching myself and that was liberating.

I held my breath and moved my fingertips over my clit while Rogan worked his dick on the other side of the wall. My mind quickly latched onto my new latitude to fantasize about Rogan.

He had me pegged against the wall, growling in my ear, tugging my hair.

"So fucking hard for you right now."

His hand gripped his cock and stroked faster and faster.

He gritted his teeth and closed his eyes, envisioning me in my nightie with my hand down my panties.

I ran my fingers through my wetness and pushed them inside myself. If only it were Rogan's fingers touching me. How would his face look as he climbed closer to his release? I could only imagine the potent force inside him coiling and tensing, ready to explode. That thought threw me over the edge, and I bit my lip to stifle my gasps as I came. The excruciating voltage in my body flashed and flowed through me in an energetic wave. As it finally eased, a serene silence overtook me. My stiff legs and arms slackened, subsiding into a listless heap on the bed.

After a splash of water in the bathroom sink, I heard the door click open and Rogan walk out into the living room. The familiar sound of him settling on the couch was the last thing I heard before the apartment fell silent.

What just happened between him and me?

If I asked my father, he'd babble out a senseless diatribe about sin and judgement.

I turned to my side to cuddle with my pillow.

I didn't have to bear the weight of unraveling the complicated musings of my father's philosophy anymore.

Simply call me a sinner and let me sleep, because I'd just shared something incredibly human with a really hot guy and I loved it.

Chapter 9

———

ROGAN HAD GIVEN ME driving lessons, but I left early for my meeting with Dallas Monroe because Boston's one-way streets and jammed traffic boggled my country-girl mind. Wouldn't taking the subway be so much easier than this? Although, if I'd be working late nights, the subway might not be the safest place, and I'd be glad I had my truck. I drove into the employee lot at Siege ten minutes early. Lux met me at the back entrance and guided me through a huge main room in the club that looked almost like an empty mechanic's garage. The walls were covered in riveted metal and adorned with art made out of screws and bolts. Above my head, private balconies shrouded by rustic canvas ringed the edges of the dance floor.

He led me to the rear of the club and up a metal staircase. He knocked on a solid black door at the top of the stairs.

"Enter," a deep voice called.

Lux let me in, and the man I presumed to be Dallas Monroe stood from behind his desk. I hesitated and my hand flew to my chest. Cyan's staggeringly large husband crowded the room even though he was the only one in it. He wore a sleek suit and tie, his dark hair slicked back. A sooty shadow covered his jaw and a jagged scar ran from his eyebrow to his hairline.

"I'm Dallas Monroe. Pleasure to meet you, Tessa. Have a seat." He pointed to a chair in front of his glossy chrome desk with a glass top. The contradiction of his ultra-modern office against the industrial look of the club threw me for a second.

I managed to gather myself and take the steps to the leather chair. "Mr. Monroe, I—"

"Call me Dallas." He sat down across from me.

"Oh. Okay."

"I could use your help here with VIP accounts. You'll be booking parties, setting up the booths before they arrive, and providing whatever they need. Here's a list of clients."

He handed me a sheet of paper full of names and dates. "Get familiar with their files. VIP hostess is a coveted position here at Siege. I trust you to keep the list and anything that happens related to your work confidential. You'll sign a non-disclosure agreement. Be careful not to let anything slip, particularly with other employees. Bring any issues to Lux. You can also come directly to Brock, Rogan, or me, but no one else."

"Okay." Wow, Dallas was entrusting me with all this responsibility, and he didn't even know me.

"Go downstairs and Jovanna will get you set up with a uniform, paperwork, and show you the ropes. You can start tomorrow night. Oh, and Tessa?"

"Mmm?" I managed to get a sound out even if words failed me.

"Set your limits with club patrons and don't hesitate to stick to them. They aren't allowed to touch you, and you aren't obligated to entertain or interact with them outside of working hours. If they give you any trouble, go straight to security personnel."

His striking blue eyes glinted as he sat back in his chair, and a dimple matching his brother's appeared in his cheek with his smile. Oh boy, no wonder Cyan said she was happy to have him watching over her. With Dallas protecting you, you'd never feel afraid.

"Okay. Thank you for the truck, and the money, as well as this chance to work here."

Dallas rose too and looked down at me with a knowing smile. "I'm happy to help."

"Why? Why would you help me?"

He rounded his desk and walked toward me. "We all need assistance sometimes. Making a change is tough. I admire you."

"Me? But I'm... I mean I'm so out of place here. I don't have any experience, and you're giving me this opportunity?"

"You worked at the drugstore—handled money?"

"I did, but..."

"You worked in a kitchen?"

"Yes."

"That's experience. You raised children?"

"Yes."

"One of the hardest jobs in the world. Taking care of little ones, raising them up healthy and strong and seeing to their needs. You'll be great at this job. The VIPs are a bunch of babies anyway."

I giggled and watched him twist his wedding ring like Cyan had done.

"No matter what they told me, I always believed there were men out there who could love only one woman."

"Absolutely. Cyan is the only woman I have ever and will ever love." He sat on the desk and crossed his ankle over his knee. "I could never lay with another woman besides my wife. I wouldn't want her to think of me with another woman, much less be forced to allow it under the same roof. It must have been difficult to see your mother go through that. And I'm glad you escaped before it became your future."

"Me too. I never wanted that life."

Wow. Dallas represents the ideal I'd always dreamed existed. A man could be loyal. He could love one woman unconditionally and support her while allowing her to be free. Exactly what I wanted. Dallas was taken, but I yearned for someone like him to love me someday.

"I know what it's like to be forced into a life you don't believe in. It's my pleasure to give you this job and get you started on your career. No one should suffer like you have."

"If it wasn't for Rogan..."

"Rogan's a good man."

"Yes. I think he is."

"I'M OFF NOW. IF YOU need anything else, Jovanna will help you." I smiled at Enrique, the handsome Latino singer I'd been working with tonight.

"Don't leave, mamacita. Party's just getting started." His eyes scanned the growing crowd in his VIP booth.

"Oh. I'm exhausted. Maybe next time. Thank you for being the ideal first client."

"You did a fantastic job. Very accommodating. I love this club. I'll tell my associates to ask for you."

"Bye."

"Adios."

And with that, I had more proof that the secular world was not filled with evil. Enrique was a kind man and there was no way he'd be going to hell.

I left the employee exit with a smile on my face. My father would hate my flirty Siege uniform— a pink-camo miniskirt and a black V-neck tee that said Siege in metallic pink letters swirling across my boobs. I loved it.

As I rounded the corner, an ominous figure emerged from the employee lot. A cold tremor shivered down my spine. I braced my feet and positioned my keys like spikes between my fingers. If he came at me, I couldn't outrun him in these heels. He stepped out of the shadows and...

"Rogan! You scared the bejeezus outta me!"

My shoes scuffed on the pavement as I sauntered past him to my truck. He followed me silently and propped his hands on his hips as I grabbed the handle directly above the door and hoisted my butt up into my seat. When I turned to wave to him, he was gone.

I surveyed the dark lot. No Rogan. As I drove out, I felt his eyes on my truck.

Chapter 10

THE BACKLESS SLIP DRESS I chose to wear to the wedding showed the scars on my shoulder, but I didn't care. I loved the wisps of flowers in golden sequins glittering around the hem and bodice. The satin belt at the waist and the pale blush fabric made it romantic enough for a wedding, but the plunging neckline showed a hint of cleavage. I'd spent hours practicing walking in these rose-colored platform pumps with matching golden embroidery.

I pulled on a sheer shrug and left my hair loose to cover the scars on my left shoulder. They were still visible when I moved my hair away, but so what if someone noticed? They'd never know I didn't scratch myself climbing a tree or something. I added amethyst bracelets and matching studs and looked in the mirror. Not bad. I liked this new me.

I watched my feet as I walked toward Rogan, making sure not to eat it.

"Jesus, Tess."

I tugged at the spaghetti straps of my dress without looking up at him. "Don't judge me, Rogan. I picked this dress because it's sparkly and I like it. I'm wearing it no matter what any man thinks."

When I stopped and looked up, his eyes were hooded and dark. Lord have mercy. Rogan's chiseled features and tapered waist were even more breathtaking in a suit. He kept his stance casual, like a dark suit with an ivory shirt and thin black tie was just another uniform for him.

His eyes caressed me from head to toe. "Wasn't gonna criticize you. You look fantastic. You'll outshine the bride."

"I doubt anyone could outshine Yolanda..." *and her enormous boobs.*

"My Sunshine could." He cleared his throat and held his hand behind my back without touching me. "Let's go."

In the parking garage below the apartments, Rogan opened the passenger door to a shiny, black four-door Chevy Silverado.

"Up you go." The skin on my waist buzzed where his big warm hands supported my weight to help me into the seat. The truck interior smelled new. Rogan may not spend money on his apartment, but he'd invested in his truck.

As we pulled away, I asked, "How long have Yolanda and Diesel been dating?"

"Three months."

"Oh. Isn't that kinda quick?"

"Yes. And stupid."

"You don't think they'll make it?"

"Not if he stays enlisted."

"Why do you say that?"

"He'll be gone a lot. The weight of separation strains a marriage. Most of them break."

"Couldn't she live on base with him?"

"Men in my unit don't live on a base. And the places he's deployed are entirely too dangerous for a wife to follow. She has to wait at home and pray each night she doesn't get that knock at the door delivering the news no wife ever wants to hear."

"I hadn't thought much about military wives before. I bet she's thrilled when he comes home."

He nodded. "Diesel thinks if he has someone waiting at home for him, he has a greater chance of making it back alive. It's bullshit. Grenades don't skip over men wearing rings. Best to stay single and guarantee you don't destroy someone's heart when you die."

"What a grim outlook."

"Reality, Sunshine."

"And every time you come back, no one's waiting for you?"

He cringed and his voice became defensive. "I don't need anyone. Just a job. I come home, go to work, no big deal."

Ah, yes, I'd struck a raw nerve. "And how many times have you been deployed?"

"Can't tell you."

"More than ten?"

He raised one eyebrow and quirked his lips.

"More than twenty?"

"Takoda doesn't always go with me. Sometimes she's here when I get home," he said as he pulled into the parking lot of an upscale golf course.

WE SAT AT THE BACK of the crowd as Diesel and Yolanda exchanged vows in a sunset ceremony overlooking the lake. A female vocalist sang of everlasting love, and I couldn't help but think about Rogan coming home to an empty apartment after risking his life in the desert or wherever they'd sent him.

Blaze looked sharp in a tuxedo as Diesel's best man, but nothing compared to Rogan in a suit. He was sexy as hell.

After the dinner at the reception, the music started and I stood up. "Dance with me," I asked Rogan.

"I don't dance."

"C'mon, be my first dance."

"No."

"I'll dance with you, Swift." Blaze rose from his seat and offered me a hand.

I took it and followed him to the dance floor. He wrapped one arm around my waist and held our hands together in the air as he guided us to a mellow song.

"You excited to move in with me tomorrow?"

"Yes, the lengthy move down the hallway."

"I'm warning you, I walk in my sleep."

"Oh, really? What should I do if I see you sleepwalking?"

"Just invite me into your bed, I'll fall right back to la-la land."

"Ha! No way. Platonic roomies. Nothing else."

"Absolutely," he said and pressed his lips together.

The song changed to a provocative beat, and Blaze moved us together to the music. The dance floor pulsed with the tension of attractive people smiling and swaying to the groove.

Diesel rocked his hips into Yolanda like he wanted to take her right there. I bet after the reception, he'd rip off his bride's dress in a hurry to be inside her. Or maybe they'd be so eager, they wouldn't even take the time to undress. They'd fuck on the floor in a haze of tulle and diamonds. She wouldn't care about stains on her dress because she'd be lost in him.

I bit my lip and Blaze pulled me closer. I caught Rogan watching us with dark eyes and stiff shoulders. Could he read my naughty thoughts? Maybe he was jealous of my dancing with Blaze. Probably not. He stood and strode to the balcony without a glance back at us.

I LEFT BLAZE ON THE dance floor and followed Rogan to the balcony. He rested his elbows on the railing as he gazed out to the lake.

"I've never seen a wedding as nice as this. The weddings back home were subdued events. The couple pretending to be in love, the other wives pretending to be happy."

He tilted his chin toward me and squinted. "What else have you never seen?"

I mirrored his position on the railing, and stared out at the darkness of the golf course, trying to see what he was looking at. "I've never seen the sun set over the ocean. I've never been to a concert. I've never traveled anywhere for fun. Lots of things others take for granted."

"How'd you get those marks on your shoulder?"

I snapped up and covered my shoulder with my hand.

"Do all the kids in Caldwell have those?"

"Only the evil ones."

His forehead creased, and his lips turned down. "Did your father do that to you?"

"He marked our transgressions on our skin."

Rogan's hands balled into fists. "And what'd you do to earn those?"

"I defied him."

"How young?"

"Don't ask me that."

"How old the first time?"

"Five."

Rogan stared out into the distance and hunched his huge shoulders. "What did he use?"

"Sugar cane. To keep us sweet."

His chest rose and fell with his deep sigh. He turned to me and held up his arm, giving me the choice. I stepped closer to him, and he enfolded me in his embrace.

I tucked my head into the safety of his hard torso and let the bliss of his closeness wash over me. He flexed his fingers over the scars on my shoulder.

"He use his fists on you?" The scruff on his chin scratched against my hair as he spoke.

"Sometimes." He rubbed his hand up and down my arm. "I'm a troublemaker. Maybe that's why my father sent me on such a dangerous mission. He wanted to get rid of me."

He raised his head, and his hands on my upper arms forced me to look at him. "Bullshit. He knew you were the most beautiful child he had. A sterling Palomino he couldn't tame. He wanted to possess you in a way he couldn't all the other women. He couldn't corral you and put you in his stable. Probably scared the shit outta him the places you'd go, the woman you'd become."

I peered up into his eyes. Rogan's compliments caressed my heartache like his calloused fingers on my shoulder.

"You should've been hugged. Often. Your parents let you down." He pulled me back into his arms. "Your dad touch you in any way besides his fists?"

"He... "

"Go ahead."

"He traveled a lot. But when he was in Caldwell, he'd spend one night with each wife. When my mom died..."

"Yeah?"

"I took her night."

"Your mom died and you took her night."

My cheek mashed against his dress shirt as I nodded. "He would... sleep behind me."

Rogan's arms clenched around me. "Sleep."

"Yes. Sometimes he—"

He squeezed me so hard, he crushed the air from my lungs.

"Uh. Too tight."

He released me and paced away. With his elbows on the balcony railing again, he spoke to the dark night. "He rape you?" His voice came out as a low rasp.

"No. It's difficult to discuss." I twisted my fingers. "He said only intercourse between married people was condoned by God."

He whirled to face me. "Really."

"He thought I carried my mother's soul."

"And..."

"He'd leave his seed between my legs to offer to God as communion with her." I covered my face with my hands. "I should've fought h— "

"No. None of this is your fault."

"He said he'd kill me if I fought him. He'd kill Milo if I told anyone."

"He's got thirty wives and still molests his daughter? What a filthy son of a bitch."

"He didn't rape me."

"It doesn't matter. What he did was wrong."

"Yes."

He curled his palm on the nape of my neck beneath my hair. "You say Takoda's brave, but you are a strong, courageous woman. Your mom would be proud of you."

"I don't know. The sister wives said I was a bad seed."

"Those whack jobs worry way too much about seed."

"They said my soul was damned."

"They were wrong. He programmed them to think that way." His fingers squeezed and twined into my hair. "You've been held prisoner. Twice. Unjustly captured by evil people. They could've killed you, but you survived. You're safe now. And you're free."

I nodded and closed my eyes. "Because of you." I could never thank Rogan enough for rescuing me from the hell in Afghanistan and the misery of Idaho.

As he drew my forehead to his chest, the hook in my heart dug in deeper. His arm around my back bound us together like a thick iron rope.

We stayed like that for several deep breaths before he spoke. "And you are not damned. You're the closest thing to an angel I've ever seen."

Chapter 11

TAKODA GREETED US AT the door like we'd been gone weeks, not a few hours. "Come with me to run her."

"Okay."

He snagged the leash off the hook, and we took Takoda down to the park around the corner. The amber streetlamps elongated our shadows on the sidewalk as Takoda sniffed her pee-mail in the bushes.

The minimal champagne I'd consumed at the wedding was enough to give me courage. "Why do men like boobs so much?"

He chuckled. "Don't know."

"Yolanda has big ones, and she shows them off."

He unhooked Takoda's leash, and lobbed one of her Kong chew toys off into the darkness. She bolted off like a rocket. We kept walking on the sidewalk.

"They're not real, ya know."

"What? Her boobs? They're fake?"

He nodded and glanced at my chest.

"Does Diesel like that?"

"Diesel's first two wives had a similar body type."

"This is his third marriage? So Diesel goes around marrying women with big fake boobs?"

"Could be."

"He does seem like he's in love with her. For more than just her boobs."

"You'd have to ask him that."

My curiosity over Tori gnawed at my insides, especially after I'd shared my secrets with him tonight. "Did you date Cyan's friend Tori?"

Rogan's pace slowed, and he angled his chin toward me. "Why do you ask?"

"She's pretty. Worldly. Mature. Carries herself with grace and composure." *All the things I'm not.*

Takoda bounded back to us with her Kong gripped in her teeth, her tongue lolling out the side. He hooked her leash, and we took her home.

As he removed his jacket and manned the alarm, I took off my sweater as I walked toward the bedroom. "Goodnight. Thank you for taking me. I loved it."

"Hold on a second."

I froze. "What?"

He stepped over to the couch and sat down. "Come here. Need to talk to you." He patted the cushion next to him.

"Oh, okay." As I sat down, our knees bumped and a frisson sparked between us like it did every time we touched.

"Don't compare yourself to other women."

He slung an arm over the back of the couch. "Know what makes you beautiful? Your stormy blue eyes, long fucking legs that'd drive any man to murder, hair for miles, fine ass, round, full *boobs*—to use your word. I could go on for days about your lips."

"Oh." Wow.

He lowered his head, and his hand cupped my neck. "But who you are defines your beauty. Not many women out there can say she's survived growin' up the way you did and came out the other side looking like a million bucks, givin' smiles to everyone she meets, not letting any of the brainwashing shit get her down. Never met a woman as brave as you, and that is fuckin' sexy." As his face edged closer, the heat of his energy invaded my space. "There's no comparison." The warm breeze of his soft lips brushed my cheek.

I held my breath and waited for him to pull away. He didn't. He lingered, and my heart launched to the sky in a multi-colored hot air balloon.

"Kiss me." I didn't mean to say it. It just came out. But it was out there now. Would he kiss me?

His other hand rose slowly to my neck, and he held me in his palms like you hold a dandelion before blowing its seed tufts away. "Drove me nuts you dancin' with Blaze."

A dangerous gust twisted low in my belly. As I inhaled to respond, he pressed his mouth to mine. His fingers squeezed my neck, and I whimpered. The tip of his tongue lapped at my upper lip. I opened for him, inviting him to invade my mouth. Yes, yes! Our tongues crashed and circled in a delicious wave. He tasted like champagne and wedding cake.

Without breaking the kiss, he pushed me to my back and hovered over me. I wrapped my arms around him and dug my fingertips into his solid shoulders. His clothes scuffed along the sequins at the hem of my dress as he gave me his weight. His hard cock pressed against my core through our clothes. God, I wanted to feel him like this with nothing between us. Just him and I naked and caressing each other.

His hand skated along my side to my knee, hitching it up around his hip. He ended the kiss and took a deep breath with his eyes closed. "So fucking sexy." His eyes opened slowly, and he focused on my cleavage. "I shouldn't. But damn." He kissed down my neck along the edge of the fabric, stopping at the lowest point with his nose between my breasts. "You smell good."

"Rogan." I tilted my hips and crushed his erection between us. He answered me with a sensual grind. God, it felt huge. "Please. Please don't stop." As our bodies worked their way infinitely closer, the heat between us fueled the air of my balloon higher and higher. My hands explored the curve of his back like I'd dreamed of for so long. His sinewy muscles felt bigger and stronger than my ultimate fantasies. My fingers stopped at the waistband of his slacks.

He raised his head. "Wish I could be the one to show you all you've never seen. The first to fuck you, erase whatever bullshit your dad planted in your head. Make you come hard. Watch you light up in my arms." He pressed his forehead to mine and his fingers curled behind my knee. "But I can't."

I gasped and tugged his shirt. "No. Don't say that." I pulled it free from his pants and ran my fingernails over the bare skin of his back. Sleek skin over taut muscles, burning hot under my fingertips. "You can. We can. Who's going to stop us?"

He growled and his body stilled. "I can't. You've had enough shit thrown at you. You don't need mine. After what you've been through, you need a man with a gentle hand. Someone whose heart is... free. That ain't me."

With one last inhale of his earthy scent, I grasped his shoulders and held tight. "No."

Don't pull away from me, please.

But my arms could never hold a man as strong as Rogan down. He broke from my grip like it was as weak as a spider web. He knifed up to standing with his gaze turned to the floor. He took a deep breath and a stunted step back.

I stared at the top of his head and panted to catch my breath.

Please come back.

"You'll be meeting plenty of influential people at Siege. Find yourself a VIP."

And just like that, the flame fueling our balloon extinguished, and we descended into freefall like we'd passed through the wall of a hurricane and sunk through the column of the eye.

He marched to the door and took off into the frigid night, not bothering to grab his jacket. Takoda and I stared at the closed door.

The basket of my balloon crashed to the ground, and I sat up on the couch. "Come here, girl." Takoda trotted to me and put a paw on my lap. As I scrubbed her head behind her ears, my deflated balloon fluttered to the earth. "Why did I ask him to kiss me, huh?"

Takoda looked back at me with a face that said, Because he's drop-dead gorgeous, you idiot. Who wouldn't?

"Too true. He is one fine man."

And a dangerously good kisser, even if he is impossible to understand. With a sigh, I gathered the nylon fabric of my balloon in my arms, carried it to my bed, and flopped on my back, burying myself in the rainbow.

The exhilarating ride had ended. My body lay on the ground, but my heart—my poor confused heart—soared through the roof, over the city, and up to the moon.

———————

WITH MY BELONGINGS in bags over my shoulders, I headed to the door. Time to leave. Rogan made it clear he didn't want me here anymore. Even if he found me *fuckin' sexy*, and let himself kiss me last night, he didn't want anything more with me.

What did he mean his heart wasn't free? Maybe Tori meant more to him than he let me see. Maybe he had another girl. Maybe he liked men. Whatever his reasoning, I needed to get away from him.

The few doors and a hallway separating us would provide a physical barrier for the persistent shame I felt for crushing on a guy who didn't want me. And for letting him touch and kiss me when I knew it didn't mean as much to him as it did to me.

"Keep your hands off her, man." I overheard Rogan talking in the hallway on the other side of the half-opened door.

"You claiming her?" Blaze asked.

"No," Rogan answered.

"Then you got no right to tell me not to touch her."

I bit my lip and held my breath to keep quiet.

"I don't. However, if you're interested in keeping all your limbs working, do not touch her."

"I hear you, but pull your head out if you want her. She ain't gonna be single for long. If it's not me, someone else is gonna take a chance at her, pretty and sweet as she is."

"Don't call her sweet. She doesn't like it."

I stepped out from behind the door. Rogan looked at me and rubbed the back of his neck.

"Need help, Tessa?" Blaze asked.

"Sure."

Rogan crossed his arms over his chest as I handed a bag to Blaze.

"Give me all of them," Blaze said.

"Oh, I can carry—"

"Pfft." He snatched my bags from my shoulder and stalked to his apartment.

I felt Rogan's heat as I stepped past him, but I didn't look up. "You can have your bed back now."

At Blaze's door, I risked a glance over my shoulder at him. His gaze drilled into me and his arms arched slightly forward, like he was asking me to walk into them. The hook in my heart tugged and twisted, but I turned my back on his lost puppy face and walked into my new apartment.

Goodbye, Rogan. I'm not waiting around for you to pull your head out.

I RAN OUT THE DOOR with my head down, my backpack over my shoulder, and my dance clothes thrown on. I bounced off a rock hard wall of camouflage.

"Whoa, there." Rogan's raspy voice sounded in my ear as he steadied me with his hands on my upper arms.

Two weeks of avoiding Rogan and pretending I didn't miss him all came crashing to a fruitless end in the corridor outside Blaze's apartment. His beard had grown back in and dark mud splotches marred his clothes.

"I'm sorry. I didn't see you."

Butterflies zipped around in my tummy, and my legs trembled. This sexy-as-sin man had put all his weight on me and kissed me on the couch. He'd pulled my leg around his hip and mashed his hard cock into me. He'd also left me turned on and breathless.

"School start today?"

"Yes."

"What classes are you taking?"

"Science. History. I have some relearning to do."

"How do you feel about that?"

"I don't mind. I want to know the truth that's been kept from me."

"And dance?" He pointed to my leggings and leotard.

"Yep. I'm excited. Dancing wasn't allowed back home."

He nodded and grunted.

I pointed at his rifle bags and the pack over his shoulder. "Where're you coming back from?"

"Visiting your cousin Falcon in North Carolina."

"My cousin? Oh right. My cousin. How is he?"

"Doing well."

"Good. Good." I stared into his eyes and tried to read him. He had that distant gaze again of a man who was focused somewhere else. "Okay then. Bye."

I stepped out to pass him, but he grabbed my arm. "Enjoy your first day of school."

"Thank you."

Darn, darn, why did I find him so attractive? I wanted to sit down on the couch with him and talk about his trip to North Carolina and then have him kiss me and tell me I was *fuckin' sexy*.

"You get the number I sent you for Natalie Sorenson?"

"Yes. I have an appointment next week. I'm a little nervous talking to a therapist."

"You can trust her. Whatever you wanna tell her is safe."

"Okay." I looked down at his hand. "I need to get to class."

He released my arm slowly.

"Bye."

"Later."

I shouldn't have looked back, but part of me wanted to check out his butt in his fatigues and another part of me wondered if he was still watching me.

Yep. He was looking over his shoulder at me as he walked toward his apartment, and his ass looked yummy in his camo.

Chapter 12

ROGAN

The bolt of my M-16 locked in place. I slipped it in the bag next to the tattered black and white wedding photo I'd taken on every mission over the last four years.

I mashed ten extra tees in the corner of my duffel bag. We'd have a long hunt for Jericho, so I packed heavy, all my scopes for any terrain.

Jericho's son, codename Timeron, was the key. Diesel had located him from videos and audiotape he'd posted online. He was being groomed to take over for his father. If we found him, he'd lead us to Jericho. He might need some convincing, but I'd get the intel from him. He'd cave like they all do. Then I'd kill him and laugh while I did it.

My phone lit up with a text.

T: Can you meet me at Siege?

Me: What's wrong?

T: Nothing. I just need your help

With that word *help* my focus shifted from killing a man to protecting her, like it did all the time now.

My flight would leave in twelve hours. Going to her meant staying up all night and giving up my last chance at shut-eye before the most important and dangerous mission of my life.

If I went now, I'd only add more memories to torture myself while I was gone.

I already had a vault of them.

Her tears in the shower the night I brought her home.

Her bouncing tits as she danced to Taylor Swift in the kitchen.

Her pert nipples poking her wet T-shirt after her shower.

The short little gasps as she got herself off while I jacked myself in the bathroom.

Her desperate pleading.

Kiss me...

The subtle rattle of her jaw and defiant challenge in her eyes. *Don't call me sweet.*

I rubbed my hand over my face and shook my head. I couldn't be the man for her. Even if my life didn't revolve around revenge, my touch was too deadly.

I'd sneak out tomorrow without saying goodbye. She'd find someone else to give her *help*.

That's where my logic always collapsed. Someone else doing my job did not sit well.

Tonight would be my last chance to help her. Her last chance to give me her sweet thank yous.

I walked to my closet to change into the suit I wore when I worked security at Siege.

What's a few more memories added to the pile?

TESSA

Me: Can you meet me at Siege?

R: What's wrong?

Me: Nothing. I just need your help

My legs trembled as I slipped my phone into my purse after my shift at Siege. Would Rogan come to Siege for me this late at night on a holiday? What if he did come and my crazy idea backfired?

Keep fighting till you find joy.

I left my purse and my uniform in my dressing room locker and took a deep breath as I walked into the main room. I'd been nervous all day, but after my first fireworks display, a new confidence took root inside me. Rogan and I were explosive together and if this went as planned, the fear would be worth it because my joy would be meeting me here tonight.

The heavy beat of the music thumped through my body like it was keeping me alive. I focused on the entrance, trying to recognize him in the ocean of red, white, and blue partygoers.

"What'd you need?" His angry voice snarled in my ear.

I spun and gasped. "Did you come in the back door?"

"What'd you need?"

He'd shaved his beard since I'd bumped into him in the corridor three days ago. My heart squeezed just as it did the first time I saw his transformation from bearded commando to smoking hot body-guard.

Oh boy. "I, uh, need a... dance partner."

His brows scrunched as his dispassionate eyes raked over my outfit. I'd changed into a short, backless dress with a slit up the left thigh. At least these black pumps decorated with trailing starbursts of rhinestones made me taller next to him. I needed any inches of courage I could find.

His gaze caressed the strings of stars on the straps over my shoulders. "I was in the middle of something, Tess. Dropped everything for you."

"I'm sorry."

"You playing games with me?"

"It's Independence Day. I'm celebrating my freedom!" I threw my arms in the air and wiggled my hips. The jewels of my diamond-encrusted dress reflected magical beams of light on Rogan's black dress shirt.

His gaze moved from my waist to the scooped neckline of the dress.

"Still think I'm a young girl?"

He ran his tongue over his teeth under his lips and closed his eyes. He bent to speak into my ear and squeezed my hip between his thumb and fingers. "A young girl doing a stupid thing."

He marched to the back stairs with his arms arched away from his sides and his shoulders angled high. Dancing bodies made room for him then replaced the space he occupied.

My clenched fists held the tears at bay. Crying in front of all these people would only make the humiliation worse. I'd made a fool of myself chasing Rogan. He would always deny his attraction to me.

A warm hand on my shoulder stemmed my public breakdown. I looked up to see Enrique, the VIP from my first night at Siege, offering me a disarming smile.

"Que paso, mamacita?"

"Hi, Enrique."

"That guy upset you? Want me to set him straight?"

"No, no. It's fine."

"Forget him. Come dance with me." He grasped my hand and dragged me deeper into the crowd.

Enrique swiveled his narrow hips to the beat and raised our hands over our heads, forcing me to spin around. I stumbled and laughed as he stabilized me with a hand at my waist.

His arm at my midriff tugged me flush against his body, and I quickly learned why Enrique Gutierrez sold out concerts and topped the charts. His velvet voice in my ear as he sang along with the song made my stomach plummet. Dancing with him perked up my mood and dampened the bitter sting of my lame attempt at seducing Rogan.

"Let's take a break. I'll buy you a drink." He placed his palm on my lower back and guided me to the bar.

My feet thanked him for helping me up onto a stool and giving them a break.

"What're you drinking? How about a mojito?"

"What's a mojito?"

"Tonight you will find out." He held up one hand, and the bartender ignored all the other patrons to come to us. "Dos mojitos diablos, por favor, con cerezas."

Enrique ordering a drink nearly surpassed the pleasure of him singing in my ear. He must have women drooling all over him, and yet he was taking a moment to dance and have a drink with me.

"Now, tell me, mamacita. Who's that pendejo who left you standing alone on the dance floor?"

"Tell me more about mojitos."

"Ahh, you care for him."

"Is there a little Mo in mojitos?"

"Life is too short to let some loser bring you down."

"Tess." Rogan's voice came at me from my right side.

Enrique stood up and faced Rogan. "Get lost, cabron."

"Ella esta conmigo." Rogan spoke in Spanish to Enrique.

"Verdad?" Enrique asked with humor in his voice as he looked at me and the space between us on the barstools. "Segura que... no."

I didn't know what that meant but telling Rogan *no* in a smartass tone couldn't be good for your health.

The waiter dropped two pink frothy drinks on the bar behind me and skittered off.

"Tess, you're dancing with me," Rogan ordered.

"What?" I stuck my head between them.

"Let's go."

"She's about to have her first taste of a proper mojito."

Oh boy, Enrique was a brave soul to challenge Rogan so boldly.

"No. She's not. She's dancing with me." Rogan reached for me but Enrique blocked his arm. Lightning fast, Rogan grabbed his wrist and twisted it behind his back.

Suddenly the bar was packed with burly men. Six men I recognized from Enrique's party stood to my left with their legs wide, knees bent, hands on their waistbands, ready to pull a gun if they needed it. Lux and four other Siege security guards took similar stances behind Rogan.

Whoa. This escalated fast.

"Stand down, soldier!" Dallas approached and yelled in Rogan's face. Rogan released Enrique, and the air in the room quickly cooled. The men removed their hands from their weapons, but they remained alert and silent as Rogan and Enrique stepped away from each other.

Enrique glared at Rogan as Dallas tried to smooth things over. "I'm sorry, Gutierrez. I'll take care of the situation. You can call off your men."

"You okay with him, Tessa?" Enrique asked me.

"Yes."

Enrique tilted his head toward me, and his guys followed him out of the bar.

Lux and the other Siege security guards resumed their positions in the club.

"What the hell, Rogan? You roughing up the VIPs now? Why? Because of her?" Dallas angled his head toward me.

Rogan kept his lips pressed tightly together.

"Never seen you lose it before. Don't cause trouble in my club. I expect more from my top man."

"I'm sorry, sir. Won't happen again."

"Make sure of it."

Rogan nodded, and Dallas marched to the back stairs that led to his office.

"What was all that about?" I asked him.

"Didn't like you having drinks with that guy. Dancing with him like you knew him."

"I do know him. I hosted a party for him my first night here. You told me to get myself a VIP, and when I spend a few minutes talking to one, you accost him in the bar."

"He made the first move. I just restrained him."

"Whatever. This is all looking very suspicious. Why did Dallas say you're his top man? Why did all those men look ready to kill? Why does Cyan have a body—"

He yanked me from the bar stool and marched to the dance floor with me shuffling behind him in my heels.

He stopped in the middle and propped his hands on his hips.

"So now you wanna dance with me?"

"I don't dance."

I huffed out a breath. This man was unbelievable.

"You're just gonna stand guard?"

The crowd moved around us. How incredibly stupid? What kind of giant man stands stock-still in a gyrating crowd?

He continued to scan the room for nonexistent threats.

"Great. I have a dance partner who doesn't dance and thinks I'm a stupid girl." I crossed my arms over my chest which pushed my breasts together, drawing his gaze to them again.

"You're not a stupid girl. Every inch of you is dangerous woman."

"Then dance with me, you idiot."

He pressed his lips together. "Fine."

I grunted as the force of his arms hoisting me up against him knocked the air from my lungs and caused my back to arch. I steadied myself with my hands on his massive shoulders. He inserted one thigh between my legs and rocked his hips.

I leaned back to look up at him. "You can dance?"

"Saying I don't dance doesn't mean I can't."

A sensuous J Lo song came on, and the music swelled inside me. All the fear and shock of the night disappeared in the erotic beat. Rogan rolled his hips, and our bodies locked in an entrancing rhythm.

I ground my sex down on his thigh, and the jewels on my dress crunched under his fingers around my waist. I tossed my head back and flung my arms wide, giving Rogan all my weight, letting his powerful arms support me. He could probably see the crotch of my undies, but I didn't care. For the first time in my life, I could truly dance uninhibited.

When he lifted my torso upright, I popped up with a smile and a huge exhale. The ringlets in my hair bounced around my shoulders.

Rogan stared at my lips. "Jesus."

His eyes softened, and the corners of his mouth turned up. His hands moved lower, and his fingertips explored the creases of my cheeks under the short hem of my dress.

"Mmm." His sultry rumble ignited an electrical fire between us like transformers exploding in loud bursts of light.

He raised his thigh and forced me to smash down harder on his beefy leg. I wrapped my arms around his neck. If he didn't let me down, he'd find a wet spot on his pants.

His hands under my ass cheeks lifted me higher until our faces were inches apart. One hand slid up to my lower spine, taking the hem of my dress with it. The palm of his other hand covered my thong. The length of his rock hard erection ground into my abdomen, pulling a rumbling groan from deep in his chest.

Kiss me.

I didn't dare to say it aloud again, but he must have read it in my eyes. He pressed his soft lips to my neck, and I arched my head back, offering him access to all of it. His teeth scraped my skin, sending bolts of lightning striking to my core.

Rogan hissed as he lowered me to the floor. His hands on my shoulders turned me so his hips swung against my back. His rigid shaft pressed between the cheeks of my ass. My body froze.

No, no, no. Not there, please.

I wrenched out of his hold and spun to face him. Did he notice my evasive maneuver?

His fists clenched and his nostrils flared. Of course he'd noticed, and he thought I was teasing him. I most definitely wasn't teasing. If he wanted to take me here on the dance floor, I would have let him and enjoyed every second of it. But my body flinched by reflex when he approached me from behind. I opened my mouth to explain, but shut it again, because I wasn't sure exactly why I panicked. Even if I knew what to say, he wouldn't hear me anyway with the music blaring so loud.

Chapter 13

LIKE A VIPER, HE STRUCK and grabbed my upper arm. My feet scuffled along as he dragged me up the stairs to the mirrored wall. With his touch, a hidden door opened, and he yanked me into a room with a U-shaped console and computer screens lining the walls. I didn't have time to figure anything else out because Rogan propelled a chair out of the way and shoved me up against the desk.

"You want this?" His hard cock rammed against my sex, making my stomach drop and my knees shake. "You want this?"

"Yes."

"*This* is more than you can handle." He accentuated the word with his hips jabbing into mine. "*This* is a fucking timebomb." His fingers dug into my waist, crunching against the jewels on my dress. "You have no idea what you're asking."

God, Rogan's wrath frightened me and turned me on in equal measure. "I want you. However it comes."

"No. You're way too fragile." His tone betrayed he doubted his statement, like a child trying to get out of trouble when they knew their excuse wouldn't hold water.

"I'm not made of glass. Be rough with me."

He stared at me and ground his teeth, war raging in his eyes. "If I let loose, I'll shred you."

"Give it to me. I need you to want me so bad it hurts."

With a guttural growl, he slammed his mouth on mine. Our tongues mashed and our teeth clicked. Finally. Finally, Rogan let his passion take over. He tasted salty and wet and warm. He palmed my breasts through the dress. Not gently, a rough squeeze that pushed them up and crunched them together. And I loved it. I didn't want soft. His demanding touch was real and potent and set me on fire for him.

He ran his lips down my neck and dipped his tongue inside the neckline of the dress, swiping over my nipple. "Yes, Rogan. God, yes!" My fingernails scraped through the sheen of sweat on the back of his neck.

I reached for his shirt buttons, but he stepped back and yanked my dress up to my hips. He kissed me again, and I shivered as his fingers worked into the top of my panties. His fingers stilled as he deepened the kiss and moaned.

The heat of his hand slipped in deeper, cupping my sex and probing my wetness. His massive palm between my legs lifted me up onto the desk, so high that my shoes fell off and clicked to the ground.

With a growl, he broke the kiss. "Brace yourself." His hands wrapped around my hips and pinned me. I planted my elbows for balance as the cold laminate smashed into my backside.

He pulled my panties down to my knees. I widened my feet as far as they would go with the panties restraining me. He hovered his face over my sex. His inhale seemed to stun him for a second, but he snapped out of it and dove in. He licked my slit up to my clit and I gasped.

"Goddamn, fucking heaven." He pulled my underwear down the rest of the way and tossed them across the room. With his knees on the floor, his tongue drilled in on my clit. He lifted my leg up over his shoulder and dove in deeper.

God.

He's feasting on me.

Totally feasting.

His lips sucked and pulled till I gasped for each ragged breath.

It all happened so fast. Rogan bombarded me with his untamed anger, his tongue sending buzzing jolts to every molecule of my body. A terrifying orgasm brewed deep in my core. It felt so good, I wanted it to last forever. He needed to...

"Slow down. I'm—"

"Fuck no," he murmured into my sex and forced two fingers inside me.

"Ahh!" A sharp twinge of something wonderful inside me swelled from his fingers and filled my body like I was floating on a life raft.

My hands scratched his head as it bobbed between my legs, unable to grab hold of his short hair.

I cried out as a climax assailed me. My insides crumbled to dust. I didn't exist. The universe was only light and Rogan as I came, groaning and gasping. He didn't let up, forcing me to spasm on his fingers again and again.

"Stop." I could barely utter the word. I grabbed his ears and pushed his head away. He resisted at first, but slowed and stopped. He stayed close and took a deep breath. I exhaled too. The storm had passed. Whew.

When he stood, his eyes had darkened to coal. A wrathful menace still swirled in them. His lips shined with my juices as he loosened his belt with rough jerks.

I was wrong. The storm had not passed. The wall of it was charging toward me full speed, no way to stop it.

He whipped his cock out, and lordy, it was huge, a dark round head throbbing and pointing at me. His hand curled behind my neck and forced me down, bending me at the waist.

"You still want this?" His voice scratched like coarse sandpaper on metal.

I tried to nod, but his unforgiving hand kept my head in place. "You know to cover your teeth with your lips?"

He didn't want me to answer so I didn't try.

I should've broken out of his demanding hold, but I was still so turned on from the dancing and my monumental orgasm, I did want it. Rough or gentle, I wanted this connection with Rogan.

"Suck." He bumped the head of his cock against my closed lips. "Suck it, Sunshine. You want it? Suck it."

His grip tightened around my neck, his thumb digging in behind my ear. The pain tripped a wire inside me, and suddenly, I didn't want it anymore. I dropped my head. I couldn't do it. Not like this.

He released my neck, and I raised my torso upright, wiping away hair stuck to my face.

"I told you. You don't want this. I warned you." He moved fast, tucking his hard cock into his pants. "Fuck!" He grunted and smacked his fist into the console. He marched away, the tail of his shirt hanging out partially in the front. The master of composure and masking emotion was a disheveled mess, just like me.

At the door, he didn't look back when he spoke. "Don't tempt me."

The door snapped shut behind him, like a crocodile's jaw. I stood alone in the strange room, my eyes stinging, stunned and naked from the waist down.

Damn. Dammit! Rogan rejected me over and over and yet I stupidly, stupidly let him.

With three deep breaths, I fixed myself up and left the room. I searched for him in the club as I stumbled to the employee lockers to get my things, but didn't see him. Good. I didn't want to see him now anyway. I just wanted to escape. I took off my shoes and raced barefooted out the employee exit, clutching my backpack and fighting back tears. My hands shook as I fired up the engine and drove out of the lot. I didn't feel his eyes on my truck like I always did. The road home blurred through the wetness in my eyes, but I made it to the parking structure for my apartment safely and found a space.

I cut my headlights and sat in my truck. The shame and disappointment poured out of me in surges of sobs so mighty I couldn't stop them. My crush on Rogan was futile. He would never fully give himself to me. He might occasionally lose control like he did tonight, but in the end, he would always hurt me.

Tori was right. I should've never chased a man who didn't want me like crazy. Well, I'd learned my lesson. I was done with Rogan forever.

Chapter 14

I WAS EATING BREAKFAST when Blaze walked out of his room the next morning. His pack and rifle case were slung over his shoulder. He wore fatigues like I'd seen Rogan wearing when I ran into him in the hallway last week.

"Are you leaving?" I set my bagel on my plate and stared at him.

"Yeah." He messed with his gear intently, like I wasn't there.

"Where are you going?"

He didn't answer, grabbed a bunch of bags, and opened the front door.

Rogan and Takoda were standing in the corridor, waiting for him. Rogan wore clean, stiff fatigues and his Army boots. I stood from the table in the nook and stepped closer to Rogan, but he didn't look at me. His face hardened into an arctic glacier. His lips looked thin and pale. Unlike last night when they were full and slick and kissing me in the most unimaginable ways. His lips had also said cruel, hurtful things that left me crying myself to sleep. I wrapped my arms around my middle to ward off the chill creeping up my spine.

Blaze glanced from Rogan to me. "Gonna load the truck." He walked out with his gear.

"Where are you going?" I asked Rogan. The hairs on my arm stiffened, like they do during the deathly lull before a storm.

He turned his head toward me, and considered me with dull, lifeless eyes. "I can't tell you."

He didn't need to. I could read the resolve on his face. "You're going to Afghanistan. On another mission."

His head tilted slightly. "If anyone asks you, you don't know where I went."

"Is the Army making you go or did you volunteer?"

"I'm going because I want to."

"Why? What could be so important?"

"Got unfinished business there."

"Are Diesel and Takoda going with you?"

"Yep. The Monroe brothers will watch over you until Diesel and Blaze get back."

"The Monroe brothers? Diesel and— Wait. You're not coming back?"

"If I survive, I won't return here. Don't wait for me." His voice softened and rasped, revealing the anguish he was feeling too. The hook in my heart tugged painfully like a fish caught on a line. "Goodbye, Sunshine. Just move on."

"Do I at least get to say goodbye to Takoda?"

Rogan looked down at Takoda and pointed one finger at me. I bent my knees, and she ran into my arms.

"Goodbye, girl. Be careful out there." I rubbed the scruff of her neck till her skin wrinkled up behind her ears. She panted and angled her head, begging for more. I kissed the top of her head. A jagged hole ripped through my chest. "You can't say goodbye and walk away."

"I have to."

A butcher's knife severed my mangled heart into jagged, bloody chunks. "This hurts." I kept my eyes on Takoda and blinked away the pain threatening to drop from my eyes.

The door clicked shut, his gear thudded on the floor, and his boots tapped out three deliberate steps toward me. When his strong arms pulled me to standing, I peered up at my blurry commando. This is not happening. I couldn't say goodbye. Not now. Not ever.

"Listen. I know it hurts now and it feels like it'll never pass. But it will. You'll forget about me. Move on to someone your age." He ran his hand over my hair like he'd done the first time he'd hugged me. "I'm sorry about the way I treated you last night. You don't deserve that."

"Older guys do stupid things too." I sounded petulant, but I didn't care. This was forever. My hero who'd rescued me and gave me my freedom was walking away and would never return.

"You don't understand." His voice cracked.

"Explain it to me, please."

"Certain acts are so heinous, they can't go unanswered."

"And you have to provide the answer?"

"We're the best team for the job."

"You're choosing to fight over love?"

He bent at the waist to stare into my eyes. "Yes."

"And have you made that choice before and regretted it?"

His torso flinched back like I'd hit him in the core. "Tess..."

"People repeat behaviors. Diesel marries women based on their body type. My father brings children into this world, only to reject them. You risk your life to wage battles far across the ocean. Battles that keep you from putting down roots."

He rubbed the back of his neck. "You could be right, but this is the way it has to be. I'm sorry."

I closed my eyes. He pressed his lips to my forehead and skimmed them over my nose, landing on my mouth.

I kissed him back, softly, inhaling his warm breath, memorizing it and storing it in my lungs like a firefly in a jar.

He grabbed my waist and pulled me flush against his torso as he deepened the kiss.

This kiss broke a promise he'd never made. The bitter regret of an unfinished verse he'd never started singing.

His husky growl and the hunger in the kiss said he didn't want it to end. But like Rogan always does, he pulled away, leaving me breathless and lost.

He picked up his rifle and his bags. "Bye, Tess."

Takoda followed behind him with one last look back at me.

"Goodbye, Rogan. Bye, Takoda." I waved at their disappearing backs. "Be safe."

The door clicking shut sheared the final strand of the cable tying me to Rogan. I stood in the middle of the room holding the loose end of a tattered rope.

Chapter 15

"HEY, SUGAR. HAPPY BIRTHDAY." Brock draped an arm over my shoulders and squeezed.

"Thank you." I didn't look up from my work preparing the VIP booth for Enrique tonight.

"Why the frown, Tessa? Not many girls get a do-over of their twenty-third birthday."

I looked him in the eye. "A do-over Rogan made happen for me. And you and Dallas too. I'm so grateful for that..."

"But?"

"I wish he were here."

He glanced around the empty club. "He leaves like this. It's only been a week. He comes back."

"He said he won't be back."

Brock didn't respond as he watched me place Enrique's orange Tic Tacs inside his booth.

"How's your dance class going?"

"Did Rogan tell you I was taking a dance class?"

"He mentioned it."

"Oh. Good. I mean well. It's going well."

"I have an idea that might cheer you up. Are you afraid of heights?"

"What? No. I don't think so."

"How'd you like to dance for us?"

"Dance for you? Like the dancers on the catwalk?"

"More like in the box. Would you like to be a box girl?"

"Are you nuts? I'm totally unqualified."

"You know how to shake that fine ass of yours?"

"Oh. I guess I'm learning. It comes natural if the music is right."

"You wanna dance up there?" He pointed to the hook hanging from the ceiling where the boxes were suspended.

Did I? Men would be watching me, lusting after me. I'd probably be wearing something even skimpier than my Siege uniform. My father would bust a gut.

"Yes! I would love it. Oh, please?"

He pulled out his phone and dialed. "Bro, get Tessa a gig as a box girl."

He listened for a second then replied. "A stunner like her needs to be in the spotlight. Not in the shadows kissing VIP ass."

Another pause. "She said she wants it."

He listened to Dallas's reply and folded his hand like the beak of a duck, closing and opening it like quacking. I tried not to giggle. Brock was brave to mock Dallas, even if he couldn't see it.

He tilted his chin away and lowered his voice. "He left it up to us."

After listening for a bit longer, Brock handed me the phone.

"Hello?"

"This something you want?" Dallas's somber tone took me by surprise.

"Yes. I think I'd love it. It's a chance to fly. The ultimate freedom."

"Then I'll allow it, but it's temporary and only once a week. Don't lose focus on your schooling."

"I promise. I won't."

"Did you pick a major yet?"

"No."

"Let me know when you do. I'll have a place for you at any of my businesses. You can be a manager, a salesperson, anything you want. But for now, the answer is yes. You start tonight. See Jovanna for wardrobe."

"Oh my goodness. Thank you!"

He ended the call, and I handed the phone back to Brock. "I'm scared and excited and oh my gosh."

"Don't be nervous, sugar. Just be authentic. The honesty rolling off you is enchanting. They'll see it too."

"Oh..."

"Have fun. I'm gonna sit right under your box and watch you spread your wings."

I laughed because I'd be spreading lots of stuff, wings included. "Thank you so much."

"One more thing." Brock handed me a white greeting card and a small box wrapped in white paper and a glittering red bow.

"What's this?"

"Present for you." He headed to the back of the club and left me alone with my present.

In a thick brushstroke of carmine red, the front of the card read,

Find a place inside where there's joy, and the joy will burn out the pain.

Inside, a message was scrawled in his orderly script.

Sunshine, happy first birthday as Tessa Harlow. Never let anyone dull your sparkle. Rogan

The box held a faceted square ruby necklace with miniature diamonds around the edges, just like the one I'd told him about stealing from the drugstore. I dangled the glittering gem from the chain and watched it glint in the light. I clutched it in my hand and pressed it to my chest. Darn him for being so thoughtful and nice on my birthday.

JOVANNA SHOWED ME AROUND and gave me the box-girl rules.

No nudity. No smashing your tits or ass up against the glass. No bodily fluids in the box.

She picked out a pink plaid skirt and white polyester shirt that knotted at my midriff.

At ten o'clock, I stuffed all my fears in my locker and climbed the steps to box three. My sweaty fingers gripped the handles of the swaying glass cube as some guy wheeled me out over the dance floor.

My stomach lurched and I swallowed back bile.

No bodily fluids in the box.

Presumably vomit would be considered a bodily fluid.

Once the box settled in place, my stomach recovered, and the music streaked through me like adrenaline. Fate had brought me a chance to dance in the air above a crowd. Fear would not stop me from seizing it and enjoying it. I closed my eyes to the blinding strobe lights and forced my stiff muscles to move to the beat. So what if I looked awkward? So what if my moves gave away the fact I grew up on a commune with no dancing? My ruby necklace bounced on my chest, I shook my ass, and I had a damn good time.

After two hours of dancing, I changed my exhausted body into sweats and carried my bag to my truck. The employee parking lot seemed extra dark without the reassuring hug of Rogan's eyes on me, but a new comfort took its place—the comfort of confidence in my body, making my own future, and finding joy, one day at a time.

SIX MONTHS LATER

Light Boston snow flurries landed on the hood of my truck as my phone lit up with a call from Cyan.

"Happy New Year!" Her jovial voice made me smile.

"Happy New Year to you too, Cyan."

"Did you make any resolutions?"

I'd read all about Christmas and New Year's and decided to embrace all the traditions I didn't even know I'd been missing out on. "I did. I want to be on time to class and never miss a day. But this snow might put a damper on that." The flurries came down thicker and clouded my view of Roxy's.

"There's a nor'easter rolling in tonight."

"I know. I'm just picking up some lunch, and I'll head straight home after class." From what I could see from the parking lot, the line at Roxy's would take me at least ten minutes.

"If you get stuck in the snow, call me or Dallas. Promise?"

"I will and thank you again for spending Christmas with me." My first Christmas. "I loved volunteering at the children's shelter."

"Those kids break my heart. I wanted to take them all home."

"I know. Me too." More like it made me want to run home to Milo.

"Dallas took the World's Best Boss coffee mug you gave him to Siege today."

"He did?" I laughed. "I had no idea what to get him."

"No. That's the ideal gift for him."

"Listen, I gotta go in and get my food before the snow gets too thick, but... Did you ask him?"

Cyan sighed before she answered quietly. "I did. He said he doesn't know."

Why did I continue to interrogate her when the answer was always the same? Dallas and Brock had no idea if Rogan was alive somewhere with Takoda, Diesel, and Blaze. Even if anyone knew, they weren't going to tell me.

"Do you think he's alive?" I asked Cyan.

"I hope so, sweetie. Rogan's become like family to us. All we can do is have faith and wait."

"I'm starting to lose heart. He said not to wait for him."

"And the only sign you've had from him was the song?"

"Yes." Six weeks after he left, Rogan added a song to the "Beyond Taylor Swift" playlist. "In Case You Didn't Know" sustained me through the rough nights when I wondered if what had happened between us was real or not. The lyrics told me it was. He'd felt it too. He just had to leave for reasons I may never understand.

"Someone else moved into Rogan's apartment," I said.

"Really? Who?"

"Some huge commando who looks like them."

"Hmm. Is he hot?"

"Cyan! Yes. I mean, he's attractive in a *silent but might kill you while you're sleeping* kind of way."

"Well, go over there and borrow a cup of sugar. Make him some cornbread."

"Maybe. I'll think about it." I couldn't imagine myself doing something like that. "I need to get going."

"Okay. Talk to you soon."

"NUMBER SIXTY-NINE!"

My Roxy's receipt said seventy-two. Three more orders till mine came up. I ignored my protesting stomach and glanced out the window of the restaurant. A cute guy in a black peacoat and a baseball cap walked by on the sidewalk. He glanced at me, his eyes widened, and he pretended like a large hook yanked his neck back as his body kept walking. He stumbled to a stop and stared at me with a goofy grin.

"Number seventy!"

I hid my laugh and kept my eyes on the food trays passing by.

The second time I checked the window, the guy walked by again—this time walking back the way he came, his head lowering as he descended imaginary stairs. At the edge of the window, he jumped down and fell below the window frame into a non-existent pit.

"Seventy-one!"

The lucky Roxy's customer holding ticket seventy-one picked up a delicious smelling tray of cheeseburgers and fries. I inched closer to the counter, ready to pounce on my order as it came up next.

"Do you believe in love at first sight, or do you need me to walk by again?"

The man from outside stood behind me, tufts of snow falling to the restaurant floor as he whipped his cap off his head. He stared at me with boyish blue eyes and mussed hair, looking eager to take me outside for a snowball fight.

"Seventy-two!"

"Uh, my number's up." I dashed away and grabbed my order, choosing a route to a table as far from him as possible. I kept my head down and eyes on my food.

"Are you my appendix? Because I don't know anything about you, but this feeling in my gut is telling me that I should take you out."

He stood at my table with a tray. His lopsided smile made him hard to dislike. "Can I join you? There's no other tables available."

My gaze flitted to the three empty tables next to us. He plopped down across from me and shook salt on his fries.

"Man, I love Roxy's. Don't you?" He sipped his shake. "I was going to impress you with a smooth pickup line, but I'll just lavish you with my awkwardness, okay?"

"Okay."

His eyes watched my lips smile. He pulled off his coat and his cranberry dress shirt pulled taut against his wide shoulders. He offered me his hand over the table. "Lance Croft. I really enjoyed our first date. Can I take you out again tomorrow, insert name here?"

I took his hand. "What?"

"If we're going out again, I'll need your name. You know, for the police reports afterward."

Hmm. Should I give this guy my name? He lost points in the suave department, but he earned extra credit for humor and effort.

"Tessa. Tessa Harlow."

"The pleasure is mine, Tessa Tessa Harlow."

I finished my food and collected my trash. "I have to get to class."

"Oh, where do you go to school?"

"UMass."

"I'm an adjunct prof at UMass. Art appreciation."

"Wow. What a coincidence."

"Are you from Boston?"

"No. I came out here to go to school. I'm from North Carolina."

"Great barbeque in North Carolina."

"Mmm-hmm." The truth was I hadn't done my research yet like I should've.

"Say, how'd you like to go to the Palace Theatre with me tomorrow? I'm reviewing the new production of Miss Saigon for the Boston Times."

"Tomorrow? A Broadway show?"

"Well, Boston's version of Broadway. I'll warn you. Miss Saigon is heavy. Have you seen it? Hamilton would make a much better first impression, but that's not till next week."

"No. I haven't seen it. And I can handle heavy." I wanted heavy. I wanted to feel things deeply, good or bad.

"Give me your phone."

I unlocked my phone and handed it to him. "Don't forget. Lance Croft." He tapped in his contact info.

"I won't forget."

He handed my phone back to me. "Text me your address." He waved his fingers over the phone.

"Like now?"

"Yes," he said slowly. "To make sure you don't forget me. And it'll make it a lot easier to pick you up for our date if I know where you live."

Could I trust him? There's no way he could know anything about me or Rogan. His puppy dog friendly routine didn't ring any internal warning bells, so I went with it.

I texted him my address, and he flashed me a white, satisfied grin. "I'll be there at five tomorrow. We'll have dinner first."

"Okay, bye." I grabbed my backpack and scurried out the door. Wow, my first first date, first Broadway show, first dinner out on the town, and all this with a handsome, funny teacher.

I ZIPPED UP THE SIDE zipper on my midnight blue long-sleeved dress. My hair still covered my scars even though I'd cut it to mid-back, but I didn't want to have to explain them to Lance on our first date.

He arrived at five o'clock, looking sharp in a gray suit. He helped me into his Range Rover and drove me to the Miss Saigon Restaurant to set the mood for the show. We ate yummy Vietnamese food and made small talk about Boston and UMass.

An employee handed me a playbill as we walked into the awe-inspiring lobby of the Palace Theatre. I clutched the glossy paper and gawked up at the grand arched ceilings with my mouth open.

"Can you hear the souls of Jimmy Durante, Mae West, Bob Hope—all the performers who've played here?"

I closed my eyes and envisioned the workers of the past raising the marble walls, carefully attaching the opulent gold leaf accents that climbed up to heaven like majestic offerings to God.

"No wonder they call it a palace."

Lance directed us to seats in the third row, center aisle.

"How'd you get these seats?"

"I've been reviewing for the Times for years."

We sat down, and the bows of the violins bobbed into view as the orchestra below us tuned their instruments. The lights went out, the opulent velvet curtains opened, and the music swept me away. I soared on a wave of notes through Vietnam and a war that was over before I was born.

The passion and the tragedy playing out on the stage blindsided me and I sobbed. I cried for the poor girl in the show. I cried for Chris, her American GI husband, and I cried for Rogan. The music said it all. Rogan had died. He wasn't coming back. Senseless war had claimed his life like it had taken so many others.

At the intermission Lance handed me a tissue. "I'm sorry if it's too morose for you. We can leave now, if you like."

"No, no. Let's stay. Just tell me, does it have a happy ending?"

"I don't want to ruin the ending."

"Does it have a happy ending? I need to know."

He shook his head. "You're going to cry through the second half too. We can leave."

"No. I won't leave. I'm not afraid to face this."

After the show, Lance stopped us on the sidewalk outside the theatre. He wrapped an arm around my shoulder and pulled me close. Rogan's arms would never be my sanctuary again. His rugged scent would never hit my nose. Lance smelled polished and clean.

"Why'd you cry so hard? I mean I know it's sad, but..."

"It reminds me of a soldier I knew."

"Can you tell me about him?"

"I think he's dead."

"You do? But you don't know?"

"I haven't heard from him in six months. Someone else is living in his apartment. And the music... I'm sure he's dead now."

"I'm so sorry. I didn't know. This was a bad idea."

I stood up straight and pulled my shoulders back. "No. I'm fine. I made such a fool of myself."

"You didn't."

He drove me home and walked me to my door. "I enjoyed your company, even if you cried. You feel things deeply. A sign of compassion."

He leaned down and pressed a kiss to my forehead. His hands rested on my hips.

I closed my eyes and concentrated on his lips on my skin, his hands on my waist. No hot air balloon ride, but a calm and safe blanket surrounded me.

"Full stop honesty here, Tessa. I'm into you. I wanna see where this could go. Let me take you out again tomorrow night. Something less depressing. I'll take you to dinner on the tallest building in Boston. Lift you up high. No more sadness."

Should I? He was offering me a healthy, normal date. No electrical storms or explosions, but maybe that was the best way to avoid pain. Maybe slow and steady, a relationship based on respect, was the way to go. An attractive guy with a respectable job and a nice car was letting me know he liked me.

"Okay. Thank you. See you tomorrow, Lance."

"Seven o'clock."

"Okay."

Chapter 16

———

ROGAN

Kabul Province, Afghanistan

"Intel from the son checks out," I said to my team as we scrutinized the topo maps and aerial photos displayed on the tables and computers at base camp.

"What finally broke him? The water or the knives?" Blaze asked.

"Takoda."

He gave Takoda a pat. "Good girl."

"Either way, Timoron is dead, and the location he supplied is credible," I responded.

Blaze smirked and looked down. "Still wish I could've been there to see her scare the shit out of him."

"It's not a show. Now, back to the location. Jericho's in the cave. One hundred percent."

I held up the image of a tall man entering a cave in the Afghan Spin Ghar mountain range. "That's him."

"Let's go then."

Fucking Blaze, always so eager to run to his death.

"No. Review the plan again. If we blow in unprepared, we'll be wasting the six months we spent trying to find him." The point of my pen marked the base of the cliff. "Takoda clears the base and takes point all the way up." My pen followed the twisted path to the cave at the peak housing Jericho. "We climb to three hundred meters and flank 'em here and here." I pointed to the west and east approaches to the main cave. "Me, Falcon, Diesel, and Blaze take the west entrance. Oz and Ruger guard the east side, catch any escapees. Warning shot to draw them out. I'll engage them as they exit. Falcon kicks them over the edge before they can blow themselves up. If Jericho doesn't surface, Takoda and I go in through the passage and engage him in there."

"You and Takoda alone?" Falcon asked.

"The goal is to draw Jericho out. If he doesn't show his face, Takoda and I go in. The ricochet inside the cave makes it too high risk for all of us to enter."

"You think we're pussies? We all go in," Blaze responded.

"If he blows himself up and we all go in, we all die. Takoda and I will clear the cave."

"We all go in or no one goes, Boggs. To hell with the self-sacrifice shit," Falcon said.

The loyalty of these men never ceased to amaze me. We would either succeed together in glory or die together in failure. "Alright. Takoda goes in first and immobilizes him. We traverse the crevice." The picture in my hand showed the narrow west entrance to the cave. "Based on surveillance, we'll encounter at most five combatants. My guess is no hostages in the cave, no women. If there are hostages, I'll assess it and make the call."

They all nodded.

"After we hit the target, collect proof of death, Blaze lights up the cave, we rappel down to the base where a helo picks us up." I pointed to a flat spot on the topo map. "Brings us back here." The men stood to pack. "Steady and slow. If the plan gets fucked, adjust on the fly. Got total confidence in this team. I'd lay down my life for any one of you and I know you'd do the same. We haven't lost one yet and this won't be the time that takes down Alpha Squadron. This'll be the mission that finally takes down Jericho. Let's go kick some ass."

———

AS WE BEGAN THE CLIMB up the mountainside, Takoda signaled with her tail she'd detected explosives and we went wide around the spot. The walls became steep, and Falcon helped me strap Takoda to my back. My gear scratched the face as we scaled the rocky cliff. We reached the cave entrance, removed our night vision, and took our positions as the first light of dawn touched the north face of the cliff.

"Firing," I said into my headset.

My warning shot into the cave pinged off the wall twice.

We waited for a reaction. After about a minute, one of Jericho's men emerged carrying a rifle. His eyes darted around, and his hand reached for a ripcord to a vest.

Fuck, I knew they'd all be wearing vests.

I shot him in the forehead. Before he fell, Falcon jumped and side-kicked him in the chest, pushing him over the edge of the cliff.

"Cover!" Falcon called.

We ducked as his vest detonated and rocked the side of the cliff.

Another militant scrambled out of the entrance to the cave. Idiot.

I planted one in his chest and Falcon kicked him over the edge. *Boom*! Another explosion blasted the cliff when he hit the ground.

We took cover on the perimeter again and waited for Jericho to exit.

After two minutes, Ruger called on the comms. "Two exited the cave on the east side. We got 'em."

"Were they wearing vests?" I asked.

"No. We're safe."

"Good. Watch for Jericho."

"Affirmative."

We waited five more minutes for Jericho to exit. "Come out, Mustafa!" I called in Pashto.

No response. The coward was going to make us come in after him.

I released Takoda and pointed two fingers toward the narrow entrance of the cave. "Get 'em."

She ran in without hesitation. That damn dog was so fucking brave. Growls and screams from inside let us know she had him and was engaging her killer bite.

Adrenaline made my skin itch as we turned sideways to traverse the entrance. I could not fail now. I had to get to my target. We reached the other side and the cave opened up. I saw him. Jericho. Unarmed. Screaming and struggling on the ground as a vicious Belgian Malinois mauled his arm.

"Out." She growled and thrashed on his arm. I knew how she felt, but she had to release him. "Takoda, out. Heel!"

She finally let Jericho go. He grunted and reached for his weapon that had fallen to the ground about two feet away from him.

I took aim at his head. "Firing." The guys dropped to the floor.

Jericho picked up a rifle and pointed his barrel at Takoda.

No way, motherfucker.

I engaged him in the head before he could get a shot off. The pink mist I'd yearned for painted the walls, but the goddamn live bullet exited his head and zinged around the cave. Jericho dropped and I rushed him. I inspected his nose, what was left of his forehead, and his eyes.

Yes!

"Got him! Jericho, EKIA." I called the words I'd repeated in my mind a million times in the last four years. Fucking enemy killed in action.

I carved off his left forefinger with my utility knife and slid it into a plastic bag. The proof of death I'd hungered for where it belonged—locked in the compartment of my vest.

We exited the cave and waited for Blaze to rig the cave to blow. A quick inspection of my team and everyone looked in one piece. Blood dripped from Takoda's left ear, but it was just torn skin. Falcon loaded Takoda onto my back. My hand pressed to the pocket of my vest and felt the finger. Yep, still there.

Blaze ran out of the cave. "Sixty seconds. Move out."

The rocks and debris from the explosion rained by our faces as we rappelled down the cliff. We ran to the waiting helo and lifted off.

Mission completed.

MY VICTORY SUN FINALLY dropped below the horizon over our base in Kabul. I pulled up the clone of Tess's phone to check for new selfies. She'd cut her hair and lightened it in the last six months. She'd gotten her teeth straightened. I kinda missed the quirky imperfection on her otherwise flawless body.

I closed my eyes and flipped through the Tessa slideshow in my head again.

The crunch of her jeweled patriotic dress as I hoisted her onto my cock on the dance floor.

Tasting her at Siege. God, her sweet taste and her little whimpers in the security room at Siege. That one stayed with me the longest.

What am I doing? I shouldn't indulge in my sparkle in the darkness. The slideshow only flared my bitter regret, and made my cock excruciatingly hard.

I took so much life today. And yet she was safe in Boston, dancing and going to school. Not being held captive by terrorists or abusive religious freaks. In some fucked up way, killing Jericho today gave her that freedom.

Maybe a combat jack would get her outta my mind. Nah. Exercising old Chester in the field wouldn't take the edge off. Only one thing could do that, and she was seven thousand miles away.

My phone alerted me to a message on her cell.

A new contact.

Who the hell was this and why was he happy to meet her?

I pulled up Brock's burner phone.

Me: Need you to check on T for me. New contact. Lance Croft 919-555-1122

Three seconds later, his response.

Brock: On it

She's moving on, finding herself another man like I told her to do. This Lance Croft asshole would be tasting her, comforting her, watching her fly.

Fuck! Why did I hold back again? What was I protecting her from? Me? She can handle me. She's a warrior. Eden's spirit had let me go a long time ago. Nothing was preventing me from loving Tess except myself.

A new resolve settled in my gut.

Operation Devil's Gate—completed.

Mission Make Tess Mine—initiated.

Chapter 17

TESSA

My phone lit up with a call as I applied my makeup for my date with Lance.

"Hey, Brock. What's up?"

"Sugar, Lance Croft is not whoever he told you he was."

I closed my lips gloss and set it on the counter. "How do you know about him?"

"I saw his text on your phone."

I picked up my cell and held it to my ear. "You're watching my phone?"

"Rogan asked me to look out for you, remember?"

My heart twisted into a knot of regret and grief. Rogan was dead and wouldn't watch over me any more, but at least Brock still cared about me.

"Croft works for the FBI. His real name is Lachlan Cutlass."

Brock's usually easy going voice turning urgent and bitter set my hair on end.

"The FBI? What would he want with me?"

"It's more like what would he want with me and my brother. Don't give him any information. How long have you been dating him?"

"Tonight's our second date."

"Cancel."

"What?" I glanced at my clock. "He'll be here in a few minutes."

"Look him up. You'll see he's not whatever he told you he is. I'll be right over."

"No—"

But he'd already disconnected.

THE SERENE BOSTON SKYLINE reflected off the panoramic windows of The Top of the Hub restaurant. The gourmet New England steamed lobster on my plate cooled uneaten as I stared at the lying jerk sitting across from me.

"I have a problem."

Lance put his fork down and raised his eyebrows. "Hmm?"

"Can you tell me why I couldn't find an adjunct professor at UMass named Lance Croft? Or an entertainment reporter from the Times with that name?"

His shoulders pulled back a fraction, but he was good at covering. If I wasn't looking for it, I wouldn't have noticed any reaction.

"I write under a pen name. And it must be an oversight on the school web—"

"No Lance Croft. No Lachlan Cutlass?"

"Tess—"

"Are you an FBI agent?"

He leaned over the table and spoke in a hushed voice. "Yes."

With a quick glance, I made sure no one was listening and leaned in too. "Are you investigating the Monroe brothers?"

"No." He lied to me with a straight face and a convincing tone like the practiced con artist I now knew he was.

My phone buzzed in my purse and I checked it quickly.

Brock: I'm in the lobby if you need me.

I ignored the text and continued my staring contest with Lance. "What's your real name?"

"Lachlan Cutlass. Special Agent for the FBI."

"Thank you for being honest with me—now at least."

"Tessa, I'm sorry I didn't tell you the truth. It's a precarious situation."

"I'm sure it is."

He looked away, and we both sat back in our chairs, ignoring our food and the elegant ambiance of the restaurant.

I'm an adjunct prof at UMass. Art appreciation.

Full stop honesty here, Tessa. I'm into you.

What a scumbag liar, trying to get information on my boss and his brother and then lying about it. Lachlan Cutlass was a fraud, just like my father, and I fell for it so easily.

The waiter cleared our plates and left us alone with the strained silence on the table.

Special Agent for the FBI.

As I glared at him, my mind orchestrated an idea to reverse Lachlan's own game on him. My days of being manipulated by men like him ended eight months ago. No more playing the victim. Time to fight for my joy.

"I might forgive you for deceiving me if you can help me."

He scrunched his brow. "Help you how?"

"I have five siblings stuck in a dangerous situation. I want to get them out."

He quirked his lips. "Tell me the details."

"HE BELIEVED I CARRIED her soul, so he left his seed with me as an offering to God."

Lachlan's eyes softened as I finished recounting my story of the abuse and the restrictive life I lived on the compound.

"How'd you get out?"

"I had a phone. I could get internet access when I went into town. I found an underground rescue organization and messaged them to help me. I snuck out through my window. They set me up with an apartment and a job in Boston." Lachlan had lied to me and now I'd lied to him. He didn't need to know Rogan rescued me from terrorists.

"So that's how you got the job at Siege? What's the name of the rescue organization?" He pulled a phone out of his jacket and tapped the screen.

Uh-oh.

"Um... My father's name is Jebediah Barebones."

Lachlan's blue eyes scrutinized my face.

I inhaled a deep breath. "The Brotherhood of God Church. Caldwell, Idaho. "

The repercussions of telling Lachlan this would ripple through my family. The compound would be tossed into disarray because I gave my father's name to the FBI. The betrayal of my promise to Rogan weighed even heavier on my conscience than calling out my dad. I had promised him not to trust anyone except the few people he'd said I could trust, and here I had given my father's name to a stranger. But he'd left me. I'd convinced myself he was dead and wasn't coming back. I had to do what I could to save my family.

Lachlan read on his phone for a minute then placed it on the table. "There's an open investigation. We've been watching them since Ervil Jeters went down ten years ago."

I nodded because Rogan had mentioned the FBI investigation when I first met him. "Watching? But no one has done anything?"

"No witnesses. They can't get an undercover agent in there. The security is too tight. No women have come forward. Those fuckers are all hush-hush about the shit going down inside those walls."

"Oh." That was the first time I'd heard Lachlan cuss.

"Transporting sex slaves across state lines is the most severe allegation we're trying to prove."

"Sex slaves?"

He put his phone back in his pocket and returned his gaze to me. "Human trafficking. Did they bring you and other women from Utah to Idaho and make you have sex with men you didn't know?"

"We moved from Utah. I wasn't forced to have sex with anyone, but the other women, yes. They were pressured to sleep with seed bearers. But no girls under eighteen. After Ervil went to jail, my father decreed no more sex with minors."

"We can still get them on rape, even if the women were over eighteen and consented. You can't coerce a woman into sexual acts with the threat of God. It's religious terrorism. How many seed bearer psychos are pulling that crap in Caldwell?"

"I don't know."

"But your father claims to be a seed bearer?"

"Yes."

"If we can get the women to testify, maybe get DNA to prove paternity, your father and any other seed bearers are guilty of rape."

"Okay."

"The bureau's also collecting evidence to prove tax evasion, WIC fraud, and child labor law violations. Will you testify?"

"Yes. To what I know." Facing my father in court would terrify me, but I'd find the strength. I would not cower to him ever again.

"One more favor?" I asked Lachlan.

He tilted his chin.

"Don't mention to the Monroe brothers I'm working with you."

"I don't speak with them. But Brock and Dallas are aware I'm with the bureau. If they see you with me, they'll figure something's up."

"Let's not let them see us together then."

"Agreed. I can't date you while the case is active anyway." He reached across the table and grasped my hand in his. "But the second this case is resolved and your father's wearing an orange jumpsuit, I'm taking another shot at you. Not giving up. You're too sweet."

I yanked my hand from his. "Don't call me sweet. My father used that word to intimidate and steal my dignity. I'm not sweet. I'm strong."

"Damn. I like that about you too. You're an amazing woman. You'd be good by my side."

"To be honest, I'll never trust you enough to date you after you lied to me the way you did—even if it was for a job."

"You said you'd forgive me if I helped you."

"I said I might forgive you. And forgiving doesn't mean I'd risk my heart with you. Making a girl feel stupid for falling for you doesn't lay a solid foundation."

"I didn't mean to make you feel... You were falling for me?"

"A little. I don't know. I'm confused."

"This sucks. I wish we'd met some other way." He rubbed his chin with his pointer finger and thumb. "I'm still gonna make a move on you after this case is over."

I laughed and challenged him with my eyes. "Go for it."

"I will." He dropped a wad of cash on the table with his napkin and stood. "Let's go. I gotta light a fire under this case."

———————————

FOR MONTHS, I'D WORRIED about Milo and the other kids back home, but I'd stuffed it down, holding onto hope Rogan would come back. After tonight, I couldn't resist any longer. I shouldn't have, but I texted my sister. Hopefully Lachlan would be able to get her out of there.

Me: I'm alive. Everything's going to be okay. Stay strong. V

Temperance: V? Thank God you're alive.

Me: Keep it secret. For now.

Temperance: OK. Luv U

Me: <3 U 2

Chapter 18

ALL WEEK, I WORRIED about Lachlan and Temperance. Not knowing what would happen to them sent my thoughts into a spiral of worst-case scenarios. At least tonight I could dance and forget for a little while. My chunky Mary Janes clomped on the metal stairs backstage at Siege. Billy, the stagehand, closed the door to my Plexiglas cube and wrenched the pulley, floating me and my box above the center of the dance floor. A few patrons arched their necks to check out the new dancer hanging from the ceiling, but most ignored me.

I bent and grabbed my ankles, stretching my hamstring muscles, and garnering more glances from the crowd below. My hands skimmed up my legs and hiked my plaid schoolgirl skirt up, revealing my boy-cut white satin panties and the bows tying the ruching at the sides.

With a tug on the knotted ties of my shirt under my breasts, I laughed as the techno rendition of an old song by Vanity 6 played over the sound system. The irony of me *shaking my ass* to "Nasty Girl" was lost on the masses below, but Brock winked at our little inside joke as he took a sip of his drink. I smiled back at him in his VIP booth. He returned his attention to the three women accompanying him tonight, and I started my dance routine.

Even with my eyes closed, the flash of the strobes transported me through a psychedelic wormhole to a simpler universe where Vanity was just a singer's name and I was just a dancer in a box.

As the hours passed, Tessa Harlow's physical body evaporated and only my spirit writhed to the beat of the music. The ultimate freedom sang in my bones, curing a bitterness deep in my tissue.

To dance with abandon, without fear of judgement or recrimination, was life altering.

In my euphoria, I felt the warm caress of Rogan's hands on my thighs, trailing up my backside and lifting my skirt, his huge palms flat on my butt cheeks. The striking heat broke my trance and caused me to seek the source.

In reality, I danced alone in my box. No one in the crowd paid me any attention— except one man sitting alone at a small table near the entrance. His cap and full beard covered most of his face. He tilted his head, exposing a pearly white grin and assessing blue eyes. I stumbled and braced myself on the walls of the box. Lachlan's black ball cap and thick beard hid his identity from the crowd, but I knew he was there for me.

A trill of flattery pinched my spine. A hot FBI agent had donned a disguise and risked exposure to come watch me dance. The high of the compliment quickly faded as I remembered Lachlan's face as he lied to me.

He may be into me, but Lachlan sacrificed his chances with me for the sake of his job. I wasn't about to get involved with another man who chose his career over love.

A half hour before closing, Lachlan paid his tab and waved up at me before he left the club.

At the end of the night, I changed into my regular clothes and carried my costume and heels in my backpack as I walked to my truck in my flat shoes.

Formless shadows lurked behind each vehicle in the lot, but I ignored them, pretending Rogan was still here making sure I got in my truck safely.

"Psst."

"Who's there?" I stopped and clutched my keys.

"Vanity." A tall man in a cowboy hat stepped out from behind an SUV. He kept his hands in his pockets and cocked one knee. His loose cotton shirt and dusty work pants looked so out of place in a big city parking lot like this.

"Zook? Is that you?" Zook Guthrie? In the Siege parking lot? I hadn't seen him in five years. Zook and I had cared for each other once. I could trust him. Right?

"It's me."

"You look so much bigger. Why're you here? How—"

"Did you think we wouldn't find you, Vanity?" My father's nasally voice hit my ears. His lanky shadow stepped around the hood of a car to my left and paced toward us. "Or should I call you Tessa Harlot?"

Oh no! How did he find me? With my truck parked just ten steps away, my only hope was to outrun them. I bolted and grasped the door handle, but I'd forgotten to unlock it. Darn, darn. I fumbled with my keys, but Zook charged and grabbed my upper arms.

"Zook. Let me go. Don't do this." I wrenched in his hold. My heart thumped so wildly, I'm sure he could feel it.

My father stepped in front of us. "You're coming home now, honeysuckle."

"No!"

I swung my arms to attempt to block him, but he seized a chunk of my hair and yanked it up. Needles stung my scalp. His heavy fist walloped my cheek, jerking my head to the side. I stopped fighting and reeled in the pain. I couldn't focus. My head, my face... Escape. I needed to escape. But how?

Zook handed me off to my father. The terror ratcheted through me as he wrapped his long arms around me and pulled me against him with my hands pinned behind my back.

"No! No!" I kicked and screamed through a haze of pain and panic.

"Get her feet," he ordered.

"Stop fightin', Vanity." Zook grabbed hold of my flying ankles.

"Never." I lost a fight like this at a street market in Karachi. Never again.

My father threw me to the ground and straddled me. He slugged my face, blow after blow. I screamed and hit him as hard as I could with my keys, trying to reach his eyes, but my hands bounced off him like failed shots at a dartboard. I grunted as he landed a vicious punch to my stomach. He stopped for a moment to wipe the sweat from his face.

I made eye contact with Zook through the mess of hair covering my face.

"I'm sorry, Van." His face contorted in anguish. He didn't want to betray me. Zook. My first love. So handsome and good. Under the control of the Brotherhood like everyone else on the compound.

Through all the chaos, my thumb found the panic button on my fob and pressed it. The truck horn blared in screeching bursts.

Blinding headlights lit up my father's back. He turned and covered his eyes to block the light. Zook's hands shook as he squinted at the approaching car.

"Oh shit." Zook took off running.

With a loud roar that emerged from deep in my stomach, I focused all my strength and stabbed the point of my keys into my father's neck.

"Ow, fuck!" As he clutched the spot I'd hit, his weight lifted from me. A muscular arm swung out and plowed into his face. In time with the blasts of the horn, the shadow of a hulking mass of man threw fast, brutal punches into my father's face. A gurgling sound emerged from his throat as he collapsed in a bloody pulp.

"Stop! Stop! You'll kill him." I tried to sit up. "Ow. Please help me."

The massive chest of my mystery hero heaved as he looked at me. He dropped the motionless body and stalked toward me. A car pulled up. Zook jumped from the driver's side, raced around, and loaded my father's limp body into the passenger seat. The wheels skidded on the pavement as they zoomed off.

Gone. They're gone. It's over. I'm safe.

My rescuer kneeled at my side. "Are you alright?"

Even in the dark, with my head spinning and the horn blasting, the scrape of the voice was unmistakable. "Rogan? What... Are you here?"

He must've found my fob because the horn blasts stopped.

"I asked if you're alright."

Yes. His voice. How could Rogan be here? "Are you dead? Am I dead?"

"What?"

"I dunno. It hurts. My head, my face. Everything hurts."

"Fuck." He slipped his arms beneath my back and knees and lifted me gently. He carried me to a truck and set me in the passenger seat. He spoke into his phone as he drove out of the lot. "T needs you. My place."

I closed my eyes as we sped away.

Chapter 19

I WOKE TO DALLAS KNEELING in front of me. He dabbed a cool compress to my temple. "Hey," he said in a comforting bedside voice.

"Hey."

As the fog cleared, my eyes focused on three dusty soldiers scowling down at me. Diesel, Blaze, and Rogan stood with their arms crossed and brows furrowed. They wore the same unmarked camo and the boots they'd worn when they rescued me in Kabul and they were covered in the same amount of dust and grime.

"Rogan." His beard covered his face, but his familiar pink lips showed through. "You're alive? Oh my God!"

He stared at me and pressed his mouth into a tight line.

"What's wrong?" They were the ones out fighting a war in the sand, and yet all their concentration drilled into me.

"You got beat up pretty bad." Dallas pressed something cold to my cheek. "Seeing a woman's face looking like yours is not easy for a man to take."

My skin throbbed and stung where he'd touched it. I took the compress from him and lowered it to the couch. Why were they all fussing over me like this? "I'll be fine. It's not the first time my fath—" Rogan growled and balled his fists. "Uh, I'll recover. I'm fine." I took a deep breath and looked around the room. Black leather couch, a card table in the nook off the kitchen. Rogan's old apartment? "We can't be in here. Someone else lives in this apartment now."

"Not anymore," Rogan responded, his voice hoarse.

"Oh. Where did he go?"

Takoda sauntered up to the couch and panted her doggie breath on me. I managed to sit up without getting dizzy and pat her head. "Takoda, I was so worried about you. You're back. What happened to your ear?"

Knocking on the door interrupted us. Rogan pulled his phone out of his pocket, checked it, and showed it to Dallas. "You know him?"

Dallas squinted and examined the screen. He pinched his nose. "I saw him at Siege earlier."

Rogan showed me the phone. "You know this guy?"

The video showed Lachlan Cutlass, still wearing his beard and ball cap, standing outside Rogan's apartment door.

"That's Lance Croft," I replied.

"Also known as Lachlan Cutlass," Dallas added.

"He was at the club?" Rogan asked Dallas.

"Yeah."

In one swift motion, Rogan opened the door, lowered his shoulder, and careened into a wide-eyed Lachlan. They collided with a grunt and tussled into the hall, thunking into the wall in the corridor.

Takoda trailed on Rogan's heels. She barked and snarled, standing alert with her hackles up, her whole body pointed and waiting to pounce.

Blaze, Diesel, and Dallas watched the brawl, but didn't move to help.

The crunch of a fist connecting with someone's flesh echoed in the hallway. "Stop! Stop!" My feeble voice didn't carry over the ruckus. I sat up, but the room tilted and I moaned.

Dallas held me down by my shoulder. "Take it easy, Tessa."

"Aren't you going to stop them?" Why was no one breaking up the fight?

"No."

"You guys! Enough! Please!" I screamed from my spot on the couch.

Rogan stalked back in and wiped his palms together. Lachlan followed him, breathing heavy and fixing his rumpled clothes. He wiggled his jaw with his hand and winced.

"Heel." Takoda sat at Rogan's feet, but her eyes dialed in on Lachlan and her ears pointed at him like monoliths.

Rogan's eyes shot bullets at Lachlan. "You freak. You go to that club and watch her dance in a fucking box hangin' from the ceiling?"

Lachlan stared at me with concern. His eyes narrowed when he saw my face and the cold compress on the couch. "Oh God, Tessa."

"You don't stay to walk her to her car?" Rogan stood between me and Lachlan.

Lachlan flicked his eyes to Rogan and side-stepped him. When he returned his attention to me, the concern was gone. Awareness and anger blanketed his gaze. "Who did this? Your father?"

"What the hell is your game? Leave her the fuck alone," Rogan said.

"I'm sorry I wasn't there." Despite Rogan's blazing anger, Lachlan kept his cool demeanor.

"It's not your fault. I'm fine. Rogan was there."

Lachlan looked to Rogan and nodded, thanking him. "She needs a doctor."

"Dallas was a medic. He's seeing to her."

"We should call the police."

"We're not calling the cops. I'll take care of Jeb Barebones."

"Do not fuck up my investigation." Lachlan pointed a finger at Rogan.

Rogan looked down at Lachlan's finger and clenched his fists like he was trying hard not to break it. "Your investigation is already fucked or you'd have swept that compound by now. Get the hell out!"

"Rogan, please. He's helping me."

Rogan looked from me to Lachlan. "Leave now. I need to talk to her."

"I'll call you tomorrow, Tessa. Rest tonight and then we'll figure out what to do next."

Rogan growled as he shoved Lachlan out the door.

———————

"TAKE CARE, TESSA," Blaze called as he left the apartment with Diesel.

"Bye, guys. I'm so happy you're back."

"I'm sorry he got to you," Dallas said to me. "It won't happen again."

"It's not your fault. My father had his mind set on finding me. You couldn't stop him."

Dallas left me alone with Rogan and Takoda.

Rogan and Takoda were back.

My father knew where I worked.

My head throbbed trying to absorb all the facts on top of the shame from the beating tonight.

For six months, I'd focused on school and forging a new future. Today two men from the past slammed back into my life and collided in a blast of violence and pain.

"I thought you were dead."

"Not dead." He walked toward me with his hands loose by his sides.

I took a deep breath to calm the butterflies that had taken flight in my chest. "I'm so relieved. I can't believe you're here."

"I'm here." He kneeled next to the couch. "I should've gotten there sooner. I knew your dad would find you after you texted your sister."

"You saw my text to Temperance?"

"I was watching your phone. Got here as soon as I could. It took us six months to find our target and complete this mission. I'm sorry I was too late."

"You weren't too late. You saved me. Again."

He shook his head.

"Forgive me for contacting Temperance. It's created so much trouble."

"You never need to ask my forgiveness. We'll take care of it."

"Is that why you came back? To protect me from my father?"

"Part of it."

"What's the other part?"

He wrapped one big, warm hand around my neck and scrunched his fingers. "Missed you."

I sucked in a breath as the heat of his touch emanated through my body. "You missed me?"

"Mmm-hmm." His fingers trailed down and stopped on my ruby necklace. "Missed my Sunshine."

Gah! I missed him too. So much. I thought of him all the time, worrying he'd been killed. Despite the relief and joy I felt at seeing him again, I had to protect myself. He'd hurt me and could do it again without a second thought. I lifted his hand from my necklace and pushed it away. "Please, don't."

"You're hurt. Let me comfort you."

"I'm different now."

"How're you different? You still my brave girl who won't be intimidated?"

"Yes."

"Still dance around in sparkly jeans to Taylor Swift?"

I couldn't help the giggle that escaped. "Yes."

"Then let me hold you. Just tonight. Tomorrow we'll talk about what else may have changed or not. Maybe tomorrow I'll leave again or you'll send me away. For tonight, be safe in my arms."

My body screamed *yes* as he leaned in to put his hand behind my head. How could I refuse him after he'd come straight from combat to rescue me? I rested my forehead on his hard chest, letting the scent of dust and man drift into my nose. I needed to feel his strength to prove he was alive. I needed his reassuring embrace after my dad's attack. I'd probably regret it in the morning, but he was right. For tonight, we should hold on to each other.

He took off his boots and lined them up under the bench by the door. His eyes were glued to me as he removed his camo jacket. He'd done the same undressing routine the first night I stayed here. Back then, I wondered what the rest of his tattoo looked like. Now I know it's an *E*. I still don't know what it represents, and I don't know much more about the man who wears it.

He looked down at himself and quirked his lips. "I'll shower in a bit. Can you handle a little stank?"

I laughed. "Sure."

He lifted me gently and reclined on his back on the couch, situating me to his side, so my forehead rested on his chest and my leg draped over his knee. His hand swept my hair from my face and tucked it behind my ear.

"You good?"

"Mmm-hmm." I was good. Rogan's warmth still soothed me like it did before he left. The shock of my father's attack and Rogan's return faded and started to become a memory. All that mattered was now. His mammoth chest surrounded me like a brick wall even Jebediah Barebones couldn't penetrate.

My hand on his hard chest found his dog tags through his shirt. I fingered the beaded string and flat metal plates. If he'd been killed, these dog tags would've come home without his warm body and beating heart.

I wasn't sure how I felt about God anymore, but I needed to thank someone for this.

Thank you, Lord, for bringing him home alive. No matter our future. Thank you for watching over him.

"I'm gonna wake you up in three hours to check you for a concussion."

"You don't need to do that. I'm fine."

"Doing it anyway. You wake up, take some pain meds, go back to sleep."

"Yes, sir."

His chest rumbled with his chuckle.

Chapter 20

———

IN THE EARLY MORNING light, I reached for my missing heater of a pillow and winced at the bruises on my face and chest. I went in search of Rogan and found him staring out the kitchen window. I approached him from behind and draped my arms around his waist. He placed one hand over mine.

"What do you see out this window?"

He lowered his head and shook it.

"Do you have PTSD?"

He looked down at me over his shoulder with an eyebrow arched into the shape of a serpent. "I don't have PTSD. The Army checks my mental stability regularly. They wouldn't trust me with million-dollar equipment if I wasn't solid."

I dropped my arms and took a step away from the menace that hit me from his back.

"Why do you tell people you're retired military if it's clearly a huge part of your life?"

He spun and nailed me with hatred spewing from his eyes. "Why do you continue to push and test and ask questions when I've made it clear I can't tell you?"

"Can't or won't?"

"Both."

"Maybe we could get you some help. If you lost friends over there—"

He clasped his head in his hands and grimaced. "Shut up!"

"But..."

He stalked toward me, anger whipping off him like fire. "You have no idea what you're talking about. If I answered your questions, a fucking flood would open up and drown you in water so deep you couldn't breathe. I'll never put a weight like that on you. I tried so goddamn hard not to unload that on you, but you kept pushing and pushing and driving me fucking insane."

I turned and paced away from him. The familiar bitterness of rejection sliced through me. Nothing had changed. Rogan thought I wasn't strong enough to handle him. He'd allow himself to hold me, protect me, but he would never open a door for me and let me carry weight for him. I could never love a man with an impenetrable barrier between us. I'd only end up hurt when he leaves again.

"Did you fuck the spook?" He spoke low and quiet, his voice rough like sandpaper.

"What?" I looked back at him over my shoulder.

His nostrils flared, like a bull about to charge at a matador. "Cutlass. Did you fuck him?"

I propped my arms on my hips and matched his demanding tone. "None of your business." His intimidation techniques might work on prisoners, but not on me.

"Did you fuck him?" He paused between each word, clearly struggling to control his fury.

"No. Okay? No. I haven't been with anybody. But even if I had, that's a totally rude question, which you have no right to ask me. Especially when I just asked you a much less obnoxious question and you went ballistic!" I grabbed my backpack and my keys, which I thought I'd dropped in the parking lot. Did Rogan bring these here? I don't care. I can't care. "Thank you for rescuing me last night. I'm thrilled you're alive. No, I really am. Because you're too awesome to not be on this earth." I slung my bag over my shoulder and gripped my keys in my clenched fist. "But you're a black chasm to me. The absence of color. The opposite of me. Life's too short to live without color. I've been there and it sucks."

As I reached for the doorknob, his quiet voice pierced the void. "Stop. Stop right there." He held out one hand but let it fall.

"What? I'm right, aren't I? You're a black void to me."

He shook his head and looked to the floor.

Gah! What does that mean?

"I'm done. Goodbye, Rogan. Don't contact me. Don't talk to me. Please. Just leave me alone."

I slammed the door shut and retreated to Blaze's apartment, leaving Rogan and all the bullcrap that came with him behind.

"I DON'T WANT YOU SEEING Cutlass anymore." Rogan said his first words to me since I'd asked him to leave me alone a week ago.

I shivered at the bitter cold as he walked by my side in the Siege parking lot after my shift.

"You told me to shut up. I'm doing that."

I tucked my coat tighter around me and wiped frigid snowflakes from my face. Idaho was cold, but Boston's winters delivered their own unique bite.

"I don't want you to go back to dancing after your injuries heal."

He must know Dallas took me off the box girl schedule while I recovered from the beating. I tried to tell him I was fine and I could cover the fading bruises with makeup, but he wouldn't listen.

"You don't need to walk me to my truck anymore. Dallas added lights and cameras all over the employee lot now."

"Don't care."

We stopped at the door to my truck. "You know, you're a piece of work. You come walk me to my truck the last four nights saying nothing to me. When you finally decide to talk on the *fifth night*, you try to tell me who to see and what to do?" I shook my head. "No way."

"Tess— "

"No! I asked you to leave me alone. You've been gone six months and now... now you barge into my life and start ordering me around? I'm not looking for someone to take my idiot father's place."

He flinched. "Let me— "

"I'm happy now. I appreciate how you rescued me and helped me start a new life. I'll always be grateful for that. I'm finding my way now. But *you*"—I poked his chest and it bent my finger back—"mess with my head. Just go. Run away and kill people somewhere, but keep your black cloud away from my happy place."

He smirked at the icy pavement as I got in my truck and drove out of the lot onto the cleared street. His flurried reflection in my rearview mirror watched my truck till I turned the corner, just like he had four nights in a row.

I SLAMMED THE DOOR to Blaze's apartment and tossed my coat and backpack on the end table. The nerve of Rogan! Following me around and then telling me what to do like he cared about me. He dangles his tantalizing carrot and snatches it away over and over, breaking my little bunny heart each time.

My phone buzzed in my purse. Probably another text from Lachlan asking me how I'm doing. I needed to respond soon or he'd show up here.

Oh—a text from Rogan.

R: Balcony

An ice block dropped in my chest as I walked to the balcony doors. Arctic air snapped my hair against my cheeks and needle-like flakes blew uninvited into the room. Wow, a foot of snow had collected on the railing out here while I'd been at work. And Lord help me, in the courtyard below, Rogan stood tall and strong in the flurry. He held a guitar poised in front of him. Takoda waited at attention by his side, her tail making little snow angels.

In the darkness, the edge of the cone of light from the lamppost illuminated his outline. His boots sunk deep into the drift. Icy slush collected on the gunmetal gray beanie on his head.

He strummed his guitar and began to sing. "*Hey, darlin', will you dance with me?*"

I leaned back with my arms crossed over my chest and laughed at Rogan singing his heart out and playing guitar out in the middle of a blizzard.

"I'll play your favorite song."

"What are you doing? It's freezing!"

"Then I'll hold you close, all night long."

Oh my God! Rogan's feathery voice drilled a pick into the ice around my chilled heart.

"Hey, darlin', can I take you out?"

"Come up here!"

He nodded but sang more silky strains as he walked inside. Takoda bolted ahead of him. I ran to my front door and threw it open. His strumming got louder as he climbed the stairs. Takoda's eager paws thumped up the steps and tromped to me. She didn't touch me with her wet paws—she knew better than that—but she jumped up on her hind legs. Ice-cold drops fell from behind her ears as I scrubbed her with both hands. "Silly girl."

Rogan reached the corridor, still crooning in his sultry voice. He looked down at his guitar, and his timbre quieted.

"Hey, darlin', let me make you mine.

Say you'll walk with me a while

Because I see our future in your smile

Hey, darlin', let me make you mine."

When he raised his head, his eyes glinted through crystalline snowflakes on his lashes, and his pink lips bent in an adorable crooked line.

"Listen..." I tried to sound stern, but his sneaky move was totally working on me. I couldn't be mean to him now after he'd put himself out there like this. I stared at him in shock, a huge smile on my face.

"There's my Sunshine," he said, staring at my mouth.

I ushered him in and closed the door. "Take off those wet clothes."

He chuckled. "Alright. That was easy."

"No, I mean your jacket and hat, you goof!"

He set his guitar against the wall and removed his soaked beanie and coat. He stalked toward me with purpose. "Time to talk." He grasped my hand and led me to the couch. "Remember how you'd ask me to forgive you and I'd tell you there was nothing to forgive?" He touched my temple and squinted at the bruises fading to yellow on my face. "Now it's my turn. Forgive me. For treating you the way I did before I left, for leaving, for saying what I said a week ago. Everything. I'm sorry." He took my other hand and held my gaze. "You wanna hear my excuses, I'll tell you, but just know I apologize, no matter why, I was wrong. I did mess with your head."

"You totally did. I'm so confused. Why'd you get so angry when I asked you questions?"

"I came straight from the airport. Hyperalert and in kill-or-be-killed mode. I run into your dad and some other asshole pounding his fists into you in the Siege parking lot... He's very lucky to be alive."

"Oh my gosh."

"The next morning, seeing welts darken on your beautiful face did not settle with me. Your pointed questions... I lost my shit. I should've contained it better."

"I didn't think..."

"You know how it bothers you when people call you sweet?"

"Mmm-hmm."

"Talking about what happens downrange triggers the same reaction in me. Particularly about PTSD. Hell yes, my friends died. My family..." He shook his head. "Simplifying it to four letters... People lose their lives in war. Yes. But the stuff I've seen affects everything I do."

"Thanks for telling me this. I understand so much better now."

"There's more I need to tell you. It's not easy for me to talk about. But I'd like to show you. We're gonna spend some time together. Alone. Away from here. And I'll tell you everything you want to know."

"Why bother? Like you said, I can't handle you."

He wrapped a hand around my neck and twined his fingers in my hair. "I was wrong. You're strong. More than anyone knows and stronger than any woman I've ever met. You may be the only one who *can* handle me."

The coolness of his touch made me shiver, but when he looked in my eyes, the warmth of a campfire glowed there and heated my skin. The magnetic field crackled between us like hot bacon in a skillet, just as it always had before, but stronger now because he was focusing all his intensity on me and looked so darn gorgeous in his blue jeans and flannel shirt. But Rogan had hurt me and I'd promised myself I'd never give him the chance to do it again.

I arched my neck to dislodge his hand and stepped away from him. "You shouldn't touch me. You lost that right."

"Listen. Before I doubted my self-control with you. When I was out there this time, I realized I can utilize my training and apply it to you. In the field, I'm calm, precise, focused. I can do it. No one has better self-control than me."

"You think you're suddenly going to be able to master whatever has been making you nutso all this time?"

"I'm sure of it." He smiled at me and oh boy, Rogan's devilish grin made my panties catch fire and get wet at the same time. "You're taking time off. Come on an adventure with me. By the end of it, you'll see I'm right."

"I can't. I need to work. My classes..."

"There's no school Monday. You'll only miss Wednesday and Friday."

"How do you know my schedule?"

"You'll catch up when you get back."

"But Siege. I'm working this weekend—"

"You don't need to work. I'm in with the boss," he said in a conspiratorial tone as he pulled a number up on his phone. "Dallas, Tess won't be in for a week. That alright with you?"

Rogan nodded and ended the call. "You're off work for a week."

"You can't just call my boss like that."

"I got you the job, I can get you a vacation."

"*You* got me the job? I thought Brock..."

"Brock did it because I asked him to."

Well, that was kind. Even though he didn't tell me he did it. Wait... "Did you buy me the truck and give me the money?"

"Yes. I wanted you to have an armored truck."

"Why?"

He shrugged. "Just in case."

"Just in case what?"

His playful eyes and laughing tone became dark and serious. "If you'd made it to your truck, your dad would've never gotten his hands on you."

"Oh. I see." Rogan protected me from the beginning? He could be so darn thoughtful. But also a cold-hearted turkey. "I want to pay you back."

"No." He stalked to my bedroom closet and picked up an empty duffel bag. "Best if you pack now. We're leaving in the morning."

Hmm. Curiosity clawed at my psyche. What did he have planned? "If we do this, it's just friends. No cuddling. No kissing."

His lips quirked up at the corners. "I think I made it clear I'm lookin' for more than friends with you, but I'll play along."

"Okay. Let's go for it."

"Bring the dress you wore to the wedding. And those cutoff shorts that show your ass. In fact, where's your schoolgirl outfit?"

"My costume for Siege?"

"Yeah, with the white stockings."

"Um, in my backpack."

"Go get it."

I brought him my backpack and pulled out my top, skirt, and stockings. "And why would I need these?"

He grabbed the costume from my hand and shoved it into the duffel bag. "Continue..." He handed me the bag and waved his hand toward the depths of the closet.

I chose a few more items and added them to the bag.

From behind me, he said, "Tess."

I turned to face him. "Hmm?"

He held up a squat, red cardboard box. "Bring this too."

I dropped the bag and stepped toward him. "What is it?"

"Open it."

The box held a petite, gilded jewelry box. Intricate mother of pearl inlay traced around vines and flower buds. The lid opened in front, held by two golden hinges along the back. Inside, red velvet compartments. All empty, but perfectly square.

"It's exquisite."

"Pack it in the bag."

"Shouldn't we leave it here? I don't want it to get damaged."

"Bring it."

"Okay."

"And your ice-cream cone shoes. A bathing suit too. And your boots."

"Boots? Where are we going? Is Takoda coming?"

"Blaze'll watch Koda. Be prepared for anything. I'm leaving now. You finish packing." He walked to the door and stopped with one hand on the doorjamb. "I'll pick you up at oh-eight hundred.

"Huh?'

"Eight in the morning. Our flight's at ten."

"Flight?"

"If you wanna see the colors of the world, you gotta fly." He tapped the wall twice, gave me a wicked smirk, and left me alone in my room.

Oh my goodness. What the heck did he have planned?

Chapter 21

———

"THIS MUST BE EXPENSIVE, Rogan."

The pilot to our private jet walked into the cockpit and closed the door. I fiddled with my seatbelt and tried to calm my stuttering heart.

"I live a simple life. Save my money. Spend when I want." Rogan's wide shoulders spread across the expansive back of the plush leather seat. His left hand balanced a worn cowboy hat on his thigh, his fingers dipping into the crease at the top like they'd spent many years there.

"Do you take fancy jets everywhere?"

"No, this is for you."

My stomach leapt into my chest as the plane lifted off and the white snow on the Boston Executive Airport shrank from view.

"Your injuries healing okay?" he asked me.

"Yes." Makeup completely concealed the fading yellow of my bruises now. "So, why're we flying to North Carolina?"

"Lived there the longest of anywhere else. Closest thing I've got to a place to call home."

About two hours into the flight, Rogan handed me a small, black velvet pouch. I opened it and dropped a bumpy black rock into my hand. "What's this?"

"Black tourmaline."

"Tourmaline?"

"In its rough state. If you're not looking closely, you might pass over this stone thinking it's coal. You need persistence and a shit ton of tumbling to get the crystal inside to shine, but it's worth it. A polished tourmaline will protect you forever."

I rolled the stone in my fingers, taking in the striated bumps and grooves of the rock.

"If you decide you wanna keep it, we'll polish it up, make jewelry out of it. Or you can discard it." He shrugged.

"Discard it?"

What an interesting gift. Why would he give me something black and unpolished that would protect me forever and then offer to throw it away? I looked up and his eyes danced. He was waiting for me to figure it out.

Oh goodness. He gave me him.

His gaze moved to my smile. "I... I'll treasure this stone." I pressed the tourmaline in my palm. "Of all the gifts you've given me, this one is the most precious. We won't discard it. We're keeping it. Polished or raw. I can't wait to add it to my jewelry box."

"Good." He leaned back in his chair and closed his eyes.

Later in the flight, Rogan reached for my hand, but I snatched it into my lap. "No holding hands."

"Tasted you already, Sunshine."

Heat rose in my cheeks. "I'm protecting myself. You're not all black anymore, but you're a dark gray mass of questions. I can't trust gray. Not till you tell me everything about Boggs."

"Is that how it is? You're extorting information outta me?"

"Whatever you want to call it. Those are the rules."

"Alright. I want to hold your hand, so I guess I'm gonna have to share something."

"Make it good."

"What do you wanna know?"

"Tell me about your parents."

His gaze wandered to a point in the distance over my head. "My dad was a redneck GI. She was a society girl. A model. He loved her like crazy. She couldn't hack the life of an Army wife, all the moving around, my dad gone most of the time. She hated living on base. When he came back from deployment, they'd fight. My mom divorced him when I was four years old."

"Did you get to visit him?"

"Yes, but not on a regular schedule. When he was in the States, I'd stay with him all summer. Spent all my vacations with him wherever he was stationed. Lots of times, that was in North Carolina."

"What happened to him?"

"Killed in action in Iraq. I was twelve."

"I'm sorry. What was his name?"

"Zander Saxton."

I turned in my seat and angled my body toward him. "Tell me about him. Are you like him?"

"I'm a carbon copy of my dad. We loved all the same shit. Huntin' and camping. He taught me to shoot when I was five. Told me all his war stories and survival tricks." Rogan rubbed his hand over his face. "He was aggressive and brave. Joined the Rangers and advanced to staff sergeant ridiculously fast. Decorated medals of honor. I never had any other ambition than to grow up and be him."

"That's so sad it didn't work out with your mom."

"Don't think he ever recovered from losing her."

"Where does she live now?"

Rogan's face went blank. He turned his head and stared straight ahead. "Overseas."

Okay. Clearly he wasn't ready to share any details about her yet. "What'd you do in the Army?"

"Did my first three tours as a sniper. Tried out and qualified for the Rangers like my dad. I got lucky and saw a ton of action on my fourth deployment. Earned myself a reputation as the Executioner. My commander recognized my skill and recommended me for an even more elite special ops team."

"What's it called?"

"Can't tell you. Most secretive unit in the U.S. military. As far as the public knows, it doesn't even exist. The missions are so sensitive, they're off the books. Totally black ops."

"Wow. Impressive."

"I served with honor."

"Is that why all the secrecy with you rescuing me?"

"Yeah. We can't draw any attention."

"You must be an excellent sniper to be chosen."

"I got the disposition, but make no mistake, I worked my ass off to make the cut. Only a slim percent of candidates survive the training."

"What did they do?"

"They weigh you down and toss you off a cliff into freezing rapids then watch and see if you sink or swim. Hard-core marches through rough terrain carrying a fifty-pound rucksack. You sit in a room full of smoke with no facemask. They basically torture you to see if you can handle the pressure."

"And you made it through?"

He nodded. "Mind over matter."

"So Executioner? You've killed people?"

"Yes..." he said slowly.

"How many?"

"Why the interest in this?"

"I'm just wondering what it's like. To kill someone."

"If you don't get them first, they'll kill you or your team."

"So it's methodical for you?"

He scratched the short hairs above his ear. "Snipers carry a lot of weight. Not just gear, but pressure to be the forward line of defense, usually ahead of your unit. When the unit loses a man, the sniper takes it on. I've heard "Taps" more times than anyone should, and each time, part of me knows I failed at my job. Logical or not. That's the way it is."

"You can't bear that all yourself. The guilt will destroy you."

He shrugged. "I harbor no remorse for the lives I took, only the brothers I didn't save."

He curled his hand behind my neck, lowering his head for a kiss.

I jerked my chin back. "You only asked to hold my hand."

He froze and stared into my eyes. "I shared a shitload I've never told a soul before. Put our country's national security at risk trusting you. Now kiss me."

I laughed. "Okay."

His palm on my neck drew me closer until our lips hovered an inch apart. I breathed him in, his proximity more exhilarating than a real kiss. I arched my neck and our lips connected. I was wrong. The closeness was not better than a kiss. Nothing was better than this kiss.

The six months apart evaporated in the moment his lips touched mine. The current between us zinged faster and more intense than ever. Before, I didn't even know him. I was a different person. Now I knew he was a calculated killer, yet he brushed his full lips on mine in a gentle caress. The tip of his tongue licked the seam of my lips and my stomach dropped, wanting more than anything to let him in.

I opened for him, and his growl vibrated on my tongue, sending a tremor to my core.

His fingers mashed the strands of my hair against the skin of my neck. He tasted more earthy and rugged than I remembered. He tilted his head and moved his mouth on mine with the hunger of a starving man faced with a buffet. I wanted to be devoured, but I angled my chin and broke our connection with a gasp.

I wiped my lower lip with my finger. "Um... Thank you for trusting me." My voice was ragged.

He sat back and his shoulders rose and fell with his deep breath. His hand moved his cowboy hat over a visible bulge in his pants, and he closed his eyes.

The black tourmaline weighed heavy in my hand—a solid, impenetrable mass. I uncurled my fingers and held the stone up to the light.

"You know, this tourmaline seems more brilliant already."

He didn't look, but the corners of his mouth quirked up. "I'm gonna take you in the back of this plane."

"What?"

"On the return trip. Taking you in the bed in the back. Adding you to the mile high club."

"Um... Just friends, remember?"

He opened his eyes and leaned his forearm on the armrest between us. "Yeah, right. That kiss? I'm taking you in the plane on the way home. You're gonna scream my name."

Lord have mercy. Heat flushed up my neck. I closed the tourmaline in my palm and crossed my arms. "We'll see."

Chapter 22

―――――

DAPPLED SUNLIGHT DANCED on the rental car's dashboard as we drove under the arching willow oaks of Wilmington. Rogan pulled onto a long, narrow driveway in a neighborhood of secluded estate homes.

"Who lives here?"

"Falcon."

Nervous jitters pricked my skin. The last time Falcon saw me, I was a weak mess, in shock from my ordeal with terrorists. "Uh, do you think it'll be awkward meeting him since I've been using his name as my fake cousin?"

"Trust me. Falcon has no issues with pretending."

"I'm nervous."

"Don't be. He probably already considers you family. Falcon takes on strays—like me. He'll love you."

At the end of the drive, Rogan parked in front of a whitewashed one-story home with tall rectangular windows. A lone Adirondack chair waited on the wide porch for someone to come out and have a sit while sipping sweet tea. A man I could only assume to be Falcon sauntered through the screened front door. Oh yeah. This must be Falcon because he had the same impossibly wide shoulders and don't-mess-with-me swagger as Rogan. Falcon squinted at our rental car as he descended the steps.

The crisp January air snapped at my cheeks as I exited the car and walked to meet my make-believe cousin—who happened to have skin darker than mine and thick, curly black hair. We'd have to work on our story because we certainly didn't look related.

Rogan stopped a few feet away from Falcon, raised his chin, and saluted him with his right hand stiff over his eye and his heels together. Falcon looked Rogan straight in the eye and returned the gesture with respect. They broke their stiff stances with a laugh and hugged each other with loud smacks to the shoulder.

"Good to see ya, brother," Rogan said.

"You too, man."

Rogan released him and winked at me. "You remember your cousin Tessa?"

"Howdy, Tessa." When Falcon tipped his chin, I noticed a tattoo of wing tips poking out of his navy blue T-shirt. I waved my fingers at him.

"Betsy ready?" Rogan asked Falcon.

"Spent all day yesterday on her. Tuned up, aired up." Falcon handed Rogan a set of keys and a knapsack he slung down from his shoulder.

"We're gonna hit Bixby Boggs. Mud good today?"

"Should be. Rained all week. You bring the sun with you or something?"

"You know sun shines out of my ass wherever I go."

Falcon laughed. "Y'all joining me tonight for some of my pork barbeque?"

Rogan nodded. "Wouldn't miss it."

"Have fun. Later, Tessa." Falcon waved and walked back up the steps.

"Follow me." Rogan led me to a rustic barn behind Falcon's house. He used the keys Falcon gave him to unlock the door and swung it wide. The barn housed a red Jeep Wrangler with giant tractor wheels. An oversized American flag hung proudly from a pole in the back.

"This is Betsy." He swayed his palm like he was showcasing a luxury car at an auto show.

"Betsy?"

"Hop in." His big hands at my waist lifted me up into the passenger seat. After he passed behind the Jeep and jumped behind the wheel, he lowered his chin and winked at me. "Buckle up."

The engine thundered in my ears and a strong rumble vibrated under my feet. He tapped his cowboy hat, put her in gear, and backed us out of the barn. After a fifteen-minute drive, we veered onto an unpaved road and drove around the outside of a gate marked "Private Property." My teeth rattled as we bumped along the rugged dirt road. Rogan drove slowly at first, but sped up when we hit a flat area. Tree branches whipped the sides of the Jeep. We emerged from the brush at the top of a cavernous pit filled with muddy water.

"I built this pit for Mitch Bixby, the guy who owns this place." Rogan's eyes scanned the horizon.

"You built it?"

"Technically, I excavated it for him."

"Were you a contractor?"

"No. I just happened to have a rocket propelled grenade handy that day and used it to excavate this hole."

"You made this pit with a grenade?"

He laughed. "Yeah, it was fun. Ready to get her dirty?"

"We're going in there?"

"Hell yeah."

My head bounced off the headrest as we thunked down the bank of the pit and splashed to a standstill at the bottom. Rogan jerked the wheel and the back of the Jeep jackknifed. Chunks of mud arched over our heads, landing in heavy thuds on the windshield.

We trudged through the muck, sinking deeper as we went. The engine revved and the wheels spun but we stayed put. The Jeep coughed and hiccupped and... stalled out.

"Oh no! Are we stuck?"

He peered out the windshield at the water rising around us. "Can you swim?"

My breath caught in my throat. "Like in the mud?"

"Betsy gets stuck, we gotta swim for it."

"Oh. I don't really know how to—"

He laughed and restarted the engine. "Just kiddin." He jabbed the gearshift into reverse. Silty water flew through the air as we slugged backward. Rogan maintained total control of his vehicle. It did exactly what he wanted it to, just like Takoda followed all his commands without a thought of disobeying. With Rogan in charge, there was nowhere to go except where he wanted you to. He shifted back into gear and forged a different path forward.

"Yee-haw!" Rogan exclaimed as we dropped from the steep incline of the bank to the flat ledge next to the mud pit. He didn't stop to regroup, just punched the gas and took off for a rocky trailhead. I clung to the handle above my window and admired him in his element, his face relaxed and his mouth... smiling. Oh my gosh, Rogan should smile more because his pink lips curved in that grin was the most inviting thing I'd ever seen.

"What color is life now?" he asked me.

"Bright canary yellow! But it's all splattered with mucky brown mud!"

Rogan sped us faster down the trail. Betsy clunked hard on the far side of a mountainous boulder, and I gasped.

"You scared?"

My heart hammered against my chest. "No. I trust you."

He took off toward another sizeable rock face.

"Your turn." He stopped the Jeep and stepped out. "Hop over."

"What? No."

"Time for that off-road lesson. C'mon."

"I can't drive stick."

"I'll teach ya. It's easy."

"Okay."

"PULL OVER THERE BY that pond." Rogan pointed to the bank of a pond with mossy green water and a lot less mud.

I cut the engine and turned to look at him in the passenger seat. "You're a good teacher."

"You're a quick learner. You did great for your first time on a stick, first time wheeling."

"I hope I didn't ruin Betsy."

"She's tough."

"That was so much fun. Can we do it again sometime?"

"Anytime. Just ask, we're here."

I stepped out of the Jeep and laughed at the coffee-colored mud covering every inch of her, including a generous spatter on the American flag.

He laid a blanket on the grass under an old oak tree and drew some food out of his pack. He handed me a wrapped sandwich. "Chicken salad."

"Yum."

He opened a tub of cut watermelon and placed it on the blanket between us as we ate in silence.

"You planned all this?"

"Planning is my forte."

"I thought shooting was your forte."

"They go together. A good shot is well planned."

"Mmm." I picked up another piece of juicy watermelon.

"I brought you a gift."

My swallow made an audible gulp. "You did?"

He fished in the front pocket of his pants and pulled out a purple velvet pouch tied with a golden tassel. "For you."

I worked the string open and extracted a loose yellow stone shaped like a pear. It sparkled in my hand. "What is it?"

"Yellow sapphire."

"Yellow sapph— What are you doing walking around with jewels in your pockets?"

A wicked grin grew on his lips. "I got lots of impressive jewels in my pocket. I'll show you sometime."

I laughed. "Sapphire? Aren't they blue?"

"This one is yellow."

"It can't be a real sapphire."

"It's real. Authenticity is important to me."

"So the ruby necklace and the black tourmaline are real too?"

"Of course."

"But the rubies I saw at Burlington Mall were so expensive."

"Don't worry about that. Do you like it?"

"It's perfect and the prettiest golden yellow, like today. Thank you."

"You're welcome."

"You're letting me thank you now? Why? What's changed?"

He took off his hat and set it on the blanket. "I'll tell you later." He curled his hand behind my neck and lowered his head. "Now give me more kisses."

I angled my chin to the side. "Presents don't buy kisses."

"Questions buy kisses?" His breath tickled my cheek.

"Mmm. Yes. Tell me about Falcon and Betsy."

Rogan leaned back on his elbows and crossed his feet at his ankles as he looked up at the clear baby-blue sky. "He's my spotter and a far better marksman than me."

"Spotter?"

"We're a two-man sniper team, three if you count Takoda."

He rolled to one hip, bringing him closer to me. I put the lid on the melon and moved the tub aside. He filled the space, and his abs brushed my knee.

"Couldn't ask for a better man at my side when I'm downrange. Anytime I'm under fire, I turn around and see Falcon at my back. He's a goddamn hero if there is such a thing."

"And why's Betsy here?"

"I come out here once a month and train with Falcon. Shooting and hunting. You comfortable with that?"

"Yes. My father and the boys would go out hunting deer."

"What kinda weapons they keep around there?"

"Mostly shotguns. They were big on preparedness."

He nodded like that meant something to him. "Anyone there have a rifle? Shoot targets?"

"There was a group of men on the compound. They called themselves the Redeemers. They'd get together in the woods and shoot at trees. They ran security patrols and scared off any outsiders who got too close. Bunch of jerks, if you asked me."

He took in all my information like intelligence data. "So, did I earn myself kisses?"

"Hmm. Seems like I did a lot of the talking. You did that on purpose."

"Me?" He touched under my chin and tugged. I eagerly responded because I'd been aching to kiss him. Being so close to his smile and his rugged strength all day teased my blood into a low boil. How could anyone spend time with Rogan and not want to mack out on his plump pink lips?

He kissed my smiling lips with a grin on his own. The second our mouths touched, the humor faded and passion took over. We opened at the same time, grasping to get deeper inside each other. His hand curled around my back and heaved me on top of him, my knees straddling his waist. I squeezed my thighs together just to feel the unforgiving strength of his muscles underneath me. I felt tiny on top of him, but powerful too. I grabbed his ears and dove into the kiss.

He flipped me to my back and pinned my hands over my head with one palm over my wrists. "Gonna feel so good to finally be inside you."

"Oh..."

He looked up at our hands. "You okay with me holding you down like this?"

I looked up too but couldn't see anything. "Yes," I answered, breathy. "I'm pretty okay with anything you wanna do."

He grinned and closed his eyes as he pressed his forehead to mine. "Good."

Something wet slid up my arm. I gasped and saw Rogan had wiped a stripe of mud from my armpit to my elbow.

"Hey!"

He laughed and reached for more mud.

"No," I screamed and squirmed, but his strong hips held me down.

He smooshed a heaping handful of sticky mud into my chest, staining my shirt and chilling my bones.

"Let me go."

"No."

"Let me go. It hurts." I lied.

"You won't retaliate?" He sat back and released my hands.

"I wanna clean up. Get off!"

He moved off me and I climbed to my feet, bending at the waist to wipe the mud from my chest. "You know there's a lot of snow in Idaho."

"Yeah."

"One thing we *were* allowed to do."

"Hmm?"

"Snowball fight!" I lobbed a chunk of mud at him as I straightened, but he was prepared for me and sidestepped my shot.

He laughed at my underhanded attempt.

"I'm a snowball champion." I crouched to gather more ammo.

"Sure you are." He stalked to me, and I landed one satisfying hit on his chest before he tackled me to the mud. We rolled and wrestled. I almost had him. Or he let me think I had a chance, but he pinned me on my back again. We were filthy and wet, just like Betsy, but he was laughing, and I loved it.

He stood and offered his hand to help me up. "Let's go, snowball champion."

"WOW. FALCON COOKS DELICIOUS barbecued pork," I said to Rogan as he flipped the lights on. "Is this the room you sleep in when you visit Falcon?"

He glanced around. "I lived in this room for a while." A wistful look crossed his face. "But most of the time we don't sleep here."

"Where else do you sleep?"

"In the woods."

"Like camping?"

"If you consider sleeping outside with no tent camping."

"Oh."

"I'll take the couch. You get ready for bed."

"Yes, Sergeant Boggs."

"Master Sergeant."

"Excuse me. *Master Sergeant* Boggs." I snapped my heels and saluted him.

He grinned and walked to the couch as I grabbed my bag and headed to the bathroom. I'd already showered earlier, so I changed into my cranberry silk camisole with matching shorts. I snuck glances at Rogan in his boxer-briefs and T-shirt on the couch as I climbed into the queen-sized bed I would sleep in alone.

Rogan turned out the light and the chirping of bugs outside filled the room. "Are you named after Bixby Boggs?"

"No. Coincidence."

"How'd you get that nickname?"

He took a deep breath and spoke softly, like he was reminiscing about the story behind the nickname. "Boggs is a codename Blaze came up with during sniper training. I was the only one in my class to remain undetected during fieldcraft. I vegged up good in my ghillie suit, stayed stock still for hours. Even the experienced trainers never found me. Boggs is some creature in a children's movie that blends into his surroundings, becomes invisible."

"Ah, a handy skill for a sniper."

"Handy ain't the word for it. Stealth is a prerequisite. They can't kill you if they can't see you. Usually."

The hum of the bugs filled the silence again. Rogan spoke so casually about killing and death, resigned to accept it as part of his job description. Though it remained unspoken, his tone imparted a deeper sadness hinting at the toll the loss of life had taken on his battered psyche.

"Tell me about the yellow sapphire."

"It's called the sundrop sapphire."

"It is? Why? Because it's yellow, like..."— oh my goodness—"sunshine?"

"Yeah."

I closed my eyes and let the rasp of Rogan's simple *yeah* wash over me. Rogan had given me him—black, raw, and unfinished. He'd given me *me*, a dazzling polished gem. I'd never had anything of value. Even color had been kept from me. Now Rogan bestowed valuable gifts like candy. Not just monetary worth—and I'm sure these jewels held worth beyond my comprehension—but he'd offered me his soul, his company, his touch—all in his unassuming way. The pain of his absence still stung. He'd abandoned me with no explanation and let me think he was dead, but he was offering me these gifts now, and I should *be smart and make the best of it*.

"Thank you. For the sapphire, today, everything."

"You're welcome. G'night."

"Night."

I tossed and turned, trying to sleep and pretend the sexiest man I'd ever met wasn't sleeping on the couch in the same room.

He cleared his throat and his voice was tight. "I've slept in a lot of rough spots, but this is one of the toughest."

Ah, he was struggling just as much as I was. "Come over here."

"Not fucking you for the first time in Falcon's guest room."

My belly flipped like it did anytime Rogan talked about us having sex. "We won't take it that far."

"I will."

"You said you had self-control."

"I do."

"Then come over and hold me."

"Fuck."

If I didn't see his silent shadow pass through a beam of moonlight, I wouldn't have known he'd moved. His weight tipped the side of the bed, and his hand landed flat on my stomach, just above my belly button, but he kept his body at a safe distance. His head inched closer to mine, and his nose nuzzled my ear. "Thought you looked beautiful covered in mud, but you in that nightie is the prettiest sight I've ever seen."

He threw one leg over mine, and his hard cock rubbed the fabric of his sweats against my bare thigh. My mind recalled the image of his angry dick pointing at my face at Siege all those months ago. His intensity paralyzed me with fear back then. Now I wanted nothing more than to take off his sweats and explore every centimeter of his glorious cock. I wanted to taste it, caress it, take it inside me.

I pressed on his lower back, urging him to sling his other leg over and line our bodies up. He shifted and centered his dick at my core. He ran his hand through my hair and kissed me at the same time he stroked his cock along my panties. I groaned as the charge flowing between us lit up like an electrical fire.

My hips surged up to meet his, mashing his hard shaft against my pubic bone. I grabbed his ass with both hands and squeezed. He was as rock solid as he looked. Rogan was an amazing specimen of a man.

He growled and froze.

"No, no, no. Don't stop."

He tore his face away from mine and peeled his body off, hovering over me on his hands and knees. "Good night. Get some rest. Tomorrow we're flying outta here."

"Ugh! You're driving me bonkers! I finally give in to you and you say good night like it's so easy."

"Trust me. It's not easy. I wanna take you right now. I'm so hard, wanna shove it in your mouth, make you gag on it."

Oh my.

"But I want your first time to be memorable, and I got more to show you. You wanna know me and trust me, we need to go somewhere first."

"Where?"

"Uh-uh. Surprise."

"You're killing me!"

"No, babe. You're living in full color. What color are you now?"

"Green. A very dark horny green surrounded by a fiery, pissed-off red."

He pressed his lips to mine. "Due time, Sunshine. In due time."

He settled at my side again and tucked my head into his chest. His giant erection still rubbed my leg. Rogan must have stellar self-control because I wanted to take care of it. Now I was in a rough spot, trying to sleep knowing he was still turned on beside me.

"Let it be." His low voice hummed in my ear.

"It's very hard."

"Could cut diamonds with my cock right now. Find sleep."

I resisted a while, but the activities of the day finally caught up with me, and I found sleep.

Chapter 23

"THERE'S A WATERFALL that looks like it's flowing from a cloud."

Rogan angled his head and peered out the window of the taxi cruising the quaint streets of the Caribbean island nation of Saint Amalie. "Mount Pintaro. It's a volcano."

The cone-shaped peak of Mount Pintaro rose steeply out of the water and disappeared into the mist.

"You've been here before?"

"A few times."

"Could it erupt?"

"It could," he said from his seat next to me in the back of the taxi. "Probably won't."

The driver pulled up to the entrance of a sprawling building tucked like an oasis inside a stand of lush palms and ferns. "Is that a palace?"

"No. The prime minister's mansion." Rogan opened the door and offered me his hand.

"Are we taking a tour?"

He gave my hand a reassuring squeeze and helped me out of the taxi. An older couple and a group of about ten people gathered at the top of the stairs. Their skin color varied from the darkest tones to the fairest shades, but all of them waited for us with expectant smiles.

A blonde woman wearing cream slacks and a chiffon blouse clasped her hands in front of her as she bounced on her heel-clad toes. Her face squished like she was fighting tears. A distinguished man with wavy brown hair placed his hand on her shoulder for a moment before she burst from the group and embraced Rogan. He bent to curl an arm around her tiny waist.

"My boy. My boy." She gazed up at him.

"Ma," Rogan said softly and kissed the top of her head.

Ma? My breath stuck in my throat. His mother?

Rogan patted her back, and she turned to face the group of people behind her.

The crowd lowered their heads and bowed.

Bowed? Oh my gosh, what in the world was going on?

Rogan tipped his chin, and the crowd straightened.

We reached the top of the steps, and Rogan shook hands with the man. A gorgeous woman with sable hair and boobs rivaling Yolanda's broke out of the group and hugged Rogan. He didn't raise his arm to hug her back.

"Hello, Rogan," she said with a giggle and a wink.

"Chantal."

She tilted her head and blinked at me, waiting for Rogan to introduce us.

Rogan's palm warmed my lower back, and his fingers pressed me gently forward. "Tessa Harlow, Prime Minister Bastien Foor." He waved his hand toward the handsome man.

"Bonjour, Tessa." He spoke with a sophisticated French accent.

"Hello."

"And his wife, Guinevere Foor, my mother."

"Umm..."

"Such a pleasure to meet you, Tessa. Call me Gwen." His mother wrapped delicate arms around me, and a floral aroma hit my nose.

I glared at Rogan over Gwen's shoulder. Surprising me with his mother!

"We have tea ready for you on the veranda." Gwen grasped my elbow, guiding me into the mansion.

The crowd dispersed, and I shot Rogan another evil look for not introducing me to Chantal. He smirked and kept walking with his shoulders back and a confident swagger.

We passed through floor-to-ceiling glass doors onto a tiered patio overlooking a sparkling lap pool and vibrant green tennis courts. Chantal took a seat on the other side of Rogan at an elaborate table set for lunch for five. A servant poured tea into tiny china cups.

"Welcome to our island. How was your flight?" Rogan's mother asked me.

"Amazing! We flew over pods of dolphins. And the reefs are extraordinary. My eyes were glued to the window."

"So how'd you two meet?" Chantal wagged her finger from Rogan to me.

"My cousin Falcon in—"

Rogan squeezed my knee to shut me up. "Morning Glory still here?" he asked Bastien.

"Yes." His voice turned up in question, and he glanced from Chantal to Rogan.

"We're gonna take her out. Now."

"Oh. We can talk more over dinner," Gwen responded.

"We'll be out past sunset."

"We can wait for you." Gwen's voice took on the stern tone of a mother, and her eyes turned cold, despite the smile she held on her lips.

A muscle in Rogan's neck twitched. "Alright."

"You sure you wouldn't like a gelding too?" Bastien asked Rogan.

"No. One horse will do."

A horse? Morning Glory was a horse?

We all stood, and Chantal's eyes followed Rogan's hand as he placed it between my shoulder blades.

"We've prepared *two* rooms for you," Prime Minister Foor said.

"Of course, Bastien," Rogan answered.

Gwen winked at Rogan, but Rogan kept his eyes on Bastien.

"We'll see you at dinner then, dear. Have fun. The weather is ideal for a ride." Gwen took Bastien's hand.

A ride? We're going to ride a horse named Morning Glory?

Rogan applied a slight pressure on my back, guiding me through the glass doors to the front entrance again.

"C'MON, GIRL." ROGAN clicked his tongue, and the spectacular Appaloosa took a steady step from her stall, following Rogan's hold on her lead with no resistance.

"She's so graceful." I ran my palm over her withers. "She's a hand taller than Traveler. Her spots are darker, but she reminds me so much of her."

Rogan tossed a bareback saddle pad over Morning Glory's back and cinched the buckles around her chest. Man, Rogan's tight butt looked delicious in his board shorts.

"Don't I need my boots?"

Rogan's eyes traversed my body in my pink sundress and black sandals. "You got your bathing suit under there?"

"Yes?"

"That's how we ride here. Take off your shoes."

We removed our shoes and left them on a bench outside the stable.

Morning Glory paced next to Rogan as we walked over the lawn to a frond-covered trailhead behind the barn. Dew made the rocky trail slick but Morning Glory didn't hesitate.

"She's comfortable with you."

"It's been about four years, but I think she remembers me."

She swayed her snout toward him and gave his ear a nuzzle with a low, soft nicker.

"She remembers you and she loves you."

Rogan chuckled and wrapped an arm under her neck. "Good girl."

THE JUNGLE-LIKE TRAIL opened up to a stretch of powdery sand and turquoise water.

"The blue!"

"Your first time on a beach?"

"Yes! The ocean is... mystical. The way it glows in the sun. And the sand, the purest white."

We stood next to Morning Glory and let the salty wind hit our faces. "Some impressive colors here in St. Amalie," he said.

"The world you know is the complete opposite of mine."

"I'm sharing it with you now."

"Hey, that reminds me." I slapped his bicep. "You surprised me, you jerk."

"Easier if you meet her first. Guinevere Foor is... hard to describe."

"What is she? The first lady?"

"Her official title is *spouse of the prime minister*." He scuffed his feet in the sand.

"Wow. How'd she meet Bastien?"

"She danced with him at a charity banquet."

"He just asked her to dance?"

"His father set it up. He's the former prime minister."

"Does your mom like to dance?"

"Yes. She's known for it. The people here love to watch her dance. It eases their worries."

"And did she dance with you when you were a boy?"

"Yes."

"Did it ease your worries?"

"Probably." His gaze scanned the horizon. "She'd bust out moves in the kitchen, in a store, wherever she was. She'd forget her cares and sway her body. It embarrassed me most of the time but also made me laugh."

I smiled up at him and squinted in the sun. "How old were you when she married him?"

"Fourteen. We came to live here."

"What a romantic story. I'm happy she found love after losing your dad. She does love him, right?"

He huffed. "Someday, you will not question if a woman loves her husband. Most people marry for love."

"Oh, right. Sorry."

"Not your fault. Yes, she loves him. The press has deemed their relationship *a fairy tale love affair*."

"And is he faithful to her?"

He took my face in his hands. "Another inappropriate question, but yes, I think so. She's happy here."

"The press doesn't follow you?"

"No. They're more interested in her. There were a few pictures in the beginning, but they've lost track of me."

"And who is Chantal?"

He kissed my forehead and patted Morning Glory's back. "Hop on up."

"Uh." She didn't have stirrups and she was tall. "How?"

"Jump up."

"Jump? Okay..."

I crouched and popped up on her back in an ungraceful belly plop. As I slid back down to the ground, Rogan's hand smacked my butt, and his hearty laugh rang out.

"Hey!" My feet hit the ground and, still laughing, he bent and interlocked his hands for me to use as stirrups.

"Just teasing. Up ya go."

He boosted me up, and the thrill of being on a horse after so long raced through me—especially a horse as impressive as this one. I patted her neck. "Good girl. How're you going to mount her?"

Rogan had me hold the reins. "Like this." He grasped a chunk of mane in one hand, swung one of his long legs back and kicked, hooking himself on the horse behind me. Morning Glory took a few steps to adjust to his weight. He settled with a grunt and slid a hand around my waist.

Panic shot up my spine, but I tamped it down.

"Yah!" He squeezed his legs around the horse's flanks, and she trotted down the tideline. The rub of Rogan's stomach against my back eclipsed my vision. The stunning coast, the white sand, the crystal blue water—everything evaporated.

"God, your ass feels good bouncin' on my cock." Rogan's sexy voice hummed in my ear.

My breath clogged my throat. This was a vacation destination and not a place to panic. But the air wouldn't come into my lungs.

I stiffened and arched my back. "I can't."

"Whoa." He halted Morning Glory.

I bent my shoulders to dismount, but he held me in place. "Hey. It's alright. Stay right there." He hopped down then wrapped his hands around my torso. He lifted me off like I weighed nothing. "What's wrong?" He pressed his palm to my cheek as he bent to stare into my eyes. "You said you rode."

"I do. Just... by myself." I stroked my fingers over the coarse hair on Morning Glory's flank.

His eyes narrowed to slits. "You mean no one behind you?"

"Mmm-hmm."

"I see."

He did his mounting trick again and slung himself up on her. He reached out for my hand.

"I don't..."

"Swing a leg over."

He grabbed my wrist, hoisting me on behind him this time. "Hold on."

I wrapped my arms around his middle and intertwined my fingers near the tie of his shorts. The strong muscles of his back pressed against my stomach and chest.

"Better?" he asked, tilting his chin over his shoulder.

"Yes. Thank you." The balmy air reappeared. Oxygen filled my lungs again, and the sea salt filtered into my nose.

"Yah!" he called, and my hair flew back in the wind as Morning Glory galloped in the sand again. Rogan steered her into the waves, and she obeyed eagerly. The warm water lapped at our ankles, and Morning Glory whinnied like she loved it just as much as we did. He glanced at me over his shoulder and reached one hand back to rub my leg. "This better than dancin' in a box?"

"Yes!"

He squeezed my thigh. "Ready to go deeper?"

"Deeper?" The waves reached Morning Glory's withers, and my legs sloshed in the water.

"Can she go deeper?"

He didn't answer, just took Morning Glory into the waves till only her snout and neck hovered above water.

"Stand up," Rogan said as he climbed to standing on her back.

"What?"

"Stand up." He pulled my hands up till we were both balancing on Morning Glory's back.

"She's so strong!"

Rogan curled his arms around me and tugged me closer, pressing his rock hard body against mine through our thin wet clothes. In his eyes, joy shimmered like the sunlight sparkling off the water we stood in.

He grabbed the back of my head and kissed me hard and wild. He tasted like salt and sun and man. I clasped his shoulders and kissed him back. Rogan's mouth consumed me. The controlled kisses from last night had turned ravenous, and our tongues warred for dominance. We wobbled, and our lips broke apart as we crashed into the water.

We both laughed as his hands on my behind forced me to wrap my legs around him.

"I can't swim." I clutched his neck like I was stuck up high on a pole.

"I got you." He carried me to the tideline. "Need you on the shore," he said with his lips pressed to mine.

Morning Glory followed us to a secluded cove at the end of the beach where Rogan lowered me to my butt on the sand. I braced my hands behind me and stared up at his dripping wet form towering over me. He yanked off his sodden tee with one quick movement behind his neck.

Lord have mercy. Rogan's biceps doubled in size while he was away. His wet tattoos glinted, and his pecs pulsed like a ferocious warrior climbing from the sea at Normandy.

"When I ate you at Siege, was I your first?" His voice scratched, and his eyes simmered like they had the night we danced at Siege. I covered my chest with my arms, defending myself from the onslaught that might ensue if Rogan lost his temper again.

"My first how?"

His brow furrowed, and he dropped to the sand with his knees on either side of me. He breathed heavy and spoke with a growl. "Don't play with me."

"Why're you so angry?"

"I'm not angry."

"You sound furious, like you did at Siege, but... Oh my goodness. Could it be?"

"What?"

"You're fighting the urge to kiss me. Holding back your desire makes your voice scratch and your shoulders tense. It looks a lot like anger, but it's not. Am I right?"

His eyelids lowered and he took a deep breath. "You're looking at a man who hasn't touched a woman in six months. That woman being you."

"And before that?"

"Four years," he said low and dark.

"Four years? What about Tori?"

His eyes snapped open, and his head popped up. "I didn't have sex with her."

"I've always thought you were angry with me for tempting you."

"No. Pissed at myself for wanting you and knowing I shouldn't take you."

"Oh."

His gaze skated down my body. "As you can imagine, I've been riding the edge of a blade for a long time."

"I can imagine. How did you manage going so long without it?"

"Mind over matter."

"Did you uh... relieve the pressure alone?"

"No. Not until you showed up. Then I couldn't stop. I had to or my balls would detonate. So, I'd like to know, was I the first man to put his mouth on you?"

"Yes, but... This is hard to talk about. It wasn't my first..."

"First time you came?"

"Right."

"You came with Zook before?" He inched closer, and his breath tickled my cheek.

"Why are you asking me this?"

"I gotta know how far I can push you."

"I see. Well. A few times Zook... gave me orgasms with his hand. I gave myself..."

"Go on."

I twirled my fingers on the sand.

"You gave yourself orgasms?"

I nodded.

"With your hand or you have a toy?"

"A toy? What kind of toy?"

"A vibrator."

"Oh, hmm." I licked my lips. The word vibrator coming from Rogan's plump lips in his deep raspy voice sounded like a delicious dessert, not a sex toy. "No. I didn't have a toy. My hand."

"Show me."

"No."

"Show me." He grabbed the string to my bikini behind my neck. With a sharp tug, the wet triangles loosened under my sundress. His eyes drank in my breasts as he yanked my wet top down. He licked his lips and stared at my nipples. "Show me."

He wrenched my dress and my bikini bottoms over my hips and all the way off.

I gasped. "I'm naked."

He searched the sand next to us, grabbed two medium-sized shells, and covered my nipples. "Now you're not. Show me how you touch yourself."

He watched my hand move toward my center. The sand scratched as my fingers skimmed my clit. I rubbed a small circle, and his eyes darkened. "Spread your legs."

I hesitated, but did as he said because his commanding voice left no room for objection.

"So sexy. My mermaid."

Rogan's eyes glassed over, and he ran his tongue over his teeth under his lip. He needed to move closer and stop watching from afar. "Touch me."

"Keeping my distance."

"No more distance."

He looked into my eyes, and his heated gaze seared into me.

"No more resistance. It's time." I held my hand out for him. He placed his fingers in mine, and I set them down on my clit. I worked my hand out so his fingers rested on me. "Touch me."

He bit his lip and moved his hand a fraction, but it was enough to send a jolt of desire through me. "More."

The seashells dropped off when I grabbed my breasts and lifted them. My fingers pinched my nipples.

Rogan growled like I'd pushed him too far. Good. I wanted him to give in again. I could handle it this time.

He shoved two fingers deep inside me and my back arched, the sand rubbing my scalp. "Yes!"

His fingers worked inside me, and his thumb massaged my clit as he kissed his way up my belly. Like the head of a sparkler on the Fourth of July, his lips lit trails on my skin. My whole body shook when he stopped to suck one nipple, then the other.

Finally his mouth landed on mine, and I inhaled him. We fell into a sensual rhythm, my hips and mouth responding to each movement of his hands and tongue. I could get lost in him for hours.

My orgasm hovered on the horizon, no holding it back. His thumb drilled relentless circles on my clit. He knew exactly how to touch a woman to make her come hard. I groaned into his mouth and clenched on his fingers. A kaleidoscope of colors danced behind my eyelids as I pulsed on his hand.

He pulled his lips from mine. Our breaths were loud and heavy as we gazed at each other. Before he could pull away, I grabbed his erection through his shorts. I cupped my palm around his hardness and pressed down. "Let me."

He untied his board shorts and popped out his straining cock. Mercy. It was thicker than I remembered, but I'd only caught a glimpse of it before. In the sunlight, I could see all the glorious details. The head flushed a dark purple, and a vein throbbed in his shaft.

"I want to suck it."

"You don't have to. If you're not ready..."

"I'm ready." I sat up and dove for his cock, but he pushed my shoulders back.

"Lie down."

"I swear. I won't be scared this time."

"Lie down."

I lay on my back and watched as he repositioned over me.

"Open."

I dropped my jaw and he fed his cock between my lips. "Suck it, Sunshine. As hard as you can."

I closed around the tip and sucked him in bit by bit. He moaned and his head fell back. "Goddamn."

He pumped into my mouth slow at first, then picked up the pace. "Your lush lips wrapped around my cock. Feels so good to fuck your mouth. Fucking heaven."

I couldn't answer so I just kept sucking.

"Stop now, if you don't want me to come in your mouth."

I put my hands on his butt and pushed him in deeper. His tip bumped the back of my throat and I gagged. He slowed down and pulled out a little, waiting for me to adjust. I squeezed his thighs to let him know I was fine. Keep going.

"Fuck."

The muscles of his ass tightened in my hands and his hips jerked out of rhythm. He froze, exhaling with a long, deep groan as his hot semen spilled into my mouth. I swallowed around his throbbing dick, tasting his salty come as some escaped and dribbled down my chin.

He withdrew and wiped my lip with his thumb. "That felt so damn good." He settled his body over me, supporting his weight with his elbows. "You're gonna have to walk around with my dick in your mouth. I want that all the time."

I laughed. "We'll see."

He settled next to me and kissed me gently. "You okay?"

"Yes. I loved watching you find your release."

"I've been wanting you a long time. So much better than I'd imagined."

"You imagined us doing that?"

"Mmm. And many other things."

"Thank you for giving that to me."

He chuckled and pressed kisses from my lips down my throat. "Pretty sure I should be giving the gratitude about now."

He lay on his back in the sand and pulled me on top of him so my head was on his chest and my leg crossed over his. We held each other, catching our breath, enjoying the stolen silence.

His pecs contracted as he did an ab curl. "There's your sunset over the ocean."

Rich carmine streaked with salmon painted the sky, ending at the horizontal line of the azure sea. "It's more dazzling than I ever could've dreamed."

He pressed his lips to my temple. "I want more of you, but we should get back for dinner with the *spouse of the prime minister*."

"Okay."

We stood and brushed the sand off. He kept his eyes on me as I dressed. As soon as I tied my sundress, he kissed me deep and hard. When he pulled away, I studied the beard growing in around his playful grin.

Each time Rogan let his guard down, his lips and face became less intense and my attraction to him skyrocketed. Now that I knew how masterful his hands were and how good it felt to suck his dick and watch him come undone, I wanted to do it over and over again.

He pressed a finger to my lower lip after my tongue swiped along it. "Later. More."

"But we have separate rooms."

A chuckle rolled from his chest as he slung an arm over my shoulder, and we walked in the sand back to Morning Glory.

Chapter 24

"THIS LOBSTER IS DELICIOUS," I declared to the Foors and Rogan at the dinner table in the mansion.

Rogan stopped eating and held his fork mid-air to watch me suck the meat from the cavity of a claw.

"Yes, caught fresh for you today," Bastien said as I blushed at Rogan's acute stare.

Rogan resumed eating slowly, but his gaze darted from my lips to my cleavage and back again as I wiped the dripping butter from my chin. We'd breached an intimacy levee today, causing steaming hot flood-waters to flow over the barriers. He'd better tone it down or his mom and stepdad would catch on. The sexy button-down shirt and dark jeans he wore to dinner didn't help with my trying to play it cool act.

Maybe talking to his mom would divert his attention. "So, Gwen, what's it like being the wife of the prime minister of Saint Amalie?"

Nope. He continued to devour me with his eyes.

"I'm very fortunate, Tessa." She smiled and touched Bastien's hand. "I live in paradise with the man I love."

"Don't paint it so idyllic, Gwen," Bastien replied as he took her hand. "The people here face unique challenges, and though we are a small contribution, we share in the global economy."

"Yes, Bastien, but Tessa and Rogan are on vacation. Let's not speak politics and world devastation." She smiled at her husband.

His eyes softened as he gazed at her. "You're right, my love."

"My mother is a decorated humanitarian." Rogan spoke up. "She fights for displaced people and women's rights."

"Speaking of which, have you heard from Marla Brightman lately?"

Rogan's shoulders stiffened at his mother's question.

"Who's Marla Brightman?" I asked.

"I thought you said we'd skip the politics." Rogan didn't look up from his plate.

"She was the director of central intelligence when I first worked with her." Gwen continued as if Rogan hadn't spoken. "She's been appointed American secretary of state. Hasn't she, Rogan?"

Rogan clenched his jaw and dropped his fork on his plate.

"He serves under her. She—"

"Mom." He glared at her.

"I'm sorry, sweetie. I should follow my own advice, shouldn't I? So, change of topic. How was your ride today?"

I coughed and took a sip of my tangy sorrel tea.

"Good." Rogan turned his gaze to Bastien. "You should take Morning Glory in the water more. She loves it."

"I'll make a point of it. If Gwen and I can't do it, her handlers will see to it."

We ate in silence for a while, everyone chewing on the subtle tension between Rogan and his mother.

"If you two get married"—Gwen smashed the silence with a sledge-hammer—"you'll have the wedding here. The Amalian ceremony is so romantic."

"Mom."

"You can't deny your mother the attendance at your wedding. Not twice."

I gulped down the bite of coconut rice in my mouth. *Twice?*

"My only son will allow me to be present at his marriage, and you will take your bride," her eyes flickered to me, "in the traditional way. She can still wear white if she wishes, but the Amalian silks are stunning. She might enjoy incorporating them with her gown."

Rogan stood and tossed his napkin over his plate. "Thank you for dinner, Mom. Bastien." He stomped out of the room, leaving me staring at his back as he headed for an exit.

Gwen wiped the corners of her mouth with her napkin. "Dessert, anyone?" She looked from me to Bastien.

"No, thank you. I'm stuffed." I glanced at the doorway Rogan had passed through. "I'd like to get some rest now, if that's okay?"

"Yes, dear. You'll sample the local sweets tomorrow. Let me show you to your room." Gwen stood and walked to me.

"Thank you for dinner, Bastien," I said as Gwen took my elbow.

"You're welcome. Sleep well."

His mother led me up the stairs. "This will be your room. Rogan's room is there." She pointed to a door at the end of the hallway. She looked back the way we came. "He's probably at the pool now."

"Okay. Thank you. I'm so happy I met you."

"You too, darling. You're lovely for him."

I waited five minutes before embarking to find Rogan. As his mom thought, he was in the pool, racing punishing laps with no breaks, not even for a breath. Each angry stroke of his arms transmitted pain and goodbye. His mom intentionally dropped a bomb that would separate us for good. Rogan was married. Our fledgling love deflated to the ground again before it could take flight. It didn't make sense. If he was married, why would his mom say I was good for him? Why had he never told me about her?

Two hours later, Rogan's voice echoed in the hall as I lay in my bed. I cracked the door open to peek out. Rogan stood in his swim trunks, dripping water on his mother's carpet. His head was bent low as he towered over Gwen standing by his side. She placed her palm on the *E* on his bicep. He tilted his head and looked at her hand. She added another hand at the base of his neck and spoke softly to him. He nodded and bent to kiss her forehead. He walked toward his room with his head down. I ducked back inside, hoping he didn't see me spying on his private moment with his mom.

I ran to my bed and pretended to be asleep in case Rogan came to see me. But the knock never came. The door never opened. He'd passed by my room to be alone in his.

Chapter 25

A KISS ON MY CHEEK woke me. Rogan had crawled in the bed and cuddled up next to me, silent and stealthy. My stomach dropped, and my body heated as his strong form inched closer. His hand landed on my belly and slid up under my breasts. I grabbed his wrist and he froze.

"Tess..."

"Who is Chantal to you?"

"She's my stepsister."

"She didn't seem like a stepsister."

His body tensed, and he squeezed my middle.

"You've been with her."

"Tess..."

"Was she your first?"

He sighed. "We were teens. We're friendly now. Don't be jealous."

"You've dated all these exotic women. Tori and Chantal..."

"No comparison." He kissed my nose. "I never wanted anyone half as much as I want you." He pressed his lips to my neck.

I ignored the shiver racing down my spine and turned my head to search for his eyes in the shadows. "But was she your first?"

"Yes." His voice was thick in the darkness.

"Tell me."

"You want me to tell you about the girls I dated when I was a teenager?"

"Yes. I want to know. I told you everything."

"Chantal and I had a brief fling when I first moved here. But she's my stepsister. We quickly fell into the role of siblings after that. No big deal."

"Your mom mentioned your wife."

He clicked on the light and sat up with his back against the headboard. "She did."

"Is that why you swam for hours?" I propped up on one elbow and looked up at him. "Are you still married?"

His brow furrowed, and he stared over my head.

"Do you love her?"

"Let it be, Tess."

"Is she who you think of when you stare out the window?"

His lids lowered, and he shook his head. "Why this? I've given you so much. Why do you need her too?"

"Because I think this is the most important part of you. Is she why your heart isn't free?"

I climbed out of the bed and pointed at him. "Why have you been chasing me if you're married? Did you think I'd be okay with sharing you? Did you think the poor girl with a polygamist father would—"

"Fuck!" He shot up and stalked to the door.

"What, Rogan? Are you gonna call me stupid and flee to the desert to get yourself killed?"

He stopped and spoke with his back to me. "Stay here. Wait for me."

I flopped back into bed and clutched a pillow to my stomach. Waiting for him was torture, even for a few minutes.

When he returned, he opened a small blue velvet bag and poured the contents onto the nightstand. "This. This is what I think about when I stare out a window, when I swim, all the fucking time."

"Diamonds?"

He picked up a ring with a tarnished silver band. A petite square diamond in a simple setting adorned the top of the ring. He held it flat in his palm. "This is her. This is my love for her."

He scooped up a handful of polished diamonds and dropped them slowly onto the nightstand. They pitter pattered, a few falling to the floor. "This is us."

"I don't get it."

"We're bigger overall. More valuable. But scattered."

"Please, tell me about her, Rogan. I want to know."

He ran his hand over my head to my neck, where he gave me a gentle squeeze. "No one can ever know the story I'm about to tell you. Lots of reasons, but mostly your safety. The people I've gone up against have a long memory. The few that are still alive could come after me. Or you."

"I promise."

He sat next to me in the bed and settled us so my head rested on his abs. "The special ops unit I told you about is called Delta Force. We refer to it as "the unit." The most skilled marksmen from all of America's military are pooled together to create an elite hostage rescue and counterterrorism team. Delta Force is above the law, sheltered by the CIA. We go where traditional troops can't. No one in the unit has a wife back home. If you do, you don't keep her long. You eat, sleep, and breathe your mission."

"Okay."

My head rose and fell with his deep breath.

"After my tenth combat deployment, my commanding officer invited Falcon and me to his house for dinner. Said he was recommending us for Delta Force as a sniper team. We were thrilled as fuck."

"So how'd you meet her?"

"Eden was my commander's daughter. Ten years younger than me. Only nineteen years old. Too young. She was wild, an Army brat. I never should've approached her, but I had a lapse in judgement. I was so full of myself, high with the thrill of the recommendation from her dad. We fell in love and got married within a few weeks of knowing each other. The timing couldn't have been worse."

"Love happens when it happens. We can't control it."

He stroked my hair behind my ear. "We'd only been married four months when I got deployed on my first Delta Force op, an extremely high risk mission in Kabul Province. She freaked out. Said she'd follow me to Afghanistan. We fought over it, and I left her at the airport with strict orders to stay put. Not three days later, I was preparing for the mission at a forward operating base outside Kabul when I received a message she was in the Stan, waiting for me at a safe house in Kabul City."

I sat up and stared at him. "She flew to Afghanistan?"

"She did. She used her father's credentials to get in through the military base."

"That's crazy."

"It is. I was so pissed, she had me questioning my decision to marry her."

"So what'd you do when you found out she was there?"

"I went AWOL. Ran nine treacherous miles to her. I had to get her on a plane back home. She wouldn't leave. Said we needed to be together. We were uh, talking, when I heard a noise out on the street. I'd been followed. They came in the front, so I sent her out the back. I never shoulda done that. I should've gone with her. But they were in the house. I had to hold them off so she could make it to the car. But they got her anyway. After they were dead, I found her car empty behind the house with the keys in the ignition. They took her."

"Rogan..."

"I searched for her for forty-eight hours, banging down every door in that village. I confessed the whole story to Marla Brightman. She was director of the CIA then. She flew to Bagram to help. We made contact with them. Their leader hated me. Ahmed Hakim Osmani. He called himself Mustafa, the chosen one. Special Ops Command assigned him the codename Jericho, the fallen one. He posted a video. He raped her, my wife. The video..."

He hung his head and smashed his forehead with his palm. "She was wearing my T-shirt."

I blinked through my tears. They tortured Rogan too. They raped him and tortured his soul. They broke the unbreakable man.

"I'm trained..." His Adam's apple bobbed as he swallowed. "I'm trained to withstand anything. Rape me. Fuck me up the ass. Cut my guts out, but leave her the fuck alone." His voice dropped to a harsh empty gasp on his last word.

A sob bubbled in my chest and erupted from my mouth in a burst of air. I pressed my hand over his heart as it thumped a frantic beat in his chest.

"It wasn't a random kidnapping. Jericho planned it out to target me. The Executioner. I led them right to her."

"It's not your fault."

"When we sign up to serve, we vow to die for our country. But not her. She was innocent. She was supposed to be outside it. She never should've been there." He rasped out his words through clenched teeth. "Jericho demanded seven million in exchange for her release. Marla Brightman tried to feed me some protocol bullshit. When I saw the rape video, I lost my shit and she had me confined on the base. I was helpless. Nothing I could do."

"What happened?"

"I escaped."

"You escaped?"

"With the help of Alpha Squadron. Diesel, Blaze, Falcon, Ruger, Oz. They busted me out. The same men who went back with me in July. They took on the mission to save her with me. Diesel pinpointed their location from the website video. We surrounded Jericho's compound. Ready to raise hell and get her back."

He paused and I gave his hand a squeeze to let him know it was safe to tell me.

"Before we could enter the compound, a random group of Afghan rebels launched grenades in there. I watched the place light up right in front of my eyes. Watched Jericho and his brothers run out of the building and escape. I charged in, praying like fuck she'd survived. Koda found her. Injured. Injured bad. Her intestines..."

He must have read the shock and pain in my face. "I'll spare you that part. I carried her out to our helo. She died in my arms in transport to base. I kissed her goodbye. Her blood coated my lips."

"I'm so sorry."

"They shipped her body back to the States. Had to watch her parents bury their daughter because she fell in love with me. They'd already lost a son." Twisted anguish creased his temple and forehead. "Her father pressured Brightman to rain down on me for all the shit I stirred. I'd gone AWOL twice, gone rogue against all kinds of orders, risked the lives of many men. They were considering the death penalty."

"No!" They couldn't kill Rogan. No!

"Brightman called me for a one-on-one meeting. She was torn up about it. The toughest woman in the White House closed her eyes and cried for my loss. We struck a deal. She granted me clemency in exchange for my future service on Delta Force. The government wouldn't persecute me for going AWOL or my other crimes if I agreed to take on specialized high risk—highly illegal—missions and be available and ready whenever they called me. If anything went wrong, I had to say I'd gone rogue and face the consequences. They wouldn't back me up. I accepted their terms with the caveat we go after Jericho, and my team and I got to kill him. She told me she'd get my request through if she was elected secretary of state and let me know when it was approved. We crafted a public story of honorable discharge. I'm still enlisted. I'm still Delta Force."

"So that's why you tell people you're retired military?"

"Yes. It took four years for her to get Operation Devil's Gate clearance. During that time, I worked for Dallas Monroe managing his personal security. He knows about my wife's death and my involvement in Delta Force. We have an arrangement where I have long unannounced periods of leave to go on missions. All the guys in the unit made similar deals with Brightman and Monroe."

"So, you shut down your whole life waiting for Brightman to get you clearance to avenge Eden's death?"

"I didn't see the purpose of trying to live again until Jericho was dead."

"That's a long time to wait."

"I'd wait as long as it took."

"Is that when you dated Tori? While you were waiting?"

"I didn't date her. She showed interest. I'm still a man and I gave it a try. I thought she might be the catalyst I needed to pull me out of the depths I'd made my home for years. On the night of Dallas's wedding, Tori ended up caught in the crossfire of an enemy of Dallas Monroe's. Totally my fault she was shot."

"I don't believe it was your fault."

"I gave up on Tori after she was hurt. I'd finally learned my lesson. When I try... with a woman, it leads to disaster. Every time. That's why I had to leave you alone. I'm no good for you." He shook his head and rubbed his hand over the nape of his neck.

"That's not true."

"Last year, five months after Brightman took office as secretary of state, she sent me Jericho's location. Operation Devil's Gate was a go. Brightman took a huge risk approving the mission. The U.S. military was drawing down in Afghanistan. Sending in a revenge team to kill a low-profile terrorist was not an appropriate use of U.S. resources. If anyone found out, she'd lose her position and face jail time. It would cause a huge scandal for the administration and the CIA."

"She must have felt terrible for holding you back when you were trying to save Eden. She was trying to make it up to you."

"I appreciate that. Doesn't bring her back but feels good to know the government did right by me."

"So, you went to get him?"

"Once I got the order, the men of Alpha Squadron assembled, and we took off on the mission to kill Jericho. A week of surveillance, we never saw you."

"They didn't let me outside."

"Right. So, we engaged the guards out front during a shift change. Blew off the front door and the roof."

"I remember the explosions. I was terrified."

"We didn't find Jericho. We killed his brother Zulu and a few of his men, but we didn't get him. Koda discovered you tied to the bed under the stairs and fuck if I didn't see Eden's face in yours. I had to fight seeing your innards on the floor, seeing you raped by some deranged jihadist who thinks he's the chosen one. I managed to lock it down and get you home."

I rested my cheek on his pec and rubbed his shoulder.

"You were a complication. The plan was to drop you off at the airport and be done with it, keep my hands clean. But on the plane, you intrigued me. After all you'd been through, you managed to make my dog smile. When you told me about the Brotherhood, I couldn't unload you at the airport like luggage. I had to protect you from your dad."

"You didn't have to, but I'm glad you did."

"After you gained your strength, you drew me in. Couldn't keep my eyes off your hair, your smile, your dancing in the kitchen. You filled that dreary apartment with blinding sunshine." He ran his hand over my hair. "I treated you like shit. I'm sorry. But you were young and starting out, ready to take on the world. And I knew I'd destroy you with the shitstorm that hurts the women I touch."

I shook my head and sat up. I traced my hand along his strong jaw, but he remained still, his gaze focused far away. I touched his lips, and he turned his eyes to mine.

"I was attracted to you too. Even the first night, when you took off your boots and talked about Takoda. I knew then I liked you. I felt the current between us from the beginning."

His hand curled behind my neck under my hair, and his thumb stroked below my ear. "Me too. The second I saw you in my tee after you showered, all kinds of need to possess you raced through me. You had a clean slate to fly, experience all the colors you'd been denied your whole life. I couldn't taint your beauty with my black."

"I see it now, why you left. I had no idea you were battling with all this."

"I left to kill him, but I was also running. Running from you."

Chapter 26

"SO, DID YOU KILL HIM?"

"Yes. Jericho and every last one of his men."

"And have you found peace?"

"No." His red-rimmed eyes filled with water. "The guilt will never leave me. She'll always haunt my steps. She died because of me." He placed his other hand on my neck and pulled my face close to his. "I've been wandering around lost in the desert. But you came along like the shade of a palm frond." I closed the distance between us and pressed my forehead to his. He tilted his head and touched a gentle kiss to my closed lips. "For the first time in four years, I'm seeing the possibility. How it could be with you. But it's gonna take some time to change the way I've been living. If you want me too, and you're patient, we can make this into something good. Something that will last a lifetime."

"I do want you. I'll wait for you. I'll help you."

His hands on my face tightened and pulled me into a desperate kiss. I wanted to heal him with the kiss. I wanted to take his sorrow from him and replace it with love.

He pulled back and stared into my eyes. "When I was out there, I looked at pictures of you, knew I'd fucked up. I'd missed my chance. You were moving on to Cutlass. I had to find a way to unfuck it, so I came back. Good thing I did because your dad had found you by then."

"I wasn't moving on to Cutlass."

"I can't promise you marriage and a family. I'm the opposite of a bigamist. I had one wife. Not sure I could ever take another. I know that's not fair to you. You deserve to be a first and only wife. You'd be my second wife."

"Wife? Let's not worry about that now. I don't know if I ever want to get married anyway. I used to dream of being an only wife, but now I know it's a fairy tale. Life doesn't fit into happily ever after boxes."

He shook his head. "I'm not making myself clear..."

"But this is not the same kind of second wife as the one I know. Yes, you loved her and think of her. You miss her bitterly and you should. She was taken from you in a brutally unjust way. Her spirit is with you, but her body is gone. Your flesh is starving. You've denied yourself too long. Humans require touch and affection. That's why I picked the name Harlow. He proved it. We can't thrive without human touch." I ran my fingers along his face, making sure to caress his cheekbones and his eyes. "I can share your heart with her. She loved you. But I wouldn't be sharing you in the flesh. I'd be the only one pleasing your body, and you'd be the only one pleasing mine. There's room for her here." I placed his hand on my chest.

He kept shaking his head as he looked down at our joined hands. I could tell he was preparing to disagree with me, but I was on a roll and charged forward. He needed to hear my side.

"I'm not saying I want you to marry me, but I'm saying I understand she'll be a part of us forever, and I don't mind sharing in that way. She made you who you are—the salt of the earth. A good man."

He looked up at me with impatience glowing through the warm amber in his eyes. "I'm not asking you to share me with her. She released me a while back. My honor wouldn't allow me to move on till Jericho was dead. I'm saying I'm yours and you're mine. I don't need a piece of paper and a ring to tell me that."

"Oh."

He pulled my body up on him and kissed me. A long, slow kiss that tasted new because the truth was between us now. He allowed me to see his weakness. He finally let me inside. Our hands moved faster. I whimpered into the kiss, needing to see and touch his bare skin to match the raw honesty between us.

He spoke against my lips. "I'm gonna fuck you now. Need to claim you as mine like I shoulda done in the beginning."

I gasped and bit my lip. My belly fluttered and dropped. "Yes."

"I'll be gentle."

"It's okay. Not sure I want you to be gentle. I want you to be who you are."

"Oh, babe. Do not say shit like that. I'll hold back—the first time."

I sat up on my knees and leaned into him. "You don't need to." I spoke with my mouth rasping the scruffy hairs on his neck. "I spent my life thinking my first time would be functional with a man I didn't love. I want this to be the opposite of that."

"We're gonna be fucking all the time, girl. Give me a little recovery time, and I'll take you rough the second time, but the first time, I'll go easy."

"Okay."

"So, go get your ice-cream shoes." His deep voice vibrated against my lips.

"What?"

"I said I'd go easy. Doesn't mean I won't go dirty."

"Oh my." The misery in Rogan's eyes melted into a dark hunger, and a purposeful grin grew on his lips. I instinctively smiled back. Why did he want me to put my heels on?

His lips widened to a white smile, and something in his eyes told me he needed this. The sad talk upset him. The shoes would change the mood quickly. He was asking me to cheer him up and bring him joy. "Is that what you want me to do?"

He nodded. Yep. He needed this. "Go to the closet. Put on those shoes."

I pushed off his chest and scampered to the closet and unearthed the shoes from the bottom of my case. I reached to close the door to change.

"Leave it open." Rogan sat on the end of the bed with his elbows on his knees, his eyes glued to me as I took off my camisole and shorts. I giggled as I changed into a bra, added my Siege schoolgirl skirt, and slipped into the dangerously tall ice-cream cone heels.

As I dressed, his shoulders relaxed, the dark cloud left the room, and we were alone together having fun. He kept his gaze on me as he tugged his shirt off with one hand behind his neck and tossed it to the floor. I gasped because Rogan's body was magnificent. Each muscle sculpted and tight.

I smiled as I sauntered to him, his eyes caressing my shape from head to toe. His easy-going grin had returned, and he looked at me with so much more than appreciation. I felt worshipped.

"Dance."

I could do that too. I danced in front of big crowds at Siege. Rogan deserved a private show. I swayed my hips and smiled at him, bending forward to show him my cleavage. I climbed up and hovered over him without our bodies touching. His hands remained motionless by his side. The sniper had me in his sight, waiting for the ideal moment to trigger. I lowered myself on his abs and ground my center into him.

His head rolled back and he groaned.

I rubbed my sex over his rock hard cock, his pants and my underwear wedged between us. With a quick twist, I unsnapped my bra, and the straps slipped down my arms. His eyes moved to my breasts as I pulled my bra away from my body and dropped it to the floor.

I laughed because it felt fantastic being in control like this.

"Umph!"

He flipped me to my back in a flash, slamming his lips to mine with a growl. He pulled away and licked around my nipples and down my belly. "Tasty."

He dragged my panties down, and his mouth hit my sex. My hands fluttered over his taut shoulders as his lips worked between my legs.

"Now, Rogan. Need you now."

"You come first."

He kept at me and I felt it rising. My orgasm crushed the air from my lungs. I cried out as it blasted through me.

I took deep breaths to calm myself, but I was high as a kite. He knifed up and tugged the button of his jeans. I sat up on my knees at the edge of the bed and smiled. My turn to watch the show, and what a show. Stark tattoos cut his rugged body, yet his face remained gentle and loving.

"One second." He stepped around me to remove a condom packet from his jeans. Over my shoulder, I watched him slip it on and roll it down. He climbed up behind me, and his cock bumped my lower back.

I tensed. I couldn't help it.

"Shh... It's okay."

He spun me to face him and lowered me down to the bed on my back.

"We can do it missionary forever for all I care." He hovered over me. "This way I can watch your face when you come."

Our bodies molded together as he kissed me, and his dick nestled at the apex of my thighs. The electric current between us revved up and drew us together like a magnet. He positioned his tip at my entrance and bit his lip as he eased his way in with short thrusts.

I felt myself stretch around him and the pressure of Rogan's massive cock filling me. He grunted as he broke through and he was completely inside me.

He stilled and kissed me. "You good?"

It felt full and good, but it didn't hurt. "Yes, don't hold back."

"Fuck." He pumped into me slowly. "So damn tight."

A delicious friction grew inside me with the speed of his thrusts. His groin rubbed my clit with each sensual slide, and soon, another orgasm formed deep in my core, threatening to break me in half.

"Love you, Rogan." I wrapped my arms around his back and clung to him to ground me or I'd take off flying.

"Love you too, babe." His voice scratched with his passion, and his arms bracketed me in a cocoon that made it safe to let go. My walls clenched around him, and a power so strong and beautiful slashed through my soul. I cried out with the overwhelming force of it.

"That's my girl." He growled in my neck. His thrusts sped up, and he threw his head back. In his face, I saw him release all the years of pain and waiting and denial. He relinquished it all into me, and I accepted it with open arms.

He panted and lowered his head to my chest, sprinkling kisses up my neck.

"Been waiting for that." A sated smile lit up his eyes.

"A really long time."

He chuckled. "Anything that holds value is worth waiting for. Nothin' more valuable to me than you."

"Oh..."

"Wanted your first time to be memorable."

"I'd call that memorable. And a lot of other things."

"Mmm." He rolled us to our sides and broke our connection. He brushed a lock of hair from my face and tucked it behind my ear.

"About what I said..."

"What, that you love me?"

"And you said it back... in the heat of the moment. You don't have to say—"

"Woman, cut it out. You're not hearing me. That's on me for planting so much doubt in your head. Let me lay it out for you; I'm crazy about you." His thumb brushed my swollen bottom lip. "I knew when I first saw this smile, I was a goner."

I smiled big for him because he said the words I'd been dying to hear for so long.

He nuzzled my ear, sending tremors to my core. "If you hunger, I'll starve to feed you." He ran his soft lips down the side of my neck and nipped at my collarbone. "If you lack, I'll go destitute till you have abundance." My skin tingled where his lips trailed down to the curve of my breasts and kissed each one, skimming and nibbling up to my right shoulder and back to my neck. "If your heart craves it, I'll break mine to get it for you." He completed his circle and pressed a tender kiss to my lips. "So, you see now, I love you."

"I love you too."

He leaned across me to grab his pants from the floor. He changed the condom and thrust up into me. I gasped as his hand slid between us and massaged my sensitive clit. My legs wrapped around his back, wanting to pull him as close as two people could be. I clawed at his shoulders as another orgasm pummeled through me. He grunted and huffed short breaths into my mouth. His eyes squeezed shut, and we both gasped for air as he came inside me again.

"Only one who might love you more is Takoda."

I giggled, and his eyes watched my lips. He moved inside me a few more times before he withdrew his cock and got up from the bed. "Be right back."

He returned from the bathroom and settled me in his arms with my head against his chest, my thigh over his hip. His hand glided up my leg to my shoulder and down again.

"Let's go home to Boston. You're moving in with me." His lids hung half-hooded, and the honey in his eyes flickered in the light.

"Wow. Okay."

"No more dancing in boxes. Calling Dallas and getting you outta that gig."

I grumbled. "Okay."

"But you can wear your schoolgirl outfit and dance for me anytime."

I laughed. "I got that impression from what we just did."

His arm around my back tightened as he reached over me to turn out the light.

"No more Cutlass." His gruff voice vibrated against my ear.

I kissed his lips and his neck.

We'd have to talk about Lachlan Cutlass later. Right now, all that mattered was our love and the sanctuary of Rogan's divine body wrapped around mine.

THE NEXT MORNING, ROGAN stayed in bed with me as long as possible. He cracked my bedroom door to check the hallway and jumped back, hiding with his back flat against the door. He blended into the pattern somehow and I could barely see him. I giggled watching the disappearing Boggs in action. He put one finger over his lips to shush me.

"I saw you, dear." As the door opened, Rogan moved with it. Gwen's head slowly appeared in the doorway. I'd never seen Rogan look scared before, but his face burned red and his shoulders stiffened like he was holding his breath. "It's okay, son. We all need to make a little whoopee now and again. It's good for the soul." She smiled at me, and I pulled the sheet up to my chin.

Rogan rolled his eyes as he moved with the closing door. "The one person who can always see me is my mom. Wish I could get some of those eyes in the back of my fucking head."

We both laughed. "Oh no. Now she knows we were knocking boots."

"Knocking boots?" He scrunched his brow and crawled up the bed to my face. "Young lady, what have you been looking at on the internet that you picked up a term like knockin' boots?"

"I don't know."

"You ever watch porn?"

"Oh my gosh. How did you know?"

"I didn't, but now I do. Spill."

"See..." How could I tell him this? "The couple I babysat for, Mr. Jensen, he farms chickens."

His lips quirked. "He farms chickens and this leads to porn?"

"He was very nice to me for years. I wanted to make him a gift for his twenty-fifth wedding anniversary. They were having a party and I couldn't go, but I felt like I should give him a gift."

"And the porn comes in how?"

"I thought I'd sew him a tie with chickens on it."

Rogan pressed his lips together to suppress a laugh. He must've seen where I was going.

"And I searched for *hen tie patterns*."

Rogan burst out laughing. "And you got Hentai?"

"I did. All these cartoons and graphic sex videos."

"And so you turned off your phone like a good girl?"

"No way. I was like what the heck is this? A whole world of stuff I'd never seen. Hentai is art. Really dirty art."

Rogan put his hand over his stomach as he laughed.

"It made me wonder what else was out there. And then all these ads started popping up linking to porn sites. I checked a few out."

"I bet you did. Did you like it?"

"Some of it, yes. Most of it, no."

"What parts did you like?"

"I liked when the girls wore sexy clothes and a guy would tie her up. I also liked watching guys tied up—their naked bodies writhing around on a table or the floor, all helpless."

"You liked to watch men tied up?"

"I did. Men and women. In the ones with a man tied up, another man would usually come in and... uh, *knock boots* with him." Rogan burst into another fit of laughter. "But the girls tied up and a man touching her, that turned me on."

"You sayin' you want me to restrain you and fuck you?"

"Oh. I don't know. Maybe? Some of that stuff I'd never want to do. And the men were mean sometimes, spanking and punishing the girls when they did nothing wrong but look sexy in their lingerie. They hit them with sticks and lashes. I didn't like that."

"I see."

"I didn't care for the group sex. It bothered me."

"I can understand that."

"But, I was intrigued by the idea of being helpless and someone having his way with me, without all the tears and terror."

"Tears and terror?"

"With my dad. I felt like he tied me down, but he just wrapped one arm around me. I was paralyzed with fear, but I wonder if I'd like it with someone I loved."

He smiled and bent down to kiss me. "Thank you."

"Now you're thanking me?"

"I was a teenager last time I laughed so hard." He kissed me and rose to standing. "And I'm definitely tying you up when we *knock boots* on the plane." He walked to the door and turned back with one hand on the knob. "Get packed. We're going home."

I PLOPPED DOWN IN THE plush leather seat in the cabin of the private jet headed for Boston.

"Uh-uh." Rogan walked to a small door at the rear of the cabin. "Back here."

My stomach plummeted, and I swallowed the air that had grown thick in my throat. Rogan was just teasing on the flight to North Carolina, wasn't he? Could he have been serious?

I brushed past him through the narrow opening and stepped into a lush room. The bed and furnishings were smaller, but still high quality.

Rogan pulled his belt from his waist and leered at me. "You sure you want me to tie you up?" He draped the belt over his palm and raised one eyebrow.

All the blood in my body drained to one spot between my legs. "Yes."

Rogan with a mischievous look in his eye, teasing me with his belt, instantly sent my body into full-blown lust. This was yet another side to his complexity, and I couldn't wait to find out more.

"Want me to spank you?"

"No," I answered, breathless. A tremor chilled my bones. Could I trust Rogan with this? Would I freak out if he tied me up?

"You say *tourmaline* if you want me to stop."

"Okay."

"Nothing happens if you don't want it." His reassuring tone evaporated all my fear.

"Mmm-hmm." I wanted him naked right now. I reached for the top button on his shirt, but he took a step back.

"Take off your clothes. Lie with your hands over your head."

"Oh..."

I felt self-conscious undressing in front of him, but the appreciation in his eyes made it all okay. "A masterpiece, your body."

That made it a lot easier too.

I lay down on my back, and he crawled on top of me, straddling my hips. He wrapped the belt around my wrists and wrenched it tight. His eyes searched the sleek surface above my head. "There's nowhere to tie you up." His gaze stopped on a handle to our right. "Slight modification." Next thing I knew, I was flying in the air, his strong arm under my back rotating us ninety degrees. We ended up lying lengthwise on the small bed, my feet dangling off the edges. He looped the belt through a handle on the wall and secured it through the buckle at my wrists.

Ooh. I liked this position even more. I watched the show as he stripped off his clothes. The cut angles of his ripped body made my mouth water. Stark stars and stripes on his chest, the *E* on his bicep, broad shoulders, narrow hips, a dusting of hair from his clavicle that got thicker as it led to his stiff cock. I closed my eyes. The sinful image of Rogan naked and preparing to take me seared behind my eyelids.

He pinned me with his chest on my hips, and took his time kissing and sucking my breasts, his hands caressing my sides and anywhere he could reach. I writhed against the belt, twisting and turning to get away.

"Not going anywhere." His voice turned dark and demanding as he moved lower and dipped his tongue into my belly button. His hands held my hips in place.

Oh, man. I'd been missing out my whole life! I'd never dreamed I'd have a man like Rogan lavishing his attention on me, teasing me and tickling me this way. Divine torture.

When he traced his tongue through my opening and swished over my clit, I froze. I couldn't breathe through the bolts of fire blasting through me. I gasped for air.

He raised his head and looked up at me. His eyes were glassy like the heat over the highway on a scalding hot day. He licked his glistening lips. "Breathe, babe. I'll take care of you."

"It's too much. Overwhelming."

"Then say the word."

"No. Don't stop. Ever. I want it to last forever."

"It will. I'll never stop wanting you like this. I'd eat you every meal of the day if I could." He dove back and sucked my clit into his mouth, twirling his tongue in relentless circles. He shoved two fingers up inside me and curled them to tease a tingly spot there.

"Yes!" For a long moment, I floated weightless as if I'd fallen off a cliff. With a loud gust of air, I came hard, and my legs trembled as I pulsed on his fingers and mouth. Heaven! As I flitted down to earth, Rogan kissed up my belly and smashed his lips to mine. Wet and warm, sweet and smooth.

He lined up his tip and edged in. "God, fuck. So tight and wet for me." I bucked my hips and he sank in deeper, filling me heart and soul. His long groan stretched to a low hum. "I gotta move."

"Yes. Move."

He pounded into me, each stroke sparking glorious pleasure through me. I had no slack in the belt to even bend my elbows. I needed to touch him so bad, but knowing I couldn't made it so much hotter. My legs were free, so I used those to wrap around him and pull him deeper into me. The way his groin mashed on my clit lined up perfectly. "That's it. Oh God. Don't stop."

He didn't stop. He picked up the pace and tilted his hips, creating a constant pressure on my clit. Add to that the pure bliss his huge cock created inside me.

Another euphoric orgasm ripped from where we were joined, tore through my chest, and pushed out through my mouth. "Rogan!" My scream spurred him on and he jackhammered into me harder and faster. His neck stiffened, his head flew back, and he let out a long low groan as he buried himself deep. His cock throbbed inside me as total rapture inundated us.

He smiled through harsh breaths as he loosened the belt around my wrists. "My God, woman. Never came so hard in my life. Never been so turned on."

"Mmm. I loved that." My hands, finally freed, flew to his back and caressed the soft sheen of sweat on his muscles.

"We need to get a four-poster bed, so I can tie you up spread eagle."

"You want to do it again?"

"Absolutely. Fucking hell, you're a sex kitten, clawing against your restraints, mewling my name, giving in and taking what I'm giving."

My body shivered, the echo of his touch still fresh on my skin. "I wasn't sure I'd like it, considering ya know..."

"Sometimes it's good to take a bad memory and turn it on its head. Makes you stronger."

"Mmm-hmm."

"I wasn't subduing you. I was worshipping you. Big difference. You were in total control. I was letting you be who you are, no constraints."

"Thank you."

"You're very welcome." He brushed his lips against mine.

"So, why are you letting me thank you now?"

His fingertips tickled my side. "When I first saw you, I wanted to give you what you needed. I didn't."

"You did."

"When we got off the plane in Boston and I took you to the gate, you said *thank you* as you walked away. I felt like shit. Thanking me for what? Rescuing you from one horrendous situation and sending you to another. That thank you gutted me. After that, every time you said thank you, it reminded me of all the things I wanted to give you and couldn't. The jewels, the kisses, my heart. I'm proud to be giving it to you now like I shoulda. Standing up and being a man."

"You are all man. Whether you're giving it to me or not. But I get what you're saying. And thank you."

"Welcome."

Chapter 27

⸻

"WHAT'S THIS PLACE?" I looked around the huge ranch house in the suburbs of Boston. "Why'd we come here from the airport?"

Before Rogan could answer, Takoda bounded toward us, her nails clicking on the wood floor. Rogan crouched down, and she pounced into his arms, licking all over his face. Her tail swung so fast, it couldn't keep up with her body.

She darted from Rogan to me and back again, not sure who to kiss the most.

As Rogan tried to calm Takoda, Diesel and Blaze walked into the room from the hallway.

"Hey, Swift. How was your trip? You get your mile high membership?" Blaze asked.

I blushed because boy did I. Rogan and I made use of every inch of the small bed in the back of the jet.

"Uh, it was great. The trip, I mean. So much fun."

They all chuckled at my stumbling answer.

"We're staying here?" I asked Rogan.

"Yes. It's secure."

"Your stuff is in boxes in the master bedroom." Diesel motioned down the hall.

"It is?"

"Yep. You just need to unpack. We moved the furniture in here." Blaze pointed to the black leather couch from Rogan's apartment. "But this place is a lot bigger. You'll need to go shopping to furnish the other bedrooms."

"Other bedrooms?" I turned to Rogan. "But a place this size must be so expensive?"

"I've been collecting two salaries for four years, not spending a dime. We're good."

"Wow. Okay, thank you guys. Let me make you dinner for doing all this."

"Maybe after your surprise." Blaze grinned like a schoolboy offering a teacher a can of nuts filled with a springy snake.

"Isn't this my surprise?"

"No." Rogan stepped into the hallway. "This is." He touched a door open with his fingertips. "C'mon."

Rogan stepped back and two women walked slowly toward me with expectant looks on their faces. Oh my goodness.

"Oh my lord! Sin!" I ran to my big sister and hugged her so hard. "Pride. Pride. Pride." I locked an arm around my other sister's neck, and she clinched me in a hug. Tears gushed from my eyes so fast I couldn't see. I buried my head in Sin's neck and wept uncontrollably. "I can't believe you're here. I can't believe it!"

We pressed our heads together and sobbed. My sisters. A fragment of home. Pieces of my soul. We'd shared a bond no one will ever understand. We'd suffered through so much and been separated against our will. I'd dreamed this would happen someday, but not so soon, not today.

"I never thought I'd find you."

After a few good squeezes, we separated to dry the mess we'd made of our faces. "You look so different." Sin's red hair draped in loose curls over her shoulders. Pride wore skinny jeans and a purple blouse with matching heels.

"I changed my name to Savannah," Sin said as she wiped her eyes.

"And I go by Jasmine," Pride said.

"I'm Tessa. Nice to meet you Savannah and Jasmine." We stared at each other for a moment before bursting into laughter. I hugged my new sister Savannah, both of us half-laughing, half crying. I tugged my new sister Jasmine to my chest. "You look so beautiful."

Over her shoulder, I caught Rogan watching us, his eyes shimmering, and his smile beaming with satisfaction. I ran to him and jumped up. He caught me by my rear. "You did this? You found them? For me?"

"I did."

"Thank you, thank you. This is the best surprise ever!"

I slammed my lips to his, demonstrating my excitement and gratitude in a greedy kiss. He slipped his tongue in my mouth, and I gobbled it up. The current between us zipped to life, still charged from our naughty plane ride. I'd never get enough of Rogan and his breathtaking body.

"A-hem."

Rogan ignored the deep voice trying to get our attention, but I ripped my mouth from his and turned to see— oh my gosh, I totally forgot— Blaze and Diesel standing there. And my sisters... My sisters were here. I lowered my legs and slid down Rogan's big body, pretending not to notice the hard ridge abrading my belly.

"Uh." My sisters stared at me and Rogan with wide eyes and open mouths. Blaze and Diesel fidgeted and looked down. I don't think anyone expected me to jump his bones and mack out on him. But this is the new me, so now they knew. I'm going to be kissing Rogan a lot, so they'd better get used to it.

"Let's all go to dinner. Catch up." Rogan drew their attention from my bumbling.

"Yes. Good idea."

———

"I'M SURPRISED DIESEL and Yolanda didn't make it. They seemed so in love at the wedding," I said to Rogan as we walked into our new bedroom after dinner.

"I'm not surprised."

"What's this?" A miniature armoire sat on top of the dresser I had used at Rogan's place.

"A bigger box for your jewelry." In his hand, he held the box he'd given me before our trip. "This one fits inside it." He opened a drawer at the bottom of the large box and slipped the smaller one inside. I opened the slender, wooden doors. Empty necklace hooks hung on spinning panels covered in black velvet.

"It's extraordinary. It's like a standing jewelry box."

"If you fill this one up, I'll get you another one." He pointed to the space next to the box. "We use all the space on top of this dresser, I'll get you more dressers."

I laughed. "I don't think I'll need that many jewelry boxes. This one is enough for a lifetime of jewels."

He curled his arm around my back. "You have fun tonight with your sisters?"

I pressed my palms to his chest and flexed my fingers in his rigid pecs. "Yes. And I'm so happy for them. Savannah is happily married to one man. Jasmine has friends and plans for the future. And they both looked so pretty."

"Only had my eyes on one woman." He bent down and kissed me, the spark between us flared to life as his arm around my back drew me up against his body. He broke the kiss and looked at the bed. "This time I'm not tying you up. Want your hands on me."

"Wait. I... uh, want to talk about something. I mean, not that. I want my hands on you too, all of you. This happened so fast, I need to touch you slowly, so I can memorize every inch of you."

"Right then, here we go."

His arm scooped behind my knees, and he threw me on the bed. He landed on top of me and kissed me.

"Ermm..." My words garbled in his kiss. "Rgnnn..."

"What?"

"Savannah and I talked quite a bit tonight."

"Saw that."

"She confided in me she can't have kids. She and her husband have been trying for years."

"And..."

"And she wants to get Milo and the others out. She'll adopt them if she can."

He scrutinized my face. "Would you be okay with that?"

"All I care about is getting them out. Savannah was like a mother to us all before she left. I'd be happy for them if she adopted them, but I'd want to live close to her and to them."

"Five of them, right?"

"Mmm-hmm. Temperance is sixteen. She's probably doing most of the work right now. Hopefully, the sister wives are helping too." I did the math on my fingers. "Philander is thirteen. Mercy is nine." Rogan winced when he heard the bizarre names. "Heathen is eight and Milo is six."

"Alright. When the FBI breaks this case..."

"I want to meet with Lachlan Cutlass now."

He slid off me and propped up on one elbow to look at me. "Why?"

"He's spearheading the investigation into the Brotherhood."

"Right. And he's sucking at it. We don't need to wait for Cutlass. I'll take out your dad."

"No. If you kill him, someone else will take his place. The whole compound needs to be shut down. Families need to be relocated. It's not something bullets can fix."

"I'd only need one bullet." He winked at me.

"I know, but still... We need the FBI to speed it up."

"They can't rush in without evidence."

"I could go home. Get whatever eviden—"

"No. You're not going back there."

"Please."

"Fuck no."

He silenced me with a kiss and pressed his erection into my hip. He climbed on top of me again, but I pushed his shoulders back.

"Goddammit."

Okay, maybe now wasn't the best time. Rogan clearly didn't like his kisses interrupted.

"Taking my father down would be the sweetest revenge. You understand, right?"

"No one understands revenge better than me."

"Then let me meet with Lachlan."

"No."

"Ugh..."

"You're asking me to work with a man who went after my girl."

"He was undercover. And I wasn't your girl then."

He glared at the closed bedroom door, and his voice rasped. "Did he kiss you?"

I pressed my fingers to his cheek, forcing him to look me in the eye again. "He kissed my forehead."

A muscle twitched in his neck. "He touch you?"

"When I cried, he hug—"

"Why were you crying?"

"He took me to a show. Miss Saigon. Have you seen that? My gosh, I'd say skip it. Anyway, it's this love story about a soldier who never returns to her. I cried for you. I thought you were dead."

Rogan closed his eyes. "I'm sorry."

"But you're not dead." I pulled his shirt over his head, exposing his chiseled muscles and stark tattoos. His dog tags hung down on my chest, and I rolled the beads of the chain between my fingers. "You came back. A warm body attached to these tags." I coasted my hands along the sinews of his arms. "So beautiful. Mine to touch."

He smirked like he didn't deserve the compliment, but he did. The arch of his shoulders conveyed undiluted strength, yet he didn't carry himself with vanity. He regarded his body like a weapon to keep him alive and safe, not a work of art to be pondered and revered.

Within a few minutes, we were both naked. My hands explored every inch of him from feet to balls to hair.

He slid on a condom and entered me, my walls stretching to accommodate him.

"Fuck. So tight, babe."

I whimpered as Rogan swamped my awareness.

He flipped us so he was on his back, and my hair cascaded over his face. He did a sit up that raised us to sitting. I clutched his broad shoulders like a lifeline. He crossed his arms behind my back and impaled me on his rigid cock over and over. I clasped him tight as my orgasm engulfed me.

He groaned and buried his face in my chest as he came, and we held each other through the deluge. He lay back with me on top of him, my ear pressed against his chest. The steadfast tha-thump of his heart helped calm my breathing.

"I was lost. Couldn't breathe I was so far under water." His raspy voice rumbled low and rough. "Now I'm found. Feels so damn good to breathe fresh air."

I snuggled my forehead into the crook of his neck and blinked a tear onto his shoulder. Somehow, I'd given that to him. But he'd given so much to me too.

"I was invisible," I whispered. He drew his hand up and twined his fingers into my hair. "You saw me."

He kissed the top of my head and tugged on my hair. "I see you." His free hand caressed down my back and paused on my ass. "You're mine."

"Yes."

"No one touches you but me."

"Okay..."

"I'll make that clear to Cutlass when we meet with him."

"What?" I pushed up, and his lips curved into a sated smile.

"You want sweet revenge, I'll see to it."

My fingertips traced the stubble on his jaw. His face had taken on a mesmeric glow from our lovemaking. His lashes seemed thicker, his cheeks a ruddy red. He'd never looked more captivating.

"Thank you." I returned my cheek to his chest.

He tightened his arm around my lower back. "Ask Savannah and her husband how they'd feel about relocating to Boston."

"Really?"

"I saw a few properties up for sale in this neighborhood."

"You think we could do all that? Get the kids out, get them to Savannah, and have them live here by us?"

"We could."

"Wow. I'd love that."

"And we'll change their fucking names."

———

I WOKE ENFOLDED IN Rogan's arms, his hot chest warming my shoulders, and his hard shaft nudging my back. We must have shifted positions in the night. My legs petrified, and my breath froze in my throat.

Not my father. No need to panic. I squeezed my eyes shut. Not my father. Rogan. I love Rogan.

He jolted awake and recoiled to the other side of the bed.

"No. Stay." I reached behind me and tugged his leg, but he wouldn't budge.

"Tess..."

"Come back."

He inched his head closer but not his body.

"It's okay. You're Rogan. You're not him."

He rested his hand over my hip as he settled his frame against my back again, bending his legs so we fit together in a lazy zigzag, but careful not to touch me with his erection.

"I don't need to take you this way." His voice scraped with the roughness of sleep.

"I want it. Keep talking so I can hear your voice."

His breath feathered over my ear as his hand moved to cup beneath my breast. "You're safe with me. I love you. You're so strong. So brave."

He closed the distance between us, and his hard cock aligned between my ass cheeks. I took a deep breath and wiggled to let him know he was welcome there.

The bed tipped and his warmth tore away from my back.

"Please stay. Keep talking. I love this. I love you."

A condom pack ripped through my desperate pleas, and his solid form encompassed me from behind again. I raised a knee and rested it over his leg, opening myself to him. He moved one arm between my breasts, clasping my shoulder and pulling me close. His other hand guided his cock to my entrance.

As he pushed in, he cooed in my ear. "You're my Sunshine, my mermaid, my golden sapphire."

I gasped and blinked through unwanted tears as Rogan filled me. His fingers brushed miniscule swirls on my clit as his hard body undulated against my back. "I'm holding an angel in my arms. My angel. Like heaven being inside you."

I bent my neck, and his lips found my ear, tickling me from head to toe. We moved together for endless moments. The love between us was as visceral as the heat and sweat on our skin. I curled forward as a decadent orgasm wracked my body. He held me close and came with three quick breaths and a stiffening of his chest against my back. He didn't grunt or groan, most likely being considerate of what my father might have done, but he didn't need to be so cautious. Peace and security washed over me, coating me in an armor of confidence. Love had won an epic battle against fear, and it felt damn good.

Chapter 28

ROGAN, LACHLAN, AND I sat at Rogan's coffee table in his nook.

"What's the delay, Cutlass? Why haven't you moved on the Caldwell compound?"

"Lack of evidence. No witnesses willing to testify. Those women are fiercely loyal, and the exiled ones rarely press charges. We believe after Jeters went to prison, he created an edict that no one under eighteen could marry, making child abuse harder to prove. If Tessa testifies, it will help, but we need real dirt on him to have a solid case."

Lachlan and Rogan stared at each other.

"Tell me what you got." Lachlan broke the staring contest.

"How do you know I got anything?"

"Your woman's in danger, you're not gonna let that shit lie."

"You serve?" Rogan asked him.

Lachlan nodded. "Navy. Retired SEAL."

Rogan's eyebrows rose. "Huh. Really. And the bureau has you pounding the pavement in Boston, following college girls around?"

"Not your concern."

"Why don't you work counterterrorism for the FBI?"

"I have obligations. I prefer to keep my feet on native soil."

"Are you married?" I asked Lachlan.

"No."

"Why were you lookin' into me?" Rogan asked Lachlan.

"Made it clear to the Monroes I was investigating their business dealings."

"Not cool moving in on Tess to get to my boss."

"Wait a minute. Did you take me to Miss Saigon to get me talking about Rogan?"

"Sorry, Tessa. It's my job. Came to like you though as I got to know you. That was genuine."

I crossed my arms and scowled at him.

"Anyway. I know you're active Delta Force," Lachlan said to Rogan.

Rogan glanced at me then back at Lachlan. "Then you'd know you shouldn't be talking about the unit in front of Tess."

"If she's gonna stand by your side, she should know you're with the unit."

"It's my decision to let her in on that, not yours."

"I know about the unit, Lachlan. He told me," I said.

Lachlan ignored me and spoke to Rogan. "As a unit operative, you must have connections I don't. What did you find on Barebones?"

"Make you a deal," Rogan replied. "I'll give you evidence to lock your case tight, you back off looking into me and my unit."

"Agreed," Lachlan answered.

"You call your dogs off Dallas and Brock," Rogan pushed.

"Not gonna happen." Lachlan shook his head. "I'll give you a bye because all's fair in wartime, but the Monroe brothers murder for blood and money. Not giving up the hunt on them."

They stared at each other waiting to see who'd cave first.

"Alright," Rogan said. "I found deposits of large sums of money into Barebones' accounts that correspond with the dates women leave with sponsors."

"What do you think's going on?" Lachlan asked. "'Cuz I got my own theories."

"You go first," Rogan said.

"I think they're collecting money, holding the girls ransom if they want to leave. Figure if they want to leave, there must be someone they're leaving for, so they contact 'em and demand money for her safe release. You thinking the same?"

"Yep."

"If we can get them on kidnapping and extortion, tax evasion and fraud, we've got a strong racketeering case on top of any rape we can prove. We could take the whole place down and put a lot of those creeps away for a long ass time," Lachlan said.

Rogan nodded and aimed his intense gaze on Lachlan. "If you nail 'em for murder, could get them life sentences."

I gasped. "Murder?"

"Spill, Saxton," Lachlan said.

"Jeb Barebones took over and claimed himself the true prophet after Yoder Burkholder died six years ago."

"Know that. He died in a fire," Lachlan replied.

"Our horses Traveler and Orion almost died in that fire," I said. "Zook rescued them just in time."

"We'd need proof Jeb started the fire," Lachlan said.

"Give me some time alone with the man, I'll get you a confession."

Oh boy, I wouldn't want to be on the other side of an interrogation by Rogan.

"We can't do that. It has to stand up," Lachlan replied.

"Okay. We'll play clean. You get his computer, you'll find he purchased kerosene two days before the fire. They don't need kerosene on that compound. They have electricity and all their equipment is gasoline powered."

"And..."

"You'll find emails with him ordering his boys to bring Yoder to the barn that night. I can get them for you now, but you'll have to have your men work on legit recovery."

"I'll get on it. But still all circumstantial."

"You get your team to lean on those pussies that helped him. They'll turn fast. They got no loyalty to Jeb Barebones, only their own asses. Tess thinks Zook Guthrie will turncoat for you."

Lachlan looked at me and I nodded.

"You're gonna need a forensics team and some digging equipment. Could be bodies buried on the property. Who knows how many Jeb has taken out to get where he is."

"Of course, Saxton, I know how to conduct an investigation," Lachlan answered.

"Then get on your fucking phone and call it in."

"We need your help," Lachlan said to me. "You'll go in wearing a wire and tell your dad you want to leave—"

"No." Rogan's stern voice interrupted Lachlan's plan.

"No?"

"She does not go in alone. No fucking way."

"It's okay, Rogan." My voice came out calm, but my heart rate was skyrocketing.

"You will not face Jeb Barebones alone."

"Come with me," I asked him.

"We can't do that," Lachlan said, shaking his head. "He's not on this case. We'll have the entire compound cased out. Saxton will be outside watching on monitors."

Rogan's fists slammed on the table. "I gave you the evidence you need."

"It's all weak without his confession."

Rogan stood and marched out the door, slamming it behind him.

"He's considering it. Give him a minute," I said to Lachlan.

He returned to the table five minutes later.

"Go ahead. Make sure she's never in danger." Rogan's voice rasped with authority no sane person would dare challenge. "If she gets so much as a scratch, it's on you."

"Understood."

"CAN WE STOP AND GET a sewing machine?" I asked Rogan as we drove home in his truck.

"We could. Why?"

"I need to make a dress. If I arrive at my father's in secular clothes, it'll anger him right off the bat. I have to return as the old me."

Rogan pulled over and looked up a sewing supply store on his phone. We went there, and I picked out four yards of champagne pink fabric and one yard of white eyelet cotton. Rogan walked past me carrying a high-end sewing machine with a computer and embroidery features. The price said fifteen hundred dollars. He placed it on the register next to my fabric and notions.

"I don't need an expensive machine. This might be the last dress I sew."

"Then you're getting this machine for your last dress."

He loaded the machine in the truck, and we drove home.

"WHERE'S THIS TUNNEL you were talking about?" he asked and pointed to the screen of his laptop. I stopped working on my dress and peeked over his shoulder at the aerial photo of the compound. A bike lay on the ground and a twinge of homesickness pricked my heart. Then I saw the guard standing at the front gate and bile rose in my throat.

"It lets out here." I pointed to the door the kids all rumored to house a secret tunnel. "I'm not sure where the entrance inside the compound is."

"How were you going to use this tunnel to escape if you didn't know how to get in?"

"I planned to explore it from the outside. But it's dark and scary."

"Are there any rooms in the church you've never been granted access to?"

"There's a private men's room back here." I pointed to the screen.

"Do me a favor. Don't tell Cutlass and his team about the tunnel."

"Why?"

He raised an eyebrow at me. "Just promise me."

"Okay." I agreed but talking about the tunnel and keeping secrets from Lachlan made me nervous.

He stood and held my face in his palms. Their reassuring warmth coursed through my tense muscles. "We'll get through this. We'll get the kids out of there. And then we'll move on together. After we get them new names."

Chapter 29

———

I FLATTENED THE EYELET collar of my dress as I walked into the living room. I tugged on the puffy sleeves and stood before Rogan.

"I'm a sick, sick man."

"Why?"

"Wanna pull up your skirt and lick you through your little girl undies."

"That doesn't make you sick."

"Doesn't it make me just as bad as him?"

"Not if I want you to do it."

"Let's go."

"Where? Should I change?"

"No. That dress is perfect."

He grabbed a duffel bag and his rifle bag and directed me down the stairs to his truck. We drove to Siege and parked in the employee parking lot.

He nodded to Brock in the bar and headed up a back staircase I'd never seen before. He opened a door and inside the room was a bed and some chairs around a dining table. He took one of the chairs and placed it in the center of the room.

"They have rooms up here?"

"Yes."

"Why?"

He pulled a pair of handcuffs out of his bag.

"What's going on here?"

"If Cutlass and I are right, there's a pretty good chance your dad's gonna treat you like a hostage. He'll probably restrain you and verbally attack you. I need you to be prepared."

"What do I say?"

"You escaped from the terrorists when they were moving locations. You ran to the American Army base and the military helped you get back to the States. My team and I did not rescue you."

"Okay."

"My name is Rogan Saxton. I work security at Siege. You met me through your job. I'm your boyfriend. I'm going to sponsor you out of there."

"Oh. Okay."

"No matter what happens, do not mention Delta Force or anything I've told you regarding my work with the unit. The FBI doesn't know how we met. None of their business and immaterial to their case."

"I won't. I promise."

"He'll pressure you and know how to get to you. Your father is a diabolical narcissist. Men like him will sink their own ship if you get them talking. The feds will be recording through the cam in your necklace."

I nodded.

"Hands behind your back."

I did as he said, and my legs started to shake.

He snapped the cuffs into place. "Sit in the chair."

I sat and peered up at him. He pulled a cotton rope from his bag and approached me. His face went blank. My heart pounded like a loud gong in the silent room.

He wrapped the rope around my shoulders, crossed it over my torso, and tied it in the back. He bound my ankles to the feet of the chair so my legs were spread under my dress.

"I won't hurt you. You're safe. If you need to stop, say *tourmaline*. I'm gonna push you. Try to stick it out till the end."

He backed up into a corner till I couldn't see him anymore. I felt his eyes on me and counted my heavy breaths.

When he emerged from the shadows, his whole demeanor had changed. A hardened warrior stood in front of me.

"Where the hell have you been, Vanity? We were worried sick over you."

I pressed my lips together, not sure how to reply.

"How did you get out of Afghanistan? I didn't pay the ransom."

"I escaped when they were moving. I ran to the American base, and they helped me."

"Why'd you come here today?"

"I wanted to see my sisters and brothers. To say goodbye." I lowered my head. Even pretending to say these words was difficult.

"Goodbye? You cannot leave without a sponsor from the outside."

"I have one. He'll sponsor me."

"You fucking him?"

My head snapped up, and I glared at Rogan. I didn't think my dad would be so vulgar, but Rogan probably knew this kind of thing better than me. He wasn't breaking character and kept his face stern and intimidating.

"No."

Rogan spread my knees and his heat warmed me as he stood between them.

"How did you meet him?"

"Through work. He's my boyfriend."

"If you're fucking him, Vanity, I'll kill Milo."

"No. No. I'm not. I promise."

"I don't believe you." Rogan wrapped his hand around my neck and squeezed.

"Please. Stop." My voice came out breathy and unconvincing.

"You're weak. Feeble children like you are an embarrassment to God. I should've killed you to keep you from this imbecile you've chosen."

His hand tightened, and I struggled to breathe. I reached deep inside and found my joy. I wrapped it around me like a cloak of armor.

"You know what, Dad? I *am* fucking him—morning and night. He makes me come so hard, I can't get enough. I suck his dick. I swallow his seed. I've tasted hell and I love it."

"Vanity..."

"He loves me and my damned soul. If this is hell, I'm staying because it's fucking heaven."

Rogan's eyes darkened. The air between us became charged with the voltage I always feel when I'm near him.

"Tourmaline," he said with purpose. Was he ending the game?

His hands gripped the sides of my head and his thumbs tilted my chin up. His scent hit me as he bent to nuzzle my ear. "You did great. You're so strong. All tied up. Under pressure. You didn't lose your composure. Made it longer than I did." He peppered small kisses along my cheek.

I turned my head to capture his mouth. He pulled my bottom lip with his teeth and I whimpered. As our tongues met, my body ignited into a raging inferno. His hands clenched in my hair and tugged me deeper into the kiss. He released my head and trailed his hands down my sides to my thighs. The fabric of my skirt mashed against my skin as he massaged my legs and slowly inched it higher, driving me absolutely wild for him.

He got down on his knees and looked up at me as he lifted my skirt to the tops of my thighs. "I wanna give you some good memories to bring in with you for strength."

He bent and licked my panties. I trembled as the hot wetness from his tongue penetrated the cotton fabric.

He unbuttoned the dress in the back and worked it under the rope, down my front to below my white cotton bra. He pulled the cups down and propped my breasts on top of them. "When you're with him, you think of this." His big hands caressed my breasts and his thumbs skimmed my nipples. "You'll never be scared."

Rogan pressed something thick and hard against my panties.

"What's that?"

With a click, an intense vibration buzzed at my entrance.

"This, my love, is a vibrating dildo. You're gonna spend some quality time with it."

He moved my panties aside and worked the dildo into my opening. I moaned and arched my neck, pulling against the ropes and cuffs as he slid it in deeper.

He shoved it all the way in, and I gasped as the buzzing spread through my body. My entire existence revolved around the vibrations at my core.

"Oh my— "

"Hush."

He rotated it and something hit my clit. "Ahh!"

"Shh." With his whisper in my ear, the heat of his presence disappeared. He left me alone with this incessant pounding on my clit.

"Rogan?"

I wiggled to get it off the spot, but that only intensified the vibe.

"Oh God!"

After the shock wore off, I realized what he was doing. He wanted me to feel alone and be brave and take it. So, I let go, wiggling till the vibe hit me just right.

I pushed my breasts out and writhed on the vibrator, knowing he was watching and he'd go nuts.

"Rogan..." My breathless plea was for him to leave me be. I loved this. Not being able to stop it, knowing he thought it was hot, and he was doing this for me.

I widened my knees as far as I could in my constraints, wrapped my toes around the legs of the chair, and lifted my hips.

See me here? I'm alone and strong and I love that you gave me this.

He grunted—the first sound he'd made since he'd left me.

In my head, he'd taken out his massive cock and held it in his hand. He couldn't refrain any longer. In the corner, he eagerly waited for me to go over the edge so he could come back and take me.

Guess what, my love? You can wait.

With a sharp wrench of my hips, I shifted the vibrator off my clit. My breasts heaved as I caught my breath.

The dildo still buzzed ruthlessly inside me, but my threatening orgasm faded.

"Put it back." His gruff voice reverberated from the dark void to my left.

"Ah, so you *are* here."

"Put it back on your clit."

"You come put it back."

The seconds ticked by with my challenge looming between us. I was about to give in when he stepped out of the shadows, stroking his cock as he stalked to me.

With his free hand, he twisted the vibe back and stared me down. "Now, babe. Come now!"

And I did. He groaned as he watched my mouth drop open and my body convulse on the vibe. He held it in place for me while I rode it out.

"Enough!" I cried.

"Alright."

The vibe clicked off, and I sighed as the incredible feeling of fullness left me. Before I could catch my breath, he uncuffed my hands and loosened the rope at my torso and legs. He pulled my ugly dress over my head and tossed it aside. One arm behind my back lifted me from the chair, the other worked off my panties and bra. I held on around his neck and helped him through kisses as he carried me to the bed. I took of his clothes and the scorching heat flowed between us like molten lava. We fell to the bed with me on my back and him on top of me. "So fucking strong. My girl." I wrapped my legs around him as his cock found my opening and thrust inside.

He pounded into me deep and steady, mashing my clit with his abdomen and kissing me while he did it. Rogan filled me. My life was full with Rogan and our love. His breathing sped up and his forceful body controlled me. I was under him and at his mercy. But he was Rogan, I could trust him with anything. Another orgasm raced through me and I clenched around him. He moaned and pressed his open mouth to my neck, his teeth digging in. His cock stayed buried to the root as he came inside me. We pulsed together in a huge mass of humanity. We held on to each other as our breathing evened out and our bodies relaxed.

He kissed me slow and sexy. "Love you, babe."

"Love you too."

WE CUDDLED IN THE BED in the room for a long time. I had a thought niggling in my mind and decided to bring it up. "About the future. I have one concern."

"Mmm. What's that?"

"You leave. When the going gets tough, all I see is your back through the door. That leaves me behind, alone—no family around—to deal with whatever happened. You take Takoda with you, and I don't even have her to comfort me. I can handle it now. I'm strong, I can be alone and I understand you need that time. But if you let me love you, then we have to face these times together. We hold each other through it. Let me have that. Can I have that part of you?"

He stared into my eyes. "Can't promise you I won't leave, babe." My heart sank. "I'm glad you get it's how I process when shit gets too close. But I can give you this. I'll come running home to you the second my feet hit the soil. I'll give you every part of me I can, but you gotta be patient too. I'm stretching. I'm trying. But leaving the way I've been for a long time isn't gonna come natural to me."

"Are you still going on James Bond missions to combat zones?"

"Brightman kept her end of the bargain. I'm obligated to keep mine."

"Forever?"

"Until they don't need me anymore. It's my skill set. I'm the best at what I do."

"I know and you're my hero, but if you're gonna give me Boggs, I don't want to lose him."

"Need you to accept me as I am. I do black ops. It's dangerous. I can get called out anytime and I might not come back. I know that sucks and it's unfair to ask, but this is my job. It kept us apart for too long, now I'm asking you to accept it."

"Of course. I love you and all that comes with you. I'm with you no matter what. Just... please think about some less hazardous options."

He kissed my nose. "I'll consider it."

Chapter 30

———

"GOOD LUCK." JASMINE gave me a hug and a kiss as she stood next to Savannah in the hotel parking lot outside Caldwell, Idaho. I was wearing my pink prairie dress, and my hair was pinned and braided the way all the women on the compound wore their hair.

"We'll be waiting here for you. We'll get them out. Don't worry," Jasmine said.

I hugged Savannah too. "We're with you in spirit," she said.

"Thank you. It gives me courage."

Rogan took my hand and guided me away from my sisters. He checked the recording device in my necklace one last time. "Be smart. Don't panic."

"Make sure the kids are safe," I replied.

"I will die before I let anyone hurt you or them."

Lachlan gave us a thumbs up from the van across the lot. An army of plainclothed agents milled around, checking equipment and preparing to send me in.

Rogan pressed me up against the wall and kissed me gently. I whimpered into his mouth. He grabbed my lower back, pulling me to my tiptoes. He deepened the kiss, growling and ratcheting up the intensity.

He may have been staking his claim in front of Lachlan, but I didn't care. His kisses rocked my world every time, and if this was to be our last kiss, it was a memorable one.

He pulled away and raised his head. "Bye."

I took a deep breath as he released me slowly. I imagined harnessing his strength and the warmth of his touch to bring with me to face my father.

"Bye."

I felt his eyes on me as I walked across the lot to Lachlan.

AS THE SUN SET AND darkness closed in, Lachlan dropped me off a few blocks from the compound entrance. My insides turned to stone with each crunch of my boots on the sidewalk. In the twelve months I'd been gone, the walls surrounding the compound grew higher and more menacing.

With each step, I walked away from the life I'd made outside and back to the one I'd escaped.

No one was guarding the front gate, so I walked right through. My throat clogged as I knocked on my old front door. Aunesty, Father's third wife, answered it and stared at me for a second. Her grew wide, and she grabbed my arm to pull me inside.

"Vanity? My word. What are you... Come in. Come in. Jeb!"

My father came out from the back of the house with three of the other sister wives. He feigned surprise and held his arms open for me. "Vanity. Vanity. My girl."

He was putting on a show for his wives, pretending like he didn't attack me at my place of work two months ago. I stepped into his arms and let him hug me. "Hello, Father."

He pulled away and focused on my necklace. Oh no. What if he made me remove it?

I took a deep breath. Here we go.

"They told us you died," he said.

"No, the kidnappers released me, and I flew home."

Milo came out of the bedroom, and his eyes bugged out. He raced to me and slung his little arms around me.

"Milo. You're so big now."

He cried so hard he couldn't speak. I cried too and stroked his head and neck. "Shh... Everything's going to be okay." It felt so good to hold him again. I should've come sooner.

Temperance, Philander, Mercy, and Heathen all came out with shocked faces. When they hugged me, I knew I was here for the right reasons. They needed me.

"You all can visit with Vanity tomorrow. It's bedtime now." My father glared at me like I shouldn't have come this late.

It was the only time I knew you'd be home.

Aunesty, Temperance, and I tucked the kids into bed.

"Nite-nite, Tee-tee."

"Nite-nite, Lo-lo. I love you. Your dreams are about to arrive."

"You're already here." Milo grinned and snuggled his teddy.

My father stood behind me as I closed the door to the room where the four youngest children slept. "Let's go, honeysuckle."

I held my breath and my spine stiffened hearing his obnoxious nickname for me again. He took me to the private men's room on the second floor of the house. I gawked at the opulence. Flat screen TVs, a modern desk, a bed with a gilded headboard.

"You live like this up here? And we starve downstairs?"

"I am God's prophet. He provides for his son."

Oh, please.

As he closed the door, I gasped. Zook Guthrie stood by the far wall.

"Why's Zook here?"

"I've had a revelation." He clasped his hands and bent forward as he walked to me. "God wants you to be with Zook. The heavenly father will take you back into the church and forgive your sins if you repent and become Zook's first wife."

"No."

"You wanted Zook, remember? I caught you fornicating with him. I realize now that was an early sign of your predestined celestial union. I was selfish and kept you for myself, but I'll let you be with him. He's a chosen seed bearer. God has deemed him worthy to copulate with you to summon his angel babies to earth."

Oh boy. My father had taken a one-way ride on the crazy train.

I stared at Zook in the corner. We'd been so close once. He was the only person I'd felt I could trust. We were teenagers in love. He looked down then, his face drawn. He was stuck in my father's trap as deep as the women were. I mustered up my courage and played along.

"Zook is a chosen seed bearer?" I examined him with a speculative stare. "So, if I became his wife, I wouldn't be forced to sleep with other seed bearers?"

"No, if you marry a seed bearer, your obligation is met. You know this. See, I thought you might prefer one sexual partner, and I know you fancy Zook."

Yes, I might like not being raped while my husband holds my hand and watches.

"But if he's a seed bearer, would he sleep with other women? Even those not one of his wives?"

"Yes, honeysuckle. Why is this so hard to understand? God revealed to me that the seed bearers shall be the only men to procreate the chosen children. Their husbands will understand, and the wives must abide or face the consequence of excommunication."

Any shred of guilt I felt for betraying my father left me at that point. He truly believed the wives should allow themselves to be raped or face homelessness and giving up their children.

"I've had a revelation myself, Father." I took a deep breath and envisioned Rogan standing strong and powerful behind me.

My father's mouth dropped open and he stared at me.

"I want to leave the church."

"Why?" His eyes flared. "Is it that man who rescued you?"

His comment threw me off. Did he know Rogan rescued me from the terrorists? No, he must've been referring to the attack two months ago in the Siege parking lot.

"Yes. He rescued me in many ways. I'm in love."

Zook's head popped up and his brow furrowed.

Yes, Zook, I love the big hulk of a man who beat my father to a pulp in the parking lot and made you run like a coward.

"What's his name?" my father asked.

"Rogan Saxton. I want your blessing to be with Rogan on the outside."

"I cannot grant you blessings. This outsider is not chosen."

"He has been chosen—by me." I raised my chin.

"His soul will rot in hell, and so will yours if you tie yourself to him on earth."

"I've decided to take that chance."

"Instant gratification is a lure of the devil, Vanity. Preparing for your eternal future will guide you to make wholesome choices in this life."

His hypocrisy knew no bounds! No one had ever put this man in his place. I'd endured the wrath of his anger before, and I knew my words would set him off. The time had come to be brave. If Rogan could charge into caves filled with evil men with guns and bombs, I could challenge my delusional father.

"How are your choices wholesome or divine? You rape a different woman every night." His head jerked back hearing me accuse him for the first time. "You have children you don't talk to except to punish them with beatings."

"Do not speak blasphemy to your prophet, Vanity. I am the living representative of God, and I do his will by keeping many wives and creating children that will ascend into the highest levels of heaven with me."

"You tell yourself that, but it's all a lie. Hurting women and children is not God's will. He wants you to love your wives and your sons and daughters. That's all they want is to be loved by you. But you're too obsessed controlling them with prophecies and threats. Your manipulation to *your will* leaves no room for love."

"I love all my wives and children." His voice was a low hiss.

"Love does not molest."

His face contorted in pain and confusion. "Molest? No." He placed a hand on my face and stared into my eyes. "You carry your mother's spirit, honeysuckle. When I lost her, I was heartbroken. I lay with you to hold a piece of her close to my heart. You are my spirit wife."

"I see it now." I stared into his beady eyes. "You're so misguided. You violated me."

"No. Don't tarnish the gifts we offered God in the name of love." He added his other hand to my face and rubbed my cheeks with his thumbs.

"It's abuse. It's illegal."

His fingers constricted and pressed into my temples. "You speak lies, you apostate. I never penetrated you. I kept you pure. Stop this nonsense now!"

"Did you threaten to kill me if I didn't allow you to leave your seed between my legs?"

"Yes, yes, blood atonement is the declared penalty of dissension. I wouldn't have really killed you, honeysuckle, but you had to believe I would. My role as prophet is to force you to see God's plan. You can't go against it or the wrath of hell will descend upon your soul."

"Did you carve scars into my shoulder to mark my transgressions?"

"Vanity. Do not push me any farther. God decrees we lay down a heavy hand on all who disobey his church. The marks I placed on your back served to break your selfish will and shelter you from sin."

"Did you kill Uncle Yoder?"

"How do you know about that?" Sweat glistened on his forehead. He was losing control.

"Did you kill him in the barn fire?"

His hands shook. "Yoder Burkholder was leading the church astray. God spoke to me and told me he should die in a pit of fire. I only fulfilled the prophecy."

And with that, he had confessed. Any jury would put this nutjob away for life.

His hands clasped my neck. "Have I failed in all my efforts to gain you access to heaven? Have you become a slut? You dance like a whore and ask to leave with an outsider? Did you fornicate with him?"

"No." I gasped for air as he squeezed my windpipe.

"You lie. The prophet can see your true intention." My father's eyes lit with venom. "Demons possess you!"

"No."

He shook my neck, rattling my head and blurring my vision. "Satan convinces you to reject the life God has spoken for you through me."

He pushed me to a chair. "Sit." He tied my arms and legs. "If you repent now, I can appeal to God to exorcise your demons. It will be painful, but he will save your lost soul."

"No. I will not. If this is the devil's work, then I welcome him to do more. I love Rogan. He's good. There's no evil in him."

My father's face reddened and smoke billowed from his ears. "Then you shall pay the price for this licentiousness. What's this Rogan person's number?"

"My cell phone's in my pocket. Call him."

He pulled my phone from my pocket and turned his back to me as he dialed Rogan on video chat on a laptop on his desk.

"Hello. Are you Rogan Saxton?"

"I am." Rogan's deep voice and handsome face greeted me from the monitor. He was here with me, digitally anyway.

"You want to sponsor Vanity out of my church?"

"I do."

My father looked back at me with his eyebrows raised. "Have you fornicated with her?"

"Have *you*?" Rogan's cool voice answered with a question.

My father's gaze snapped back to the monitor.

Oh goodness. Not a good start.

"Two million. Cash." My father's spoke in his angry wrath-of-God tenor.

"No problem. Where do you want that delivered?"

My father tilted his chin at Rogan's casual response to his outlandish demand. "Do you plan to marry her?"

No, no, no. Rogan won't say yes. This could ruin everything.

"Yes. I want to marry her. I want that more than anything. I'll take good care of her. Got a ring right here." Rogan dropped to one knee and held out a blue velvet box. He opened it and revealed a huge, sparkling diamond ring. Was he pretending? Had he changed his mind about marriage? This must be part of the act. I stared at the image of Rogan on one knee, something I never thought I'd see. "I want her to wear my ring so every man who covets her beauty will know she's mine and I'm hers alone. I'll never cheapen her by loving another in spirit or in flesh."

My father's fists clenched. "You brazenly insult me at the same time you ask me for a favor? She is at my mercy."

He turned and stalked toward me with his fist poised to strike. I closed my eyes and let the thud on my face pass through me. The familiar sting of his swift hand tingled in my cheek as my head flung back.

As I straightened my neck, Rogan's voice became more urgent. "Hey, Jeb! Jeb! Listen here."

My father turned his back on me and focused on the screen again.

"I'll bring the money to the drugstore in Caldwell by tomorrow noon."

I lowered my head to cry. To antagonize Rogan, my father would strike me over and over. This beating would be his worst ever.

Chapter 31

———

A GIANT HAND GRIPPED my mouth.

"It's me. Relax," a deep voice whispered in my ear.

Rogan. Rogan? How could he be here if he was on the video?

Before I could react, the ropes around my hands and legs loosened, and Rogan lifted me under my arms till I was out of the chair. He carried me to the back of the room and placed my feet inside an open hatch in the floor.

My father spoke to the video image of Rogan on the computer. "No. Meet me at the old saw mill on Fuller Road."

"I'll be there," Rogan's video image replied. This was too weird.

"Make sure you come alone," my father said to video Rogan.

I slipped on the first rung into the tunnel and gasped. The noise caused my father to look back. He caught us just before we made it down the hatch.

"Stop right there or I'll shoot her." My father pulled a handgun from inside his jacket and pointed it at me. Zook raised a gun too and aimed it at us.

Rogan angled his body in front of me and aimed his rifle at my father. "Have to get through me first."

"Rogan Saxton?" My father looked back and forth between Rogan in real life and Rogan on the screen. "How are you here and there at the same time?"

"Turns out I *am* chosen. God gave me magic powers to appear in two places at once. Now drop the gun."

"You lower yours first."

"I'm calling the shots here, Jeb. Drop it."

Zook dropped his shotgun and raised his hands in surrender.

"You'd risk your life for a wicked sinner like her?" My father swiveled the barrel of his gun, and Rogan countered.

"Give up, Jeb. It's too late. We got your confession. You're going to prison for the rest of your days, and I pray to God you get fucked up the ass every Sunday by a really big tattoo artist named Jesus."

"You set me up, you little whore?" My father stepped to the right to glare at me, but Rogan shielded me.

"Hey, Jeb. You afraid of dogs?"

"What?"

Rogan pointed two fingers at my father.

A growling Takoda appeared from a dark corner and jumped to bite my father's gun arm. He yelled and fired his gun wildly. The loud pops deafened me and muted my father's screams as Takoda gnawed and thrashed at his arm. Rogan pushed me down into the hatch, but I poked my head up to watch. Rogan fired one shot. My father dropped his gun and grabbed his thigh, falling to his knees with a shocked grunt. Takoda tugged him until he was laying on his side on the floor.

"Out." Takoda snuck in one last thrash before she let go and backed away, barking excitedly at him as he groaned on the ground, blood seeping into his pants.

Rogan turned his gun on Zook who had stood frozen during the whole encounter. "You wanna try your luck with the fates too? Or you gonna cooperate with the FBI?"

"FBI?"

Rogan didn't answer Zook's question. In a whorl, he grabbed me and jumped down through the hatch. He landed on two feet and took off running as he hoisted me up over his shoulder. Behind us I heard men shouting. "FBI! Don't move!"

Rogan's shoulder pummeled my stomach and my legs dangled uselessly as he ran with me through the tunnel. Cool air hit my face as we emerged outside the walls of the compound. Rogan lowered me into the back seat of a black car.

Dallas sat at the steering wheel, and Cyan smiled at me from her seat next to me in the back.

"You're safe." Cyan wrapped her arms around my shoulders.

"I'm what?"

"You're safe. They got their evidence, and Rogan got you out."

Rogan held binoculars to his face and scanned around the car. "I'm going back in for the kids."

"What? No!"

"I'll be back in five." He spoke to Dallas in the front seat. "If you're spotted, leave without me. I'll meet up with you later."

"Ten-four," Dallas replied in a casual tone.

"No!"

But he was already gone. I looked out to watch Rogan and Takoda jog back in, but in true Boggs fashion, they were invisible in the night.

My already thrashing heart threatened to explode. I didn't want him to go back in. Who knows what other Redeemers were up there fighting with the FBI guys? It could be a bloodbath.

I huddled in Cyan's arms and chewed on my nails for what seemed like forever.

Dallas stepped out of the car and pointed a gun down the road.

I gasped as Rogan appeared next to the car. He carried Milo and my other four siblings ran behind him with Takoda following in the rear. He opened the door and handed me a frightened Milo.

He whimpered in my arms. "It's okay, Milo. Shh..."

Through the back window, I watched Rogan and Takoda guide the other four kids into a black car behind us. Dallas jumped back into the driver's seat and revved the engine.

One of the big F350s the Brotherhood used for security patrols approached from down the road. A loud pop pinged off the car.

Oh no! They're shooting at us!

Dallas didn't flinch at the two bullets that thunked against the back windshield. The glass splintered but didn't break. The bullets just bounced off.

"Holy shit," Cyan said.

"Exactly," I replied.

Rogan ran back to our car and crouched behind the open passenger-side door. He took aim at the approaching truck. "Get down!" I ducked down in the seat. "Falcon, pass on our left."

The black car from behind us streaked past in a cloud of dirt.

"Rogan!" Terror rocked me at the sight of my man facing gunfire with only a door to protect him.

"Stay down!"

Rogan shot a series of loud pops.

He plopped in his seat. "Got 'em. We're clear."

Takoda barked at the windshield like she was telling Dallas to go!

I peeked out through the back window and saw headlights fading in the distance.

"Stay down," Rogan said to me again.

I hunkered down lower and covered Milo with my body.

"Did you kill them?" I asked.

"Nah, shot their tires." He looked over his shoulder at me. "You want me to kill 'em?"

"No!"

He sat back and laughed.

"SO YOU RIGGED THE VIDEO feed?" I asked Rogan at the post-action meeting at the hotel. Jasmine stayed with Milo and my other siblings after settling them into beds after their frightening evening. Savannah and Rogan sat on either side of me. Cyan, Dallas, Diesel, and Falcon sat opposite us at a table in a conference room that had been converted to a base camp for the FBI.

"We pre-recorded responses anticipating what Jeb would say," Falcon replied.

"Did you know about this?" I asked Lachlan.

"No." Lachlan's voice was grumbly. "Brilliant idea. Wish I'd thought of it."

Rogan grinned.

"Will my dad survive?"

"It looks like it," Lachlan answered. "Gunshot wound to his leg will slow him down on his way to court, but he'll stand trial."

"And the confession I got was good enough?"

"It's excellent. Well done."

"I'll testify to what I know," Savannah added. "My sister Jasmine will testify too."

"Zook Guthrie already started singing," Lachlan said.

"That kid nearly shit his pants staring down my rifle," Rogan said.

Lachlan and Rogan chuckled. "We'll be in contact, Tessa." Lachlan gathered his papers and phone.

He nodded at me as he left the room.

"You were very brave." Cyan stood and hugged me.

"Thank you so much for being there tonight." I returned her embrace.

"She wouldn't have it any other way," Dallas answered as he curled his arm over Cyan's shoulder.

"I had to take my girl's back." Cyan winked at me.

"Of course," Dallas said with a smirk.

"Hey, if you tell me Rogan and Tessa need help rescuing some kids, don't expect me not to hightail it to Idaho." She smacked his pec and he laughed. "Anyway," Cyan continued, "if any of those kids end up lost in the shuffle, you let me know. Our hearts and home are open to them."

"Most of the kids today will lose a father, but they'll still have their mothers. The mothers will need help relocating and adjusting to life outside."

"Tell me what they need, and they'll have it," Dallas said.

"Thank you, Dallas."

Dallas and Cyan waved as they walked out.

Savannah was the only one left in the room with me and Rogan. "I can't believe we're going to get them. Do you think the courts will grant me custody?" she asked.

"Things are looking in your favor right now," Rogan replied.

"I'm so happy."

"Tessa talk to you about the property next to ours?"

"Yes. We're in escrow," Savannah said with a smile on her lips.

"You are? Oh my gosh! We'll be neighbors. I could watch the kids whenever you'd like." I hugged Savannah.

"I'd love that." Savannah hugged me back.

"We could be a family again."

"Yes. But this time free to love and have fun and enjoy life."

"Yes. It'll be fantastic."

"I CAN'T WAIT TO GET this awful dress of— Oof!" Rogan grabbed me and pushed me up against our hotel room door, slamming his lips on mine and pinning me to the door with his hips. One of his hands dug into my waist, the other messed with the buttons at the back of my dress.

I froze, shocked by the sudden onslaught, but the adrenaline still pumping in my veins ignited between us. I squeezed his biceps and urgently ran my hands over his neck and arms. I pressed my palms to his chest to feel his heartbeat.

Alive, safe, breathing, kissing me. My Rogan.

"Fuck," he mumbled against my lips. "Never again. Never letting you go again."

He tore the buttons off the dress and yanked the top down my front. My head hit the door as he latched onto my nipple through my bra. I freed my hands from the dress sleeves and held his head to my breast. "I'm okay. I knew you wouldn't let him hurt me."

He stood to his full height and pierced me with his golden gaze. "Nothing will ever hurt you."

He wrenched my dress down over my hips and dropped to his knees to lick me through my panties. He raised one leg over his shoulder and growled as he bit down, attacking the fabric separating us.

Rogan was on his knees for the second time this evening, the first his fake proposal, this time, worshiping me and desperate for me.

"Take off your clothes. I need your skin on mine." I tugged the collar of his shirt.

He stood with a grunt and took off his pants while I worked on his buttons.

"You sort out the birth control?" He stepped out of his briefs and freed his erection that was pointing straight at me.

I pushed his shirt over his shoulders, and he tossed it to the floor. His abs flexed as I ran my fingers down the curled waves on his stomach. I followed the trail of hair on the defined *V* of his waist to the base of his cock and grabbed hold. "Yes."

"Goddamn." He lined his cock up at my entrance. "Nothing separates us."

We both groaned as he entered me. He hitched my knee on his waist, and the rigid muscles of his abdomen slammed into my clit as he rocked into me. "I'm in you. On you. All the time."

"Yes."

He pumped into me, slow at first, but soon the inferno raged between us and exploded. My clenching around him drew a moan from deep in his throat. He buried his face in my neck and followed me over the edge.

As our breathing calmed, he moved slowly inside me, treasuring each slippery slide in and out. I rubbed my hands up and down the curves of his back.

"He'll never strike you again. No one ever will." He caressed my cheek where my father's fist had landed. "You'll never shake in fear again." He removed the band at the end of my braid and worked my hair loose.

"You were in the room when he hit me."

He closed his eyes. "I was. Took all my strength to aim for his leg instead of his forehead."

"I'm glad you didn't kill him. I wouldn't want that weighing on your conscience."

"No weight at all." He removed the clip holding my hair at the top of my head and grinned as he watched it fall free of its bondage.

"If you shot my father, no matter how evil he was, you wouldn't feel guilty?"

His fingers gripped my hair and draped it forward over my shoulder. "I'd worry you'd hold it against me, but no, no guilt."

"Huh."

"Anyway, doesn't matter. I didn't kill him, and I'm gonna enjoy watching him grow old in a jumpsuit and four concrete walls." He slid out of me and wetness coated my legs. "You okay?"

"What do you mean?"

"My *seed* on your skin."

"No, it's different. I'm over it. I love you."

A smug grin grew on his lips. He grabbed his pants from the floor and hoisted me up with my legs around him, tossed me on the bed, and landed on top of me. From the pocket of his pants, he withdrew the blue box I'd seen in the video.

"I love you too." He placed the box on my naked chest. As he opened it, a stunning princess-cut diamond rested against the velvet blue cushion. The huge center stone and the dozens of tiny square diamonds surrounding it emitted brilliant light beams like the disco balls hanging over the dance floor at Siege. He traced his hand down my left arm and brought our clasped hands up between our faces. "Does it sparkle enough for you?" He worked it onto my left ring finger.

"Oh my gosh, yes. It's absolutely breathtaking." He'd chosen a glamorous ring, the kind a movie star should wear. Not me. "But... you don't have to do this. I know you were putting on an act to trick my dad."

He pressed his lips to my palm. "No act. I'm marrying you. I'll be your first husband. And your last."

"But Eden..."

His eyes sliced to mine. "You'll be my only wife." His voice hummed with conviction.

Shock and disbelief warred with excitement and joy inside me. Could this really be happening? "Are you sure? I come with five children now, ya know. Even if Savannah adopts them, they'll be a huge part of my life."

"Plenty of room for five kids at our ranch house. More if you want them."

"More?"

"You want more?" He tightened his fingers around my left hand and leaned in to touch a kiss to my lips.

"I don't know." I hadn't thought about having kids of my own. I'd been so concerned for my siblings and the other children on the compound.

"You want horses?"

Horses? "Yes, Traveler..."

"We'll get Traveler and Morning Glory together on our ranch."

"I'm kind of a mess. I don't know what I believe about God anymore. The trial is going to be stressful for me."

"I'll be there with you. I have baggage to sift through too. We'll find our way together. Say you'll be my wife."

"I'll be your wife."

He kissed a tear from my cheek. "My only wife."

"Yes. Your only wife."

When he pressed his lips to mine, he sealed the promise between us. Rogan and I would be together forever. It seemed too good to be true. A wicked apostate from the compound had turned her life around and found her dream man. How did I get so lucky? When we broke apart, he settled me beside him and I rested my head on his chest. "I want to help the women and children left behind from the Brotherhood. They deserve a chance to find joy like this too."

"Alright."

"It'll be difficult for them. The boys will need tutoring. Some of them can't even read. They'll all need counseling. Maybe Natalie can help with that."

"You can use the ranch as a base. Dallas said he'd support you too. With the men of Siege behind you, no way you can fail."

"Thank you."

Chapter 32

"*Renmen se vre*." The Amalian guests at my wedding sang a rich, melodic song, filling the air with rising notes.

"*Renmen pout tout tan*." The second refrain echoed the first verse, but lilted lightly down.

Rogan and I sat side by side on our knees. Gwen draped a purple cord loosely from my neck to Rogan's, lassoing us together.

She bent to kiss my cheek. "What does it mean?" I asked her.

"*Renmen se vre*." The crowd sang the words in haunting unity.

"Love is true," she answered softly in my ear.

"Renmen pout tout tan."

"Love forever."

"It's beautiful."

"So are you, my love." She hugged me and returned to Bastien's side.

Chantal approached Rogan and me on the raised dais at the center of the reception hall. She sang, "*Renmen se vre*," as she added a royal blue cord over the purple one.

"*Renmen pout tout tan*." She squeezed Rogan's hand where it rested over mine. "Welcome, sister."

One by one, the guests approached and added a new cord to the collection of bands tying me to Rogan. The golden one Savannah slipped over our shoulders strapped our torsos together. Each new cable forced us closer until my back pressed against his chest and he supported my weight.

"Bo, bo, bo, bo!"

I arched my neck to peer over my shoulder at Rogan. "What do they want?"

"They want us to kiss."

"Oh."

I twisted in my bindings, and Rogan bent his neck until our lips touched. The guests cheered, and I laughed into the kiss. The ropes hid most of our bodies and the long train of my dress covered my bottom half. I'd chosen a mermaid gown in eggshell white that was covered in thousands of small crystals. Rogan ran a hand furtively up my leg under my dress. He stared at me with wide eyes while his fingers explored the garter belt clips at the tops of my stockings. "What the everlovin' hell?"

"Cyan's idea."

"Holy shit." With a whoosh, he flipped me around on his lap. His tongue probed deep in my mouth, and his fingers caressed the curve of my ass. Thank goodness for all these sashes giving us some privacy.

The cheers got louder and perhaps someone whistled, but I didn't hear it. I was lost in my husband, his massive hands placing my body where he wanted it, his luscious lips kissing me.

When his fingertips snuck between my butt cheeks, I pulled away. "Um, Rogan, these panties are kinda thin and..."

He growled and ran his hand lower. I gasped as he dipped his finger in my wetness. "Lick it, Sunshine." He tapped his finger on my lower lip. I angled my head so no one could see and sucked it in, tasting myself on him. His eyes heated, and his arm around my back tugged me closer, arching my chest against him. "Mmm." He hummed in my ear.

"We should uh... People are watching."

His groan thundered deep in his chest. He freed us from our tangled cords and lowered me back to my spot next to him.

Rogan watched me straighten my tiara and, after I'd wiped my lipstick from my bottom lip, his gaze darted back up to the tiara. "Still crooked."

I glared at the zipper of his tuxedo pants. "Still hard."

He chuckled.

"Can we leave now?" I asked him.

"No. Guinevere Foor wouldn't let us leave the wedding early. I have a surprise anyway."

"Another one? The tiara was more than enough."

Rogan had the gems he'd given me worked into a shining platinum tiara. Rectangular baguettes of black tourmaline lined the headband at the bottom. Sharp spinels rose from the base, topped with flowers made of white diamonds. The yellow sapphire swung from the peak of the tiara like a sundrop over a field of flowers. I'd given him a thick sterling silver wedding band engraved with one word. *Forever.*

As I resecured the pin holding my tiara in my hair, Falcon approached us carrying two guitars. He handed one to Rogan and stood behind us holding the other one. Blaze followed Falcon with a square amplifier and some cables. He connected the speakers and set up microphones for Rogan and Falcon.

"Can we get some chairs?" Rogan asked.

Diesel brought us three chairs. Rogan sat opposite me on the dais. Falcon took a seat behind Rogan's left shoulder.

As the sun was setting behind him over the Amalian coast, Rogan strummed an intro on an acoustic guitar, and Falcon chimed in with bass guitar playing backup behind him. Rogan sang that I'm his whole world and how our love would grow from this day forward. His voice was smooth as velvet and filled with heartfelt emotion. His version of the song was a million times better than the original.

Through my blurred vision, I saw the female wedding guests dabbing at their eyes. Rogan's Army buddies didn't cry, but their strong jaws were meaningful with pride. Rogan rose from his chair, handed the guitar to Falcon, and offered me his hand. "Dance with me."

We joined hands and stepped off the platform, making our way to the middle of the dance floor. He kissed me, and we danced for the first time as a married couple to a sweet Carrie Underwood song about a mother trusting her daughter's choice in a husband.

I gazed up into Rogan's loving eyes. "You are good." He shook his head. "You are. Salt of the earth."

"Thank you. I'm glad you see me that way. Makes me wanna be that for you."

"My momma would've loved you," I said to him. "She'd think you're gorgeous, and she'd be happy for me that I got out and found a solid man who would let me fly."

"And you will soar. I guarantee it."

"With you by my side, I will."

I tucked my forehead into his chest and inhaled the scent of my rugged man's crisp white dress shirt.

"My father would adore you like I do," he said to the top of my head.

I nodded and blinked away tears. I didn't look up when I asked him, "Would Eden be happy for you?"

He bent down and dipped his chin to whisper in my ear. "She would."

He wrapped his palm behind my neck and kissed me. I closed my eyes and savored the goodness of knowing our lost loved ones were smiling down on us tonight. His tongue probed deeper and his hand moved lower on my back.

Please, Rogan. Let's leave now.

He pulled back and touched his finger to my lips. "In due time, love." And he used the same finger from earlier, so it didn't calm me down at all.

Other couples joined us on the dance floor, and I took a deep breath to center myself.

Dallas in a tuxedo and Cyan in her sequined bridesmaid's dress stole the show. I averted my gaze when he kissed her because it seemed like a private moment between them.

Rogan's mother swayed gracefully in her gown and tiara as she danced with Prime Minister Foor, and the Amalian guests watched with appreciation.

Savannah danced with her husband, and Milo and the other kids stared at them with the same wonder on their faces I'd worn on mine at Diesel's wedding.

Brock swayed to the music with Jasmine in his arms, his hand drifting lower over the open back of her bridesmaid's dress. Oh no. Brock would not be good for her. I'd warn her after the dance.

The slinky silk dress Chantal chose to wear had caught the attention of both Blaze and Diesel, and the three of them chatted at the bar. Blaze dropped a cherry down Chantal's dress and dove his face in to retrieve it.

She threw her head back on Diesel's shoulder behind her and laughed as Blaze took his time coming out of her cleavage with the cherry. He chewed on the cherry and tied the stem with his tongue before handing it to her.

Lord have mercy, Chantal was going to gorge on commandos tonight. And from the glare Bastien was sending over to them, he did not approve. I imagine if he didn't want Rogan and I to share a room before we were married, he wouldn't want his daughter flirting with two guys at his stepson's wedding.

Rogan had invited two other men from his Delta Force team. Ruger and Oz mingled with the Amalian guests. I didn't remember them from the night they rescued me. After I talked to Jasmine about Brock, I'd ask Rogan to introduce me to them again.

My gaze flitted over to Falcon sitting at an empty table. "Falcon doesn't have anyone?" I asked Rogan.

"What do you mean?"

"He seems like he's always alone."

"His choice."

"And were you always alone before me?"

"Probably. Or with Falcon."

"He's too nice to be alone."

"I tried to convince him about love once a long time ago. The last four years, I've been sitting on his side of the fence. Wasn't till you came along, I even considered jumping."

"So he just needs the right woman?"

"It'd have to be one hell of a woman to break down Falcon's fortress. It's covered in explosives and barbed wire. And hundreds of ornery guard dogs."

I laughed. "Well, Takoda is supposedly a mean guard dog and look how she melted for me."

"Yep, Takoda loved you first. I was right behind her."

He bent down and kissed my ear as his arm around my waist pulled me up against his chest.

As the song changed, Bastien and Gwen walked over to us. "Shall we trade?" Bastien held Gwen's hand in Rogan's direction.

"Only for a minute, then I want my bride back," Rogan replied.

Bastien took my hand and guided me in circles next to Rogan and his mother. "You make a resplendent bride, Tessa."

"Thank you." I felt like a princess from head to toe. My dress and jewel-encrusted heels flashed when the light hit them. The amethyst sash made of Amalian silk tied around my waist made a decadent bow that flowed along with the train of my dress. The fact Gwen had worn it at her wedding made it extra special as my something borrowed.

Bastien twirled me and Rogan's appreciative gaze drank me in. Gwen spoke to him, and he turned his attention back to her as they danced. Hopefully, she was telling him she was happy for him and she approved of me. He bent down to hug her at the end of the song. As soon as he straightened, he zipped straight to me. His hand found its place on my lower back, and he leaned in to kiss my ear.

"We're going to our room now."

"You said Gwen wouldn't let us leave early."

One corner of his mouth quirked up. "I convinced her."

"Is that what you were talking about with her? Not sharing a poignant mother-son moment?"

"We did that too. But at the end, she told me we should go *make whoopee*."

ROGAN AND I RAN HAND in hand down the corridor of the five-star resort hotel. He swiped his key card and scooped me up behind my knees. I laughed as he carried me through the door and launched me onto the bed.

"Dress off." He placed his hands on his hips to watch.

"You carry me."

"What?" He climbed up the bed and poled his arms to support his weight over me.

"So many times. From the terrorists to the helicopter, from my dad's clutches to an escape hatch, over the threshold of this room. From captivity to freedom each time." I trailed my fingers from his temple to his shoulder.

His eyes softened. "I'd carry you across the Sahara if that's where you wanted to go." He kissed my nose. "But make no mistake, you rescued me. You're stronger than me. You carry the weight of my ruck and your own."

"Rogan..."

"Till death do us part."

"If there is a heaven, I'd like to believe we'd find each other there too."

"Yeah. Now let's *knock boots*."

I rolled to my stomach. "Help me."

He paused. "There's a million buttons on this damn thing."

"Those are faux buttons. There's a zipper hidden beneath them."

"Thank fuck."

Rogan removed my dress and his tuxedo. He stared at the garter and stockings for a long time. "I'm not even going to attempt taking those off."

I peeked up at him over my shoulder. "You have to remove them to get my panties off."

He set his brow and grinned. He yanked the sides of my bridal underwear and tore it off. We laughed and made love for the first time as husband and wife. I didn't feel any other presence between us.

He'd let Eden's ghost go. His sole focus was on every inch of me and pleasuring me, his only wife.

Epilogue

Rogan's palms grabbed my ass and squeezed. "Hey! I'm trying to concentrate here."

I lined a chunk of Rogan's hair between my fingers and snipped off the ends. "You're finally letting me cut your hair. I want to do a good job."

"Your tits are in my face."

I bent to look into his eyes as he sat in a chair in the backyard. "I know. I feel your eyes and your breath on them."

He chuckled and his laugh echoed inside my heart.

"I think I'm gonna love cutting your hair. It's incredibly sexy."

"Oh really? Let's do this inside." He flicked open the top button of my jeans.

"No. Let me concentrate for one minute."

"No." He went for the second button of my jeans.

I clicked on the electric razor and buzzed it next to his ear. "Hands off or you'll lose an ear, Boggs."

He dropped his hands, and I grinned while I carefully shaved the hair around the nape of his neck. "I have a theory about Dallas and Brock."

"I thought you were trying to concentrate."

335

"I am. I can talk, just don't touch me."

"Lots of rules for this haircut."

"Please cooperate."

"Sure. So what's your theory?"

"They're secret princes."

He chuckled. "Uh-huh."

"They are. And they live a normal life in Boston, but have body-guards because their country has sent them here for their safety during a huge civil uprising."

"All that, huh?"

"Am I right?"

"Uh. No."

"Tell me."

"Dallas and Brock have a history similar to mine, but grander on every scale. Higher up in the military, black ops they can't talk about. Dallas runs a network for vets to find jobs when they get discharged. Brock is his right-hand man."

"But why did Lachlan say they kill for blood and money?"

"I wish he hadn't said that in front of you."

"Do the Monroe brothers kill for blood and money?"

He took a deep breath and spoke slowly, choosing each word carefully. "The kinds of jobs soldiers are best at aren't always on the top side of the law. I can't tell you any more, and it's best you don't ask." Rogan held up one finger and lifted his phone to his ear. "Boggs."

Oh, he never answered the phone that way.

The longer he listened, the lower his shoulders fell. His gaze flitted to Takoda's spot where she rested in the sun. "Thank you. I'll get back to you."

He ended the call and looked up at me with crestfallen eyes. "Brightman wants to retire Takoda."

"She does?"

"She's earned thirteen thousand combat hours."

"Wow. Really? Would we get to keep her, or would she go to some doggie retirement home?"

"We'd keep her."

"That's good." I set the razor on the table to focus on him.

"I've been awarded a silver medal of honor," he said in a flat tone.

"Wow. You're not happy with that?"

"Not interested in accolades for doing my job." He placed his hands on my hips.

"But still. They want to recognize your service."

"In my line of work, I don't wanna be recognized."

"For your safety?"

"For *yours*." He pulled me closer so his lips were on my belly over the open button of my jeans.

I held his head and rubbed the newly exposed skin on his nape. "Oh."

"And Savannah's kids. Cyan, Dallas. Anyone associated with me is at risk."

"Hmm."

"She wants me to come to the White House for some ceremony." He dipped his tongue in my belly button.

I ignored the flood of desire to jump his bones. "That would be exciting."

His lips brushed my stomach as he shook his head. "Not interested."

I bent my knees to crouch down in front of him and placed my hands on his neck. "What's wrong, babe? This all sounds like good stuff."

"She's disbanding Alpha Squadron. Offered me a position as commander of a new Beta Squadron. Same missions as before, but a different team."

"Would you want that?"

He shook his head slowly. "Don't feel confident putting my life on the line without Takoda or my unit taking my six. There might've been days I'd take that risk, but now—no."

"What're your other options?"

"Honorable discharge. Everything forgotten—going MIA, disobeying orders, escaping confinement—all pardoned like it never happened. Make the fake story true."

"Wow."

"She's offering me an out because of you." He brushed my hair behind my ear.

"This is about me?"

"In a lot of ways, I think it is. She's still trying to make it up to me. Giving me freedom to be with you."

"Whatever you choose, I'll support you."

"A man needs purpose in his work."

"Is there some meaningful work you can find as a retired vet?"

"I could work for Monroe, but like I said, the work he does crosses the lines of civilian laws." He chewed his lip and stared into my eyes. "I've been thinking of starting a private security firm here. Have the guys from Alpha Squadron work for me."

"So, go out on your own?"

"Yeah. It'd be harder in the beginning, but more autonomy in the long run. I could do things my way. Really help people. Keep it legal."

"Would that give you purpose?"

"Yes."

"Then that's what you should do."

"I need to get in touch with Falcon. He probably got the same phone call I did."

"Go call him." I blew the shavings from his neck and kissed him. When I pulled away, I combed his hair into place with my fingertips. He stared at my chest for several deep breaths.

"You okay?" I trailed my fingers down his shirt and pressed his dog tags to his heart through the fabric.

He looked down at my hand, reached under his collar, and pulled the chain over his head.

"C'mon." He grabbed my wrist and led me inside to our bedroom. He stopped at my jewelry box and opened the door.

Slowly, he hung the chain on the hook and closed the door.

"How does that feel?" I asked him.

"In a way, it's giving up. Something I never thought I'd do."

"Life takes us on journeys we can't always predict."

"But closing this door also opens a new one. I'm free to love you. To build a new life. To work for a new purpose."

I kissed him, and he unbuttoned my pants with one hand while curling his fingers into my hair with the other. Then he made love to me, with renewed purpose. And as usual, he succeeded because I came four times and fell infinitely deeper in love with my man.

ON A DUSKY FALL MORNING, at the Idaho courthouse, Savannah's palm sweated in my hand. She stood on my right and Rogan was on my left. Timandra—who'd changed her name from Temperance— Jasmine, Mercedes, Phillip, and Milo flanked us on both sides as a silent courtroom waited for the verdict.

"With regards to the count of murder in the first degree, we the jury find the defendant, Jebediah Barebones, guilty."

Rogan squeezed my hand and a collective exhale from all of us filled the silence. Tori, who had fought hard through the whole trial, dropped her head and her beautiful red hair covered her face. She didn't want anyone to see the hard-nosed attorney cry.

"On count one of aggravated sexual assault, guilty." The juror continued to read guilty verdicts for all his accused crimes— twelve other counts of aggravated sexual assault, human trafficking, tax evasion, WIC fraud, bigamy, racketeering, child labor law violations, everything.

Lachlan Cutlass pumped his fist in the air. He gave me a thumbs up and a reassuring smile that said everything's going to be okay. And I believed him. This was a new beginning for me and all the women who had left the compound to start new lives on the outside. The sister wives and witnesses gathered at the courthouse clapped and cheered. My father called out, "This is religious persecution," but no one paid him any attention through our celebrations.

At the sentencing two days later, the judge sternly handed down three consecutive life sentences with no chance of parole or early termination.

Tori came to me and hugged me. "Good job, Tessa. It's done. They're free."

"Yes." All the stress of testifying was worth it.

Zook Guthrie negotiated a plea bargain for two years for his charge of sexual assault, reduced from five years because he provided critical information leading to the murder and rape convictions. My heart ached for Zook because I knew he never would've raped Lyric if my father hadn't forced him to do it. Four other seed bearers were convicted of aggravated sexual assault and given maximum sentences.

ROGAN

"This cornbread is the bomb," Blaze said.

"It's spoonbread, man," I replied.

"Whatever. It's good."

I shook my head and took the last bite of my Christmas dinner. When I stood and raised my glass, the chattering stopped and all eyes turned to me. "I'd like to make a toast." They picked up their glasses too and held them in front of them. "This Christmas is a first in some way for all of us. For Timandra, Phil, Heather, Mercedes, and Milo, it's their first Christmas." It felt good to call them by their new names. Milo chose to keep his. "For Savannah, the first as their mother. For some of us, it's our first Christmas married to our soulmates." I bent to press a kiss to Tess's temple. "But for all of us," I swung my glass past Falcon, Diesel, Blaze, Brock, Dallas, and Cyan, "it's the first as a family. We may not have been born into this family, but we sure as shit are one now."

Milo covered his mouth and giggled at my cuss word. "Uh, damn." I always forgot. "And cursing is part of life, so fucking get used to it." Tess coughed next to me, but everyone laughed. "And as a family, we celebrate freedom. Freedom to live and love as we choose. I choose to love this angel right here." I looked down into Tess's shimmering eyes. "I'd like to thank my brothers for taking my back with the new business and making Z Security a huge success in its first year. And let's all thank Tess and her sisters for preparing this kickass meal."

Everyone mumbled *thank you* and *really good*.

Tess stood next to me. "I'd like to thank you all for supporting my charity to help Brotherhood families get settled and start new lives."

I nodded because Tess had collected enough money to provide homes, clothes, tutoring, medical care, and a ton of other supplies for the families left behind at the compound. Soon, she'd expand from Idaho to Utah to help other women in similar situations.

"We all know what it's like to go without," I said to the group. "Not a soul here takes the gift of this day for granted. So I raise my glass to you all. May life offer you a colorful bounty, and may you be smart enough to take it."

FIVE MONTHS LATER

My Harley hummed between our legs, and the Carolina wind whipped our faces on the ride to Wilmington National Cemetery. Tess's hands wandering up my chest made it a challenge to focus on the road, but it felt good having her on my bike and pressed up against my back.

Crowds milled about the grounds on this Memorial Day weekend.

I held her hand and walked her through the grass to section two, space forty-five. Zander Saxton's gravesite.

"Pops, this is Tess. My wife. She found me and brought me back." She squeezed my hand. "Been twenty-two years since you gave your life. Always thought I'd join you here by now." I scanned the array of white memorial stones. "But looks like I have some living to do. This woman right here," I held up our joined hands, "gives me a new purpose. And I'm gonna fight like hell to be the man she needs."

"You are, Rogan. All I need."

"Doesn't seem fair. Me walking away breathing, with all my limbs still attached. But that's the way this mission played out. I gotta roll with it, like you always said, things get fucked, adjust on the fly."

Tess placed a bouquet of red, white, and blue flowers at the base of his stone. "Say hello to my momma. Tell her I love her." She sniffed and wiped her eyes. "Tell her the kids are happy and free. Tell her I found my joy."

I pulled her up against me. "Tell her I did too, and I'll take care of her girl. If she ever loses sight of that joy, I'll help her find it again."

She smiled through her tears. "You think my mom and your dad could be up in heaven knocking boots?"

I laughed and lifted her up for a kiss. "Could be."

I set her on the ground and tugged her hand to the south corner of the lot.

Tess placed a bouquet of violet roses on Eden Langbow Saxton's gravesite where she was buried next to her brother Nathan Langbow.

"Hello, Eden." Tess blinked back tears.

My throat clogged and I couldn't move. Staring at that stone hit me different this time. It always obliterated me, but now the hollowness at the bottom of the grief had a solid bottom. The endless chasm I'd always dropped into was finite.

"I figured if I came here often enough, the pain would lessen," I said to her. "It never did."

Tess wrapped her arms around my waist and squeezed.

"Not till today."

"Thank you for taking me here. And for sharing Eden with me."

I tucked my wife into my chest and held her tight.

Thank you, Eden. For letting me go so I could love her.

BANG-BANG-BANG! The headboard of our four-poster bed banged against the wall. Her wedding ring glinted in the lights I'd installed in the ceiling for exactly this reason. Tess struggled like a trapped doe in her bonds, and I wanted to see it bright and clear.

"Take it. Stop wigglin.'"

She was on her knees facing the headboard, hands tied wide to each bedpost. I liked her that way. Tits totally free for me to play with. I was on my back between her legs, pinching her nipples hard and tugging.

She stilled and looked down at me.

"Good." I spread her knees till her sweet cunt smashed to my lips. The second my tongue hit her slit, the board started banging, and she squirmed like crazy again.

That's okay. I liked her wiggling on my face. I plunged my tongue deep inside her, enjoying the tease, knowing she wouldn't come like this.

"Ahh! Please, Rogan. Lick it where I need it."

"Nah." I kept at her entrance and moved one hand to her ass, sweeping in the crack and brushing her hole. "This is too much fun." My other hand pinched harder and lifted her tit up.

She threw her head back and moaned.

"I'm gonna leave you tied like this all day so I can take lazy sips from you whenever I want."

She growled. "No. Want your cock. Please."

"In due time. Tilt."

She tilted her hips, giving me optimum access to her clit.

I worked her where she wanted it. She screamed and pulsed against my lips as she came hard. My girl always came hard for me.

"Now you get my cock." I slid out from under her and pulled up on my knees behind her. "You ready?" I probed her slit with the tip. She was soaking wet for me.

"God, yes. Fuck!"

"Oh, she's cussing now and takin' the lord's name in vain. That means she's ready."

"Yes!"

I entered her in one swift thrust. "I'm in you. On you. All the time."

"Yes."

I pumped into her slowly and looked down to watch my cock disappear inside her. "My Sunshine, my mermaid."

"Faster. Deeper."

I reached down her front to feel my cock sliding between my fingers in and out of her sweet pussy. "I'm taking my time. Enjoying the beauty in front of me." My palm smashed her clit. "You should feel our connection. Oh wait, you can't. Your hands are tied."

"Gah! Please, more."

"As you wish, my love." With one hand on her hip, the other grasping her cunt, I drove in to the hilt. I pummeled her over and over, each stroke a taste of heaven.

"You need to find it, babe, because I'm there." I ran my finger up and down her clit and drilled in on my target.

"Ahh!" She clenched and came all over my cock.

"Beautiful." I slammed in a few more times, trying to make it last, but it was too good. It overtook me and I let it all go inside her.

I curled around her back, and her head fell back onto my shoulder. I kissed her sweaty neck, smoothing the hair from her face. "Sublime fucking you. Better every time. Never get enough."

I untied her bindings, and she collapsed on her stomach. Keeping my dick buried in her, I rolled us to our sides, her back to my front. No more fear. We could sleep with her curled in front of me every night, and my wife would feel safe. I brushed my lips over the tattoo she'd made out of her scars, a fence with a dancer leaping over it.

"Brock gave me something tonight."

My arm clinched around her waist. "Woman, do not say another man's name when I'm still hard inside you."

She pulled away and my dick slipped out as she grabbed an envelope from the drawer of the nightstand and held it up.

"Oh shit."

She peeled open the flap. "A letter you gave him the night before you left. You must have written this after our dance at Siege. I dunno, maybe you wrote it before."

"Fuckin' hell." I scraped my hands through my hair.

She read my own words to me.

"If you're reading this, I'm already with my dad.

My father gave his life for our freedom, and I've always been prepared to do the same.

But if I don't come back, you need to know one thing,

I loved you.

I was too fucked in the head to show it to you like I should've, but I loved you.

And if I die out there, I'll die with one regret; I never made love to you.

Now, if I do make it back, I promise you I'll be fucking you long and hard every sunset and sunrise of each day we spend together, so I'm praying like hell right now you'll never read this letter.

Anyway, I hope you find joy because you're an exceptional woman. Strong, smart, beautiful, brave. You deserve it. You brought a shit ton of joy to my life in the short time I knew you. The man who gets to call you his will be the luckiest man alive.

I wish it could've been me, but I was stupid and got blown up.

Live your life free and in full color. Maybe spend a minute thinking of me on Memorial Day, but on other days, focus on the beauty in front of you."

She put the letter down and twisted to kiss me over her shoulder. "Thank fuck you made it back."

I chuckled. "I'm making good on my promise too. Sunrise and sunset."

"You are. And I'm lovin' the beauty in front of me." She trailed her fingers over the *T* on my left bicep. "And behind me."

"Love you, Sunshine."

"Love you too, babe."

"That fucker," I said.

"Who? Brock?"

"He gave me his word he wouldn't give the letter to you."

"He lied."

She rested her head on the pillow and smiled as I kissed her neck.

"It's all still true. I loved you then. Love you more now. Gonna keep loving you sunrise and sunset till the day I die."

"I'm pretty sure you'll find me in heaven and knock boots with me there too."

"Damn straight."

———————————

Become a VIP

SIGN UP TO BEX DANE's VIP reader team and receive exclusive bonus content including;

- Free books

- Behind-the-scenes secrets no one else knows

- Deleted scenes

- Advanced Reader Copies and first look at cover reveals

Visit bexdane.com

33825096R00210

Made in the USA
Middletown, DE
18 January 2019